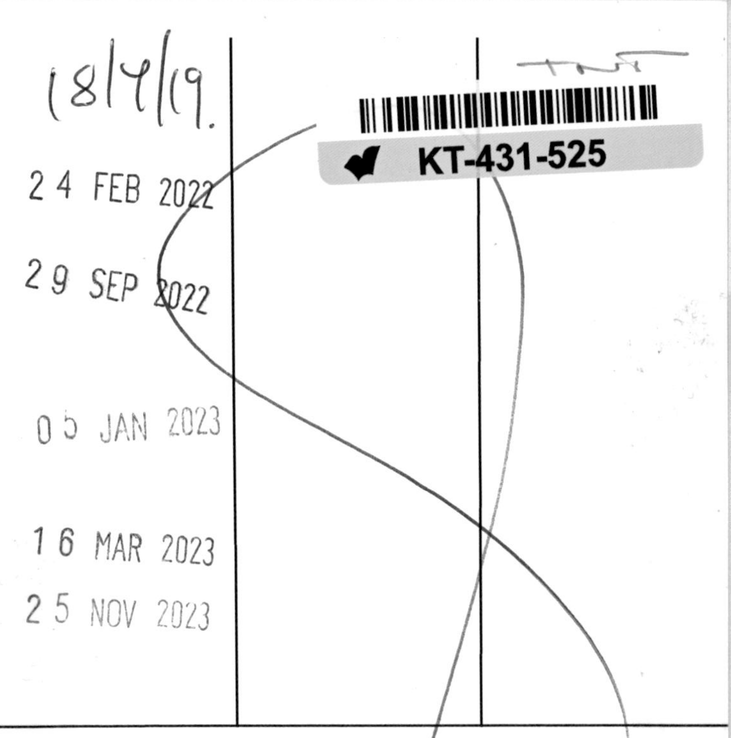

18/4/19.
KT-431-525
24 FEB 2022
29 SEP 2022
05 JAN 2023
16 MAR 2023
25 NOV 2023

CUSTOMER
SERVICE
EXCELLENCE

CSE

Kent
County
Council
kent.gov.uk

C334279404

By the same author

Daughter

The Drowning Lesson

How Far We Fall

JANE SHEMILT

PENGUIN BOOKS

PENGUIN BOOKS

UK | USA | Canada | Ireland | Australia
India | New Zealand | South Africa

Penguin Books is part of the Penguin Random House group of companies
whose addresses can be found at global.penguinrandomhouse.com

First published by Michael Joseph 2018
Published in Penguin Books 2018
001

While the hospitals and research facilities mentioned in the text are well known institutions of great renown, in *How Far We Fall* all the staff referred to as working within them as well as the patients, clinics, wards, operating theatres and laboratories, including animal laboratories, are fictional.

Set in Garamond MT Std
Typeset by Jouve (UK), Milton Keynes
Printed and bound in Great Britain by Clays Ltd, Elcograf S.p.A.

A CIP catalogue record for this book is available from the British Library

ISBN: 978–0–718–18090–4

www.greenpenguin.co.uk

To my beloved family

Fair is foul and foul is fair.

Prologue
Hampstead Heath

At twilight, London has a fairground glitter.

At this distance, the small streets and rows of houses fade from view. The graffiti and the gangs, the drunks and marauders, the foxes at the rubbish bins, everything vanishes in the dusk. What you see is not what you get, what you see is less than half of it.

There are women, four of them gathered together under the trees. They share a joint; light slides along a silver piercing, highlights the tip of a nose, guilds tattoos.

They don't talk much; they don't need to. The plans were laid years ago.

It's a question of timing. It's a question of life and death, especially life. What they will save, and who they won't. They huddle and whisper; ruin is in the air. Smoke rises from their mouths.

Their dogs are restive, their wet coats stink. They pull at their leads, anxious to be off.

Wait, they are told. Your turn will come.

London glitters, a web smudged by weather.

Act One

1

London. Late Summer 2015

It starts with a glance. Beth wonders, as her glance hardens into a stare, if she should turn away, leave the party, abandon the possibility of complications and disappointment, return unscathed to the bedsit above the dry cleaner's, to the empty wine glass on the dressing table, the cup in the sink, grainy dregs tracking to the rim.

Though there is a choice in that moment, it becomes too late to make it. It was too late weeks ago. She should have ignored the invitation pinned to the board in the coffee room, and never left the flat; she might have stopped at the door of the conference room or left before the unknown man stepped from behind Ted. Now she has seen his face, she is held.

She stands with colleagues, half listening to their chatter. Stephanie's Yorkshire accent is comforting; Beth has at times imagined laying her head on that pillowy chest and telling her everything. Helena is thin-haired and muscular; she represents the nurses' union. In the birdlike movements of her head she seems to be watching, gathering information, a little sly. Beth met them outside by chance and came in with them, smiling as though her courage hadn't ebbed at the door. Other nurses join them, mostly mothers. All week the gossip circled around what they would wear, how to persuade husbands to babysit, how late they might stay. She had listened, saying nothing. She had wanted to see Ted again but at a distance, watch him with his family. Her deepest motives are folded in shadow, though punishment is the greatest of them, his regret and his punishment as yet unshaped.

Banners have been strung across the ceiling. There are balloons in primary colours taped to the backs of chairs. Music plays from invisible speakers. The long table has been pushed against the wall and covered with paper tablecloths. Already there are damp patches of wine, fragments of scattered lettuce, the tang of coleslaw and the sulphur of boiled egg. Bottles with beaded green necks stand in ice and three girls walk around with trays of glasses, brim-full of wine. They offer these unsmilingly. Beth feels judged by their downcast eyes, ashamed of her giggling friends who scoop glasses off every passing tray.

The room fills rapidly, the heat and noise increase. The consultants are in a group at the centre, a couple of women surgeons among them, glamorous in silky dresses, the marks of exhaustion on their faces. Most of their colleagues are men in prosperous middle age. Younger doctors hover at the edge of these knots, rocking on their heels, fingering phones, eyeing each other. Unnecessary stethoscopes are linked around their necks. In the Serengeti with Ted years ago she'd seen adolescent lions circle the older ones, watching them, wanting inclusion first, supremacy later.

Some of the men glance over to her group; their collective gaze travels past her friends and settles on her. Their faces become serious, she recognises intent. Her look tonight is exotic, seductress rather than nurse. Her dark hair is heavy on her shoulders, she wears black lace to her neck, black eyeliner, a red slash of lipstick. Her cheekbones glimmer. Her friends in low-cut silk are a little older, less precisely groomed; they exclaimed when they saw her, as if her appearance had been conjured by magic rather than craft. She feels sharp-edged amidst their softness, glowing inside the circle like a knife.

She noticed Ted immediately; he is easy to notice. Tall, blond, the way he stands. She edges nearer, hidden in the crowd, an outsider, looking in. His wife is close to him; his hand holds hers. Beth stops, recalculates. He never used to hold Jenny's hand. Eight years ago, when she first met him, husband and wife were at opposite ends of the room. Today, Jenny's clothes are loose and grey; her frame seems swamped by cloth. The wild hair is gathered into a knot and streaked with white. Beth sees the blue glance flick towards her then away. Jenny knows exactly who she is, has probably known for years; she would by now have found a place to put the knowledge. Their twins are here, she recognises Ed. He is standing beside his parents, darkly angular like his mother, from whom his head is turned, as though straining away. Ted always said the boy was closer to him than to Jenny; he took credit for getting his son through rehab, it never occurred to him he was part of the problem. A red-headed girl in green dungarees stands beside Ed, her hand is around his waist, pressing close, shy. Next to them her male mirror image scans the room closely; her delicate features are sharpened into a muzzle on his face, he resembles a fox. He turns to chat to Ed who nods and laughs. A group within a group, easy to decode: Ed, his girlfriend, her older brother who seems close to Ed; at a guess he came first, introducing the sister. Ted's once shambolic, drug-taking son has shored himself up against his successful father. Theo, the photographer brother, loose-limbed and fair like Ted, lounges at the corner of the room with a camera round his neck. Their daughter is not here, of course.

Ted is the gravitational centre of the room, a king holding court. The group of young doctors nearest him jostle for attention. His eyes are clear; the puffiness has gone. He must have stopped drinking. He has the gleam of a man who has won his battles, past grief buried deep. He bends to whisper in Jenny's ear, she smiles; so he has repaired his marriage, he is hard to withstand once he has made up his mind. She was persuaded, once. A bitter taste is in her mouth, sweat prickles her neck. Ted straightens and smiles, he knows all eyes are on him though he won't guess at her presence, uninvited and no longer part of his life. She toasts him silently. After his daughter went missing, family disaster took centre stage for a while. When war reporters talk of collateral damage, she recognises the word.

The wine tastes salty, expensive. His favourite. In the early years, they used to drink it as they undressed at the end of the day, before he went home. Tuesdays and Thursdays. She smiles with her friends, but other losses crowd in. Her mother's tipsy laugh echoes from the shadows; her parents hover near at parties. Twenty years dead, self-absorbed and frequently drunk, there'd been no room for anyone else, hardly any for her. They would have been fighting before the crash, fighting and screaming as usual. The other loss is lodged more deeply; Ted's second daughter, the child he never saw.

Ted is listening to a broad-shouldered man with curly auburn hair who is half hidden behind him, though Ted's eyes also sweep the crowd, the consultants, the nurses and junior doctors, the anaesthetists and radiologists. He is watching everyone watch him; that he is taking pleasure from the moment is evident in the way he holds his mouth, pursed with triumph. New vanity, unappealing. His shirt strains over a paunch, his hand goes to his back when he straightens. There is white in his hair, deeper lines on his face, cruel ones by his mouth. He'd be sixty now, more. She is less than half his age.

If you can fall in love across a room, you can fall out of it too, falling as from a height to land in a different place with a jolt that shakes your mind. Perhaps she has been mistaken all this time. Perhaps she doesn't want him after all, never really wanted him. She wants what he has: family, safety, money. Love. The simple, unimaginable things. His sons are smiling at him; his wife holds his hand.

A camera flashes twice; Theo is crouching against the wall, grinning and snapping fast. Champagne has replaced wine on the circulating trays. The auburn-haired man has moved forward and is tapping a glass with a knife. Heads swivel at the clash of metal on glass, the chatter quietens. The shoulders and the colour of his hair are familiar. She has seen him at a distance in the car park talking to Ted or walking rapidly through the corridors of the hospital, head bent, surrounded by a group. A man in a hurry who leaves a stir in the air. Now he is clearly revealed, fresh-faced and handsome. He wears a kilt, a tweed jacket slung over his shoulders; the colours glow next to Ted's black suit. His frame seems broader than most, high cheekbones, wide-set eyes. Norse or Viking. He has the air of a soldier before a fight; calm and battle-fit. The freckles make him look very young.

'Ladies and gentlemen, a few moments, please.' The voice is confident, Scots.

'We are here to celebrate the achievements of an

extraordinary man. Thanks to the Professor we are developing cures for some of the world's most debilitating conditions.'

His shoulders shift as he talks, his feet step away and back; if he was an animal he would be a horse in peak condition, energy coming off him like heat. Ted was like that once.

'There are some special investigations going on, with exciting developments ahead,' the young man tells the room. 'Since the National poached Ted from Bristol four years ago, our department has gone from strength to strength.' A patter of clapping. 'He has looked after me since I started a couple of years back. Friend, mentor, the best teacher I've ever had – it's an honour to be part of his team.' He sounds as sincere as a child. He raises his glass. 'First a toast to Jenny; you know what they say, behind every great man is a great woman . . .'

Two women. For seven years it was she, Beth, who had stood in the shadows behind Ted, closer to him than Jenny. As if on cue, Ted turns to the slight figure of his wife, puts his arms round her, pulling her close for a kiss. Ed looks away before the laughter resumes and a small cheer goes up.

'I give you Professor Edward Malcolm, the new President of the Society of British Neurosurgeons.'

More applause. Ted holds up his hands in mock protest and steps forward. He flattens his hair, his chin lifts and he begins to speak. The words follow each other smoothly, he acknowledges the young man's praise with a self-deprecating grin, he makes several jokes and pauses for laughter. He nods at members of the audience with appreciative smiles that seem personal. He thanks his team, his wife, his boys. The performance is masterly.

Beth has manoeuvred herself to the front, near where the young Scot is now standing close to Ed. The man's features have softened as he watches Ted. He would be a middle-grade registrar, working the academic part of the rotation perhaps, hunched over a microscope in the laboratory. Clever and ambitious, Ted only employs people like himself. Oxbridge usually, though this man looks as if he travelled a tougher route. In profile his nose dips at its bridge; there is a triangular scar on his temple, a jagged one on his chin.

Ted's voice rises; he is coming to the end of his speech. '. . . so here's to Baird McAlister, a star in the making.' He raises his glass to the young man. 'And to the next generation of doctors, who will take this research forward to places we can only guess at.' He smiles at Ed who would by now be qualified; his son is frowning at the floor, red-cheeked with embarrassment. The foxy friend murmurs into his ear and Ed raises his head with a grin. Beth is close enough to catch their conversation, turning her head away to avoid recognition.

'. . . family dynamics on display; so interesting.'

'Shut up, Jake Valance.' Ed sounds irritated. 'This isn't copy.'

'Could be. Famous father, rebellious son; perfect for the *Sunday Times*.'

'You wouldn't dare.'

They laugh. Ed's close friend is a journalist then; a trained observer, that glance around the room had been narrow-eyed. She takes a step away as Ted rejoins his family to prolonged applause. The music becomes louder and the lights dim. Several nurses start to dance together in inward-facing circles. A couple of doctors from Casualty, thick-necked rugby players, begin to walk towards her. She moves nearer to Baird McAlister. His hair is the colour of fire; if she reached to touch him, she has the feeling that her hands would be warmed. As if he can sense her near him, he turns towards her. She notices his irises first, grey streaked with orange, like glowing ash, and then her reflection in his pupils: pale face, encased body. Intent.

'Quite a speech,' she says, lifting her glass.

There are green, blue and yellow threads in his jacket; close up he smells of fresh towels and antiseptic. He shakes his head but his face flickers with pleasure. His eyes crease, her reflection vanishes.

'My boss's was far more accomplished.' He indicates Ted who is now downing glass after glass of champagne as if to make up for lost time. Theo is taking photos in quick succession, the Casualty officers have disappeared. 'He's a natural at this kind of thing.'

He isn't. He practises; she knows this. He paces up

and down, practising until he is word perfect. There would have been nothing remotely natural about that speech. She wonders if Baird had noticed her already, as she had him, and if gossip might have placed her with Ted. She had let people think there was a boyfriend in the background, a successful business type, often abroad. When rumours of Ted's affair began to circulate no one suspected her, remote, preoccupied Beth. She turns her back on Ted's group; she doesn't want her face in his family album.

'Yours was better.'

The blush spreads to his hairline; a moment of silent appraisal passes between them, then he smiles. He smiles with his whole face; his mouth opens, his eyes dance, even his ears shift slightly. It's hard not to smile back.

'You seem fond of Ted.'

'Of course. I owe him everything.'

'Owe him?' Her voice is light as if amused but she knows how he feels; she'd felt like that once.

'In every way. He's given me opportunities most registrars would kill for; I've been under his wing from the start. I made a stupid mistake early on and he took the rap.' A swift sideways glance at her face. 'I shouldn't have shared that; don't tell anyone.'

'Nothing to tell.' She smiles up into his eyes. 'Scout's honour.'

He grins back, he looks relieved. There is something of the boy scout in him; words like innocence and loyalty would apply, so would goodness probably. Naivety perhaps. No wonder Ted fastened to him, someone he could mould, whose devotion would enhance his ego. Her successor; maybe she should warn him.

'I swear I've seen you somewhere before.' The grey eyes search hers. 'On a ward maybe. Are you one of those newly qualified doctors who are coming to take my research forward?'

He's noticed her then; she wants to tell him she might have been a doctor had there been more money, had her parents been sober enough to save some. He's the type that would listen.

'I'm a theatre nurse,' she answers, lifting her chin. 'Orthopaedics.'

'Tough job, that.' It sounds as though he means it. He couldn't know how tough it's been to stand there as handmaiden, passing over chosen knives when she would rather make the cut herself, delicate, precise. She has watched so often, sometimes she thinks she could do it in her sleep.

A waitress approaches, carrying a tray of steaming Yorkshire puddings, miniature cups with a slice of red meat in each, blood seeping into batter. The girl is young for this, mid-teens at a guess, a platinum blonde with tilted eyes the colour of water. Her mouth is turned down; she is doing this on sufferance. She is dressed in black with a frilled white apron, as if acting the part of a maid in a play, appropriately costumed.

Her face is expressionless; she would rather be someone else in a different drama. The hand holding the tray trembles, there is a tiny inked mouse at the base of her thumb.

'Pretty.' Beth smiles.

The girl twists her hand to support the tray from underneath, the thumb becomes hidden. The marks under her eyes are greenish, a tired schoolgirl helping out. Baird McAlister has noticed this too; he takes a pudding, then another and another. He puts them into his mouth and they vanish like magic.

'How did you know I was starving?' he jokes, but the girl steps back as if found out in some trickery. Beth sees the other two waitresses hovering. They look older. One is tall, late twenties with a slant-eyed stare and thick grey hair pulled back from a bony face; the smaller girl has bold brown eyes and a turned-up nose; with her red curls she has the appearance of a tortoiseshell cat. Despite their different colourings they are similar; stepped versions of the same girl. A family business. Beth is held, riven as she always is. Sisters. It would have changed her life.

'There's something about roast beef that restores one's self-belief,' Baird McAlister says, leaning a little towards Beth. 'Have one.'

'Food and a beautiful woman. How the hell do you do it, Albie?' A pale youth has appeared from behind Baird; a cloud of dust-coloured hair froths to the collar of his purple jacket. 'I'm Bruce.' The narrow eyes glint.

'Beth,' she replies, unsmiling.

'Me and Albie, we're brothers in arms. We compete for resources, like our lab rats.' He leans close to put a soft mole paw on her arm. 'Now where exactly did those food-bearing lovelies disappear to?' His face turns like a burrowing animal coming up into light, questing for food.

'Vanished into thin air, they must have seen you coming,' Baird McAlister tells him, an edge to his voice.

A good moment for her to leave too. Baird knows her name and where she works; let him find her, it works better that way. As she says goodbye, his eyes shift to someone behind her and his face breaks into a wide smile; turning, she sees Ted staring down at her, his mouth strained into a half-smile.

'I see you've met Albie,' he murmurs under his breath, as if they still share secrets, as if nothing has changed. His voice trembles.

A warm sense of triumph floods her throat; she moves past him, smiling faintly. Anyone watching would think she hardly knew him, was uninterested, a little bored.

She doesn't notice the walk to the station or the train back home, she doesn't pick up the glass on the dressing table or wash out the cup in the sink. She lies in bed but doesn't sleep. She stretches her hand across the strip of light that falls over the bed from the street lamp outside, spreading the fingers as wide as they can go, as if trying to grasp the bar of brightness between the soft edges of shadow on either side. The face of the young surgeon glows in her retina like an after-image of the sun, eclipsing Ted's completely.

2

London. Autumn 2015

The stage. A Player, his victims. The witness. Ambition, Fate, Destiny, etc.

Witness: to see, hear or know by personal presence and perception.

The witness can be a bystander, an enemy, a lover. A beholder. It can be someone you don't even notice at first.

Ambition: hovering in the wings.

Fate: announced by drum rolls from the pit.

Destiny: directing proceedings, having it all her own way.

The cages are stacked along three walls in the animal room on the tenth floor. They are numbered and lined with sawdust and ribbons of paper. Four rats in each. Muted squeaks and scuffles fill the room, along with the dusty, sweetish scent of food pellets.

The new laboratory assistant hasn't arrived. Albie hunches his shoulders, the blue lab coat constrains his arms. He noticed last week that an unclaimed white one was hanging behind the door, a larger size than most. *Professor Malcolm* was written on the plastic parking permit in a pocket, *lower ground, consultants only*. Albie had held the coat in both hands as though assessing its size and then replaced it. Ted wouldn't mind, but Bruce would. He'd mock him, a pretender. Bruce should be here now, working to complete his PhD; he's late as usual. He will claim some colourful sexual adventure the preceding night, then pull a crumpled sheet from his pocket, a brilliant analysis of results, scrawled in green biro, completed on the bus journey in. A threat and not a threat; as a child, the story of the tortoise and the hare seemed just to Albie; the profile of a small grey tortoise, lidded eye gleaming as he trundles past the supine hare, comes back to sustain him on long nights in the lab.

Minutes pass, no technician. Albie opens cage number eight and gropes inside. The long white animal twists in his hands. He lifts it out, holding the shoulders and tail firmly. In the operating room he places it in the red anaesthetic box and presses a button; the rat folds gently to the floor. Limp, it feels heavier. He injects ketamine into the tail vein then positions the animal in a clamp, sliding metal bars into its ears so the head is stabilised. Opening the narrow jaw, he pushes another small bar into place up against the hard palate. He scrubs up for several minutes to avoid contamination; these rats have grown up in sterile conditions. The irony is uncomfortable: they are kept and operated on in scrupulous cleanliness so they can survive to be studied as victims of the fatal disease he will give them. He doesn't pause in his preparations, the irony is familiar. Once gloved and wearing a face mask, he incises the scalp down the midline, retracts the soft flaps of skin, then drills down into the small skull. He straightens to relieve the ache in his shoulders then, taking the syringe, he slides the needle smoothly into the brain, and expels four microlitres of fluid, cloudy with tumour cells. He'd met a child with this tumour yesterday. Ted called him over to his clinic in the hospital outpatients. The father was a wealthy businessman used to control; his notes of her symptoms lay on the desk, graphed as if charting the disease would give him power over it. His little girl was curled on his lap, a tooth missing in her smile, gauzy wings pinned to the pink cardigan. Put on her feet, she lurched to one side, staggering as she walked across the room. One eye rolled inwards. The scan showed a tumour the size of a walnut in her brainstem. She would die within seven months. Ted phoned after his clinic.

'What are your thoughts, Albie?'

His voice was searching. He was after more than a rundown of treatment options; he wanted to know what Albie was feeling.

'Pity. Anger,' Albie replied slowly. He searched for words to convey the surge of determination he'd felt as he walked back to the lab.

'Go on.'

'If we carry on where we're going, we'll be able to help kids like her. It brought it home. It made me feel . . .' He was unable to convey the sorrow and certainty that had pulled at him, afraid to sound emotional.

'That everything you are doing is worthwhile,' Ted finished for him.

Ridiculously he simply nodded down the phone.

'Good man,' Ted said into the silence. 'I've always thought we dream the same dreams, you and I.' He paused and then, briskly, 'I've booked the squash court. Friday eight p.m. Try not to be late for once.'

The conversation had recharged Albie. If he had a chance against this wretched disease, the late nights and risible salary were irrelevant. He'd keep going for as long as it took.

The rat is still limp. He sutures the skin at the crown of its head, and replaces it in its cage. When the girl enters the room, he registers her overalls and cap out of the corner of his eye; the new lab assistant. Her glance flicks to his face and away, shy. His mind has been stamped with Beth's face these last three months, her mouth and her eyes; there is little space for others, so who this girl reminds him of slips away even as he reaches for it. He murmurs a greeting then turns back to rinse the soap from his hands. Her predecessor, Amil, left a fortnight ago. His mother was ill, his hometown of Aleppo engulfed by war.

Amil had explained the Middle East to him in their coffee breaks, but since he left, Albie has lost track of which side holds sway over which smoking heap of stone. Life and death on such a scale is hard to take in. The news is like a violent film rolled out nightly; horror bereft of meaning. The killing in the lab is controlled and painless. The scale is minute; it saves lives.

A stifled gasp breaks these thoughts. The girl is staring at the curled body of the rat, the sawdust is red and damp in patches. Her eyebrows are drawn; sharp lines crease the pale skin between them.

'Blood?' Her accent makes the question both emphatic and lilting. She could be Norwegian or perhaps Finnish.

'There's bound to be a little. It was a routine procedure.' He opens the cage and picks up the sleepy animal, checks the sutures then replaces the rat, who crawls groggily to the bars of the cage, pink snout twitching, before collapsing again in a little heap. 'He'll be fine in half an hour.'

She moves to the other cages, crooning a song, the words incomprehensible.

'Could you clear up in the operating room while I jot down a few observations?' His voice sounds ridiculously hearty. 'I'll come through in a moment.'

She edges round him, her shoulders dipping from side to side as she walks, a hefty gait for a slight girl, like a workman. He watches as she disappears out of the door, then picks up the pen, flips open the notebook and writes fast, notes as distilled as the poems on his bedside table; sometimes he thinks poetry might bring him more cash.

Rat 8: Operation × 1 09.30 hours September 2015. Anaesthetic: ketamine. Insertion of needle to brainstem target (9mm). Delivery of 5 microlitres tumour-enriched fluid. Site closed. Minimal blood loss. Rat returned 10.30. Observations: 10.40 bleeding stopped. Rat mobilising gradually.

In the operating room she is staring at the clamp. There is a smudge of blood on the surface below it, she should have wiped that away by now. Something in the slow look she gives him stirs the sediment of memory again.

'Feeling okay?'

She nods but her skin has the chalky pallor of paper.

'You're new to this?'

Her eyes are lowered; she seems to be studying the clear tubes where the gases are delivered.

'But you must know what we do?' he persists, exasperation threaded with pity. Lab assistants don't need qualifications or even experience, but they are vetted for efficiency; sentiment would be unhelpful.

'I am interested in your work.'

Your work. A rush of pride follows her words. He's modified a virus which now has the power to kill tumours, a significant breakthrough; all the same, researchers rarely get the credit. Ted is head of the lab; research is usually identified as his. Albie pulls out a stool for her from under the bench.

'I didn't catch your name.'

'Skuld.' She sits down.

The word reminds him of cool places, inland water. The far north. There are names like this where he grew up, Jura names. He smiles at her.

'Would you like me to explain this project to you?'

'I know you use rats . . .' A pale hand indicates the clamp.

He nods. 'We're working on a treatment for cancer using viruses. Brain cancer in children.' He tears a sheet from the pad kept by the anaesthetic box, picks up the stub of pencil beside it and sketches a rapid oval for the skull, a circle inside that for the brain and a cylinder beneath the circle.

'This is the brainstem.' He taps the cylinder. 'The main highway. It carries all the information from the brain to make the body work.' He draws a dark egg shape inside the cylinder, nearly touching the edge. 'Here's the tumour and this . . .' – he pencils a slashing diagonal through to the egg-shaped tumour – '. . . is the catheter, down which we inject the treatment.'

'You do this on your own?' Her eyes linger on the sharp line cutting through the skull and penetrating the brain.

'Prof Malcolm is officially head of research but he's

often away. Bruce and I carry out all the work.' He rises at five thirty, beating traffic to examine the animals and begin the tasks of the day. If he stops for a moment, his limbs grow heavy, exhaustion can overwhelm him. He sleeps as soon as he sits down. He slept through an entire play on Beth's birthday. Every day is the same – the same room, the familiar smell of the animals, the hours spent examining slides under the microscope.

'What were you doing just now?' She glances at the bloodstain under the clamp.

'Infusing tumour cells; it's part of some new work I'm doing, involving viruses. I'm writing it up for my PhD.'

'You give rats a tumour?'

He nods. 'Rare childhood ones. The tumours grow in fourteen days but I've found a way to destroy them.' He waits for her response but the lines between her eyebrows have reappeared; she shakes her head, apparently confused. He straightens; his tiredness has vanished. This is work he pioneered; he could talk about it for ever.

'Think of it like a war, cancer is the invader. The tumour in the brainstem is the enemy base camp.' He indicates the dark oval. 'Tumour cells spread from here to the rest of the brain, infiltrating like terrorists. With me so far?'

She nods silently.

'I've adapted a strain of the chickenpox virus which targets the tumour. We infuse it into some of the rats, it destroys the base camp and here's the clever thing . . .' He nods excitedly. 'The virus switches on the rats' immune system which attacks the migrating tumour cells; it's like recruiting the locals to take out those terrorists. It seems to be working. The tumours shrink away.' He puts the pencil down and smiles; the miracle is new to him each time.

'You said some of them. What will happen to those rats who don't get the virus?'

'They don't survive, but we make sure they don't suffer. They are euthanised when they develop symptoms.'

'And the ones whose tumours shrink?' She is watching him but her expression gives little away.

'We sacrifice them after two months. It's important that we compare the brains of the treated and untreated groups to see exactly what effect the virus has had.'

Her eyes are opaque, deep ponds in a Norwegian wood. When he first arrived, Amil had shown him round; in the animal room he had tenderly slipped a little animal from palm to palm. Albie returned later on his own; the rats were sleeping in a soft, white pile, long tails tangled together. He watched them, wondering if he had the right to interfere with their lives, end them. He'd seen children die and families suffer; even so there wasn't a clear answer, or one within his grasp. Back then he was conscious of going through a gate on to a track, and since then he'd simply kept walking, looking straight ahead. If anyone had asked him, he'd have said on balance this seemed the right thing to do. He drew away from further analysis, aware that he might become mired in choices and time would be lost.

'We follow the procedure set by the Home Office to minimise suffering,' Albie tells her. 'Euthanasia is rapid, you wouldn't be expected to assist.'

Her stool wobbles; she puts out a hand to grip the table, revealing a tiny blue mouse, perfectly drawn on the joint at the base of her thumb. The girl with the roast beef. 'I knew I'd seen you before. You were helping at Prof's party a few months ago.'

'One of my sisters works in the kitchens here, she organises events. I help if they're short of people. Extra money.' Her hands disappear into her lap. 'It won't affect my work.'

He recognises those short sentences, defence and shyness, both. He has no idea what she earns but it wouldn't be much; he doesn't earn much either. He doesn't envy Ted his luxurious flat or the Mercedes; holidays in his Greek villa would bore him. All the same, it would be good to mend the roof in Jura, repair the windows. The rewiring is years overdue. He smiles at the young girl sitting before him, her shoulders hunched as if to ward him off.

'So you're the scientist of the family?'

She shakes her head. 'My eldest sister's a technician in the large animal lab. My mother works with animals at another hospital. I came straight from school but I know about animals.' A note of defiance has crept into her voice. 'We keep stray dogs. Mum taught me everything I need to know.'

'We know about animals too.' He feels his way carefully. 'But this is a research facility—'

His phone vibrates; a list of questions from Beth appear on the screen: What time is supper? How many others? What should she wear? She seems less certain than usual, vulnerable even. Perhaps she's allowing herself to come closer at last.

'I need to go.' He takes off his gown. 'Our lab manager Bridget will run through the other procedures. The person who showed you round left out a lot. Who was it?'

'Bruce.'

'Ah.' Someone should warn her about Bruce; she is very young, a little fragile. 'I'm Albie. Albie McAlister. Let's catch up again soon.'

'I know your name.' She stands up, ethereal despite the bulky lab coat. 'They talked about you.'

'They?'

'Some consultants and the Professor.'

Hospital gossip; inescapable rubbish mostly. There will be no truth to this; all the same, his interest is piqued by the mention of Ted. 'When was this?'

'Yesterday, at the monthly planning meeting.'

'Really? You were there?' The consultants' meeting is a high-ranking affair – departmental strategies are outlined, research considered, future appointments discussed.

'They needed help setting out the food, pouring coffee, those sorts of things. My sister asked me specially.' Bright spots of colour burn in her cheeks. 'I was there the whole time, I heard everything.'

'So what did they say?' he asks more gently; she's just a kid out of school, easily hurt. He smiles encouragingly.

'They want to hire someone ahead of the Professor retiring, to take over his jobs when he goes. Your name was mentioned. He said you are a brilliant surgeon and that . . . um . . . he was very proud of you; you will make a difference. You are very . . . uh . . . innovative, and you hide your light under a bushel in the lab here.'

'Kind of them.' He grins. He doesn't buy any of it – too many pauses, too elaborate. She has made it up to flatter him or else muddled what she heard. 'I expect they have plans to spare for all of us: me, Bruce, Bridget, everyone.'

She pulls her cap off with a fierce jab of movement and shakes her hair into a bright nimbus that collects the light around her head. 'Bruce was mentioned, as a matter of fact.' The note of defiance is back. 'He'll make a mark of some kind, they said.'

He laughs. 'No one could ever forget Bruce, that's for sure. Tell me, exactly who said all this?'

'The Professor, I told you. Consultants, various ones, I don't know their names. They don't speak to me and I don't speak to them. I listen, that's all.'

The last words ring true. A listener, other-worldly, the kind of girl who keeps her distance. She has taken off her coat now, revealing running clothes; a crop top shows her pale midriff, a window of tight flesh. She is older than he thought, finely drawn. Her small breasts are outlined against the clinging fabric. A child and not a child. She stands very still; they are inches apart. She looks towards him expectantly as if waiting to see what he will do next. In the sun now pouring through the skylight of the small room, he can see a dusting of fair hair along her arms; her skin has the grassy scent of the very young. Her mouth is slightly open, showing the edges of small white teeth. He thinks of snow, Norwegian woods in snow, unsullied. Why has she told him all this? Outside a door slams and there is an explosion of chatter, startling him. He glances at his watch. Lunchtime.

3

London. Autumn 2015

Bruce is in the lift when it arrives on the tenth floor.

'Leaving already?' he asks. 'Or is it lunchtime?' His pretty face is as pale as a moth, the eyes sunk between red folds. A sour smell comes from his creased clothes. 'I'll come down again then. God, what a night; the girls get younger and younger. Why not join us next time?'

'I couldn't be less interested.' Bruce's sexual adventures are fantasies designed to shock. His stories, worn thin, are derided behind his back. 'We need to talk. We're running out of rats; you're supposed to keep the stock replenished.'

'I'll do whatever you want,' Bruce replies wearily. 'Provided we discuss it over a pint.'

'It's a deal.' Albie presses the ground-floor button. Lunch is usually sandwiches in his office – anything more seems a waste of time – but this way he can ensure rat numbers are steady; he needs a constant influx.

They walk through the doors of the Institute into blinding sunshine. Bruce puts a shaking hand over his eyes. The National Hospital for Neurology and Neurosurgery is to their immediate left, the Victorian architecture graceful next to the Institute's brutal facade, but for Albie, the Institute is the place of greater magic, the hidden brains behind the face. He is reluctant to leave, even for lunch.

Ted is by the front entrance of the hospital, his blond hair bright in the sunlight. Albie halts; an unexpected encounter, all the more welcome. Ted should be in clinic at this time, he doesn't usually get to see him in the day. He waits by the railings. Bruce waits too, sighing impatiently. Ted is shaking the hand of a tall man with a tan and a neat grey crew cut, whose Midwest drawl carries easily in the still autumn morning. They seem to be congratulating each other. The man laughs and disappears into a waiting taxi. Ted waves him off then turns to go back up the short flight of steps that leads to the hospital doors. He is still smiling when he glances up and sees them. The smile vanishes and his thick eyebrows slant together; close up they are flecked with white, frost on a hedge. Ted is getting older; he hadn't noticed.

'Albie; the very man. Can we have a quick word? Excuse us a moment, Bruce.' Ted takes Albie's arm and draws him inside the hospital entrance. 'You'll hear soon enough, but I wanted to tell you face-to-face.'

Ted's tone is the serious one he adopts when about to convey bad news to a patient. Albie feels hollowed out on the instant. He should have been expecting this; grants get withdrawn at short notice. He'll need to apply somewhere else to finish his work, maybe outside London. He is surprised by the sorrow he feels; there'll never be another boss like Ted. What about Beth? His house?

It takes a while for the words to filter through the noise in his head. '. . . a clinician I can trust to step into my shoes when I'm away in the States for a year, starting from January.' Ted is still frowning. 'That gives you three months to finish your thesis and a couple of weeks to settle in before I go.'

Albie's eyes burn. He's not being sacked but rewarded. His heart has begun to beat very fast.

'The thing is . . .' Ted glances over his shoulder; Bruce has followed them in and is studiously reading the lists of consultant names engraved in gold on oak panels at the back of the lobby. Ted moves closer, dropping his voice. 'The thing is, you need to start operating again, for the sake of your career, so you can be ready for, well, let's say for opportunities when they arise.' The blue eyes gleam. 'I don't mention this often and perhaps I should, but I'm proud of you, Albie; you're the kind of guy who will make a difference.' He puts his hand on Albie's shoulder; the wide palm is very warm. 'The truth is you're a brilliant surgeon; innovative. You're hiding your light under a bushel in the lab here.'

Skuld's words echo in his head. She'd relayed exactly what had transpired after all; he should have paid more attention. He ought to have thanked her. He feels light-headed, as if he were somewhere high up and the ground far below his feet. If this locum is to ready him for future opportunities, it tallies with his name being mentioned as the heir to Ted's jobs in the meeting. Opportunities . . . jobs . . . It could mean he'll inherit the lab and the consultancy one day. His career has been planned out by the department already; it's all he can do not to hug Ted and punch the air. His thoughts soar. As a boy he'd gazed at the stars from the cliffs in Jura, convinced he was destined to travel that far; now he will. He'll go further, there's uncharted territory to map, new therapies to create, different viruses to try out. His heart is pounding fiercely, he can feel it in his mouth.

Footsteps ringing on stone pull him back to earth. Bruce is pacing restlessly behind them but Ted is watching Albie, as focused as if dissecting a tumour from the brain.

'Sorry, Ted, I'm a little . . . I didn't expect this. Well, maybe I did. I knew, one day, I hoped, naturally . . .' He is gabbling, scarcely aware of what he is saying, drunk with excitement. He makes himself speak slowly, though his smile is so wide it is difficult to form the words. 'I'd be honoured. I accept, of course. I'll work hard, I won't let you down.'

Ted pumps his hand. 'Do you think I don't know that?' His grins mirrors Albie's. 'Of course you won't let me down.'

But he had let him down once – could Ted have forgotten? A couple of years back when he was still new to the job, he operated on a pituitary tumour to save a patient's sight. Ted had been watching. The optic nerves were tightly stuck to the tumour, like Sellotape binding around an untidy parcel. Albie burnt the small, twisting blood vessels on the surface to ease dissection; keen to impress, he began to hurry. Ted asked him to stop, but, unable to resist one last vessel, larger than the rest, he quickly burnt it through. As he rinsed away the blood, the white surface of the optic nerve appeared, the neatly divided artery lying on its surface. He had destroyed the blood supply of the entire optic pathway; the patient was now completely blind. Ted took over in silence and Albie went home, distraught. He had wrecked a man's life. He would be sued, deservedly struck off. He'd have to leave, sort out a non-clinical career, hospital management perhaps. He was halfway through a bottle of whisky when Ted's anaesthetist phoned up. Owen's gentle voice revealed that Ted had been to see the patient and taken all the blame on himself. The family had understood, forgiven even. There would be no legal action. Albie was expected to operate on a meningioma in the morning.

'You've come a long way.' Ted could be reading his mind. 'I trust you, Albie.' Then, turning towards Bruce, 'We're tossing ideas around over here, Bruce. Come and join us.' Bruce walks towards them, his face set in rigid lines. 'I've been thinking about your PhD on glioblastoma cell lines,' Ted continues cheerfully. 'It could be expanded to cover more ground. Why not use Albie's new virus technology? Come by my office, we'll talk it through.'

Albie tenses; his work. What if Bruce uses it to make his mark, as Skuld intimated? The hare could overtake the tortoise yet; then he relaxes, nodding agreement. Ted has been generous; he can afford to be generous too.

'We'll catch up when you're back in post,' Ted murmurs to Albie. Then, louder, 'Congratulations, both. Make it a swift one.' He walks rapidly away down a corridor.

'I overheard everything – tossing ideas around, my arse.' Bruce stares at him accusingly. 'How the hell did you swing a consultant locum?'

'Cheer up.' Albie claps him on the back, 'You heard what Ted said. Talk to him, use my work if it helps.'

'Don't patronise me. I'm not a fucking child.' Bruce shrugs him off. 'Look, I'm thirsty, can we just go?'

They walk through the garden square in front of the hospital. Papery leaves have drifted into yellow piles that crackle underfoot. Two young women sit on a bench, their faces turned to the sun. An old man in a green woollen hat stretches out on another bench, dozing on a mattress of yellowed newspapers; empty cider bottles litter the grass. They pass the metal statue of a mother holding a child. Albie glances around as if unsure which world is real: Queen Square gardens in the heat of mid-week London or the quiet laboratory behind him, the universe of cells down the microscope.

In the Queens Larder, the airless hum envelops them immediately. They push through a close-packed crowd to the bar, and when their drinks and baguettes arrive they take them outside.

'For someone whose pay packet has just tripled, you seem remarkably calm.' Bruce glares across the wooden table. 'Did you have any idea that this was on the cards?'

The hesitation is fractional. The less Bruce knows about what he overheard, the better. 'No idea at all.'

'Just the hand of fate, then, tapping you on the shoulder . . .' Bruce's eyes track his. Albie gazes at the glowing plane trees in the square and shakes his head, although that's exactly what it had felt like. Bruce stares down into his beer; the anger has gone. He looks miserable.

'Our new lab assistant overheard some chat about you, though,' Albie tells him, relenting. 'Apparently you'll leave a mark.'

'The little blonde?' Bruce looks up. 'I tried my best but I couldn't get very far with her.'

Typical of Bruce to flirt with a young girl. If he'd come across aggressively it would explain a lot. Skuld had been watchful at first, wary even. She might have been anxious he would pounce like Bruce, and then relaxed when he didn't. Unwittingly he'd earned her confidence.

Bruce sips his beer. 'Perhaps I ought to start working more seriously.' He looks thoughtful.

Albie feels a stab of regret at what he'd let slip and then remembers his resolve to be generous. Bruce will be like the meteors he used to watch as a child from those cliffs, a brief trajectory in the night sky then the precipitous fall towards the sea. Bruce's inertia, his very lifestyle will do for him. They chew their baguettes in the warm sunshine. Albie taps a text to Beth:

Promotion. Better things to come. Tell you more this eve. Can't wait. Just us.

4

London. Autumn 2015

Beth turns right out of Belsize Park underground, hurries past the Royal Free Hospital and, following the map on her phone, takes another sharp right downhill into Pond Street. Hampstead Hill Gardens is the first turn to the left. The sudden peace is tangible, the kind of deep quiet that is available only to the very wealthy in a capital city. She could be a hundred miles from her narrow road in East Acton, where the motorbikes roar between lines of cars and rubbish drifts in the gutters. The double-fronted Victorian mansion is halfway down the crescent on the right: Albie's grandparents' home, now his. He lives in the basement, letting the ground floor and two upper storeys to tenants for cash. The curtains are drawn and the imposing house has a bleak, forbidding air.

Albie opens the door seconds after her knock, as if he'd been waiting the other side. He draws her in.

'Welcome.' He kisses her lips, her face, her neck. 'You're here, finally. Finally!'

They've met so far in restaurants and parks for picnics, at the theatre or cinema. She has been elusive when he suggested his flat or hers, wanting an escape at the end of the evening. She has watched as his impatience built, waiting until she was sure of his feelings. Now she is caught too, a little scared.

It's cold in the dark hall, colder than the street; the musty air smells of dog. Envelopes marked with paw prints are beached along the skirting board; a fat black spaniel clatters to meet them, his plumed tail fanning as he noses her leg.

'Poor Harris. I haven't time for a dog but he belonged to my grandparents. At least there's a garden at the back.' Albie's hands stroke the dog's ears and massage his neck; she shivers as though her own skin is being stroked. He takes her hand. 'The kitchen's warm,' and he leads her down the hall, grit crunching underfoot. Harris wheezes as he pushes between them; they follow him through the open door at the end of a corridor, and down steep stairs leading into a hot kitchen. The table is heaped with papers, paintings cram the walls – watercolours of the sea, as far as she can tell in the dim light. Books are stacked in toppling piles on several chairs. A large photograph hangs over the sink: Ted, with his arm thrown around Albie's neck. Ted faces the camera, eyes screwed up as if against the sun; Albie is to one side, head turned towards the taller man. The background is layered cliffs and sea: Dorset. Jenny must have taken the picture. Beth can't ask, of course. Albie has noticed the direction of her gaze; it's too late to pretend she hasn't been looking. He moves closer to the picture.

'A present from Ted. I got it enlarged and framed. We'd just run a race along the shingle near Bridport. Have you ever tried to run on pebbles? He won by a long way. Amazing bloke.' He laughs but she remembers the weight of Ted's arm round her own neck. He probably stood centre stage in their photos too, it's hard to remember; she'd ripped them to shreds the night he left. She turns away, picking up an ornament from the dresser at random. A carved stag, beautifully done though the wooden eyes stare blindly at her and the antlers feel very sharp; she puts it down again.

'My father made that.' He hands her a heavy tumbler of dark gold whisky. 'There are thousands of deer where we grew up in Jura, he was obsessed by them. He ran a deer-stalking business.' He stands so close that their bodies touch, he is trembling. The moment stretches until he gestures at the crowded room, the piles of paper and the stacks of books. 'Sorry about this mess,' he says a little wildly. 'I got back late, I haven't had time to tidy.'

The disorder looks permanent despite his words; he is only noticing now because he sees it with her eyes. He begins to pace between table and stove, pushing up the sleeves of his shirt, clearing papers, stirring pots and lighting candles, recovering his equanimity. He spreads a cloth on the table, smoothing it out with careful hands, large hands that would feel warm and very gentle. She bends to examine his books, afraid her feelings will show on her face. They are mostly poetry, well thumbed. Kathleen Raine, George Mackay Brown. Hugh MacDiarmid. A large leather-bound notebook has been left open on a chair, revealing a sketch of rats asleep in a cage, perfectly executed. She can sense the softness of the fur, almost hear the peaceful breath sounds. She turns pages, glimpsing a human brain dissected, meticulous drawings of lab equipment, mauve and pink cells like a splash of bright art, notes in an italic hand alongside.

'Not very technical, I'm afraid.' Albie looks over her shoulder, spoon in hand. 'Ted says I should design on a Mac but I think better with a pencil in my hands.'

A screen would suit Ted, she can see that, the anonymity of the text, the ease of deletion; there is passion in Albie's pages for research, for his little laboratory animals, for the brain itself. 'These drawings are extraordinary, Albie.'

He blushes. 'Oh, they just help me think about what I'm doing. There's a section further on for operation notes; the plans for research are at the back.'

She flips to the end and sees rows and columns, drawings of equipment, aims outlined, methods discussed; and here and there pencilled rats scurry up the margins or peer from behind a column of numbers.

'Where did it come from, this talent?' She points to a sketch of Bruce in a margin, a tiny likeness of his friend asleep by a microscope.

'My mother.' He draws her to a faded photo stuck to the fridge, standing behind her to point to a slight woman with wild hair, a freckled boy leaning against her. A taller boy plays with a dog nearby, conical mountains rise in the background. A grim-faced man stares out from another photo, his foot on the neck of a dead stag. Albie jabs a finger at his face. 'That's my father. He made us stalk with him, hours of crawling through wet heather, watching and waiting.' He puts his arms round her. 'Mother was different.'

'In what way?' She lets herself lean back; his chin grazes her head as his arms tighten around her. She can feel his heart beating through the cotton, his skin warming hers.

'She was a poet and a painter. Mysterious, like the sea.' He pauses, then, with a little rush, 'You remind me of her.'

'The sea on a sunny day or in a storm?' she asks lightly.

'The dangerous kind. Unpredictable, I was often out of my depth.' She turns at his voice and he stares at her as if trying to penetrate to the deeper, darker places. A moment passes then he laughs and releases her. 'Suppertime.'

He has cooked scallops with fragments of bacon; they taste of summer and the sea. His eyes follow her fork anxiously; when she praises the food, his face relaxes into a smile. 'The scallops are big as eggs on Jura.' He tells her about the island, the beaches, the birds and the deer, about his mother's stories, suffused with ancient magic. He believed everything she said, followed her everywhere. 'I'm still following her in a way. Neurosurgery has its own magic. The more we know about the brain, the more extraordinary it becomes.' He pours wine. His face is bright in the candlelight, flames dance in his eyes. 'We are exploring at the edge of what we know. There are so many discoveries to be made; Ted trusts me to make them with him. It's a thrilling time for me.'

Be careful, she wants to warn him. Don't trust him back. Don't believe his promises; if you do, he'll break your heart.

'Today he asked me to be his locum, while he goes to the States.' Then he laughs, a short, embarrassed laugh. 'The oddest thing happened. Our new lab assistant told me this morning she'd heard them discussing me as his future replacement in the consultants' meeting. I didn't pay much attention, but five minutes later he offered me his locum. I think it means I'm being lined up for the job when he retires.' His colour heightens. 'I can't help feeling fate is smiling on me, that this was meant to be.'

'A scientist, and you believe in fate?'

'My mother did,' he replies, joking and not joking. 'She thought fate was responsible for what you get in life.'

Fate doesn't give you what you want, it usually takes it away. If you want something you have to work for it, suffer for it. Albie's eyes are sunken, his cheeks hollow. He doesn't need fate; beneath the excitement there is a deeper story of duty and routine, early mornings and late nights. Iron self-discipline.

'So now you have to prove yourself to your boss?'

He nods, his eyes shining. 'That's what I want to do more than anything.'

She smiles though her heart clenches. Ted could use that, twist it. Ted is marvellous company, he makes people feel important; they trust him and love him and then he betrays them; he betrayed her as easily as he once did his wife. It could happen to Albie.

She gets up and walks round the table, puts her hand on his shoulder and leans to kiss him. 'I'd love to see more photos of where you grew up.' He takes her hand and they leave the plates on the table and sit on the floor next to the radiator in his bedroom. He wraps a cashmere rug round her shoulders, the wool is motheaten but warm. The gold-leaved pages of the worn photo album are loose, the binding has been chewed by mice; like the cracked leather of the chairs in the kitchen, the threadbare Persian rug and the chipped bone china, everything was good once. She likes this rich shabbiness, its texture and colour. She can hear the echo of old wealth sounding through the darkness and cold; it's as though her long dead grandfather had taken her by the hand and told her it would be all right. Everything would be all right now.

Ted thought the lack of clutter in her flat was restful. He'd told her Jenny's paintings were piled on every surface at home, that the boys' football boots tripped him up and their spaniel got in his way. The emptiness in her flat wasn't a choice, though; her grandfather's wealth had been squandered on parties and drink. She'd watched her aunt's dogged progress through the barren house after her parents' funeral, searching for something to salvage for her niece. Beth had leant against the wall as she watched, nine years old, thumb in her mouth, bereft. Caroline took her in. She was a librarian in Reading and ran an allotment, her life was tranquil. Beth started to heal; as time passed she began to feel happy. There was no money for university so they chose nursing, but in the first term her aunt died, hit by a bus as she cycled to the library. The past sank out of sight, a lost city frozen under ice until Ted hacked his way through; the affair lasted seven years. He left when she was pregnant and went back to his wife; the money for a termination arrived later, online. If she puts a hand on her abdomen, she can still conjure the low-down burning anger that pulled her through.

She leans against Albie as he talks, carried by the flow of words which slide together with the ease of a song. She follows his finger as he traces the map stuck into the front of the album: Jura, a long island cut almost in two by the sea, off the west coast of Scotland, above Islay, below Mull. The deer-stalking business ended with his father's death, the estate passing to Jamie, the elder brother who spent lavishly to turn the house into a hotel. The weather was bad for three summers, debts accumulated. They had to sell everything except Dunbar, the gamekeeper's lodge, the last house on the track to the north. He points to a square white building facing the sun and the sea, the windows flung wide open. She bends to look more closely; the sounds of the wind and the waves would wash through those sunny rooms. When her parents died, the police discovered her in the flat two days later on her own in the dark. Silence can frighten her still.

'I promised Mother I'd keep Dunbar but I can't afford the repairs, it's becoming run-down. The locum will help, thanks to Ted.' Then he smiles, pointing to the smudges of brown and gold behind the house. 'See that bracken? If we were there now, we'd hear the stags bellowing.'

'Do stags bellow?'

'It's autumn, the rutting season has started. They warn off competitors.' He puts a hand on her thigh and leans to kiss her, 'Battling for a mate.'

She puts her hand over his, making her decision. 'You don't have to battle.'

She wakes later, her face stiff with cold. The slippery eiderdown is on the floor. She moves closer to Albie's sleeping warmth. He stirs and pulls her to him. 'If you were a dream, you have just come true,' he murmurs. Their mouths touch and open.

Later, he pulls on a plaid dressing gown and pads out; she moves to lie in his place, sliding her legs downwards in the warmth. She feels different, lighter, as if she has put down something heavy she'd been carrying for a long time. When Albie returns, he hands her a cup of coffee and begins to talk while she leans her head on his shoulder. He describes his research, and how that will shape his future, how the locum has focused his thoughts. He tells her that he loves her.

As she listens, possibilities unfold in her mind, like the fresh sheets she spreads out for her patients, ready for any weight, any wound. Every now and again, she turns to press her lips against his shoulder, as if to know him by the texture and taste of his skin, as if to assess the resilience of his flesh.

5

London. Winter 2015

'Hey guys, coffee or tea?' Owen leans against the wall of the small coffee room, as relaxed as usual, despite the long list of patients still to anaesthetise. Albie thinks of surfers whenever he looks at Owen, or a child's version of Jesus. The man's serenity is famous; Ted has been known to refuse to operate on difficult cases without him. The red lips smiling through the dark beard recall the edges of a wound made by an imprecise knife. Albie glances away; too much operating, too many incisions, each lipped by bloody skin.

'Tea, please, Owen.'

'Coffee,' Ted raps out.

A routine morning in neuro theatre; the operations have gone smoothly. Ted has just implanted an electrode in the brain of a patient with Parkinson's disease; he paces restlessly while the position is checked in the scan.

Owen hands tea to Albie and then gives Ted a mug of dense black coffee, downed instantly. Albie inhales the smoky scent rising from his cup; it takes him back to childhood, always. Jura. Ten years old, drinking the tea his mother brought to the garden at five every day. Gulls crying, waves slapping on rocks, his body sprawled on grass, tingling with anticipation for the life ahead. No one knew why he was so different from Jamie. His father had watched, baffled, as he grabbed at opportunities like a starving child for food; only his mother recognised he was going about his destiny. He passed everything, won everything, but there is one more prize to claim. He closes his eyes and presses his fingertips together as if praying. Beth slips behind his eyelids, exquisite, mysterious as if guarding secrets. There are places he can't go; beyond childhood her past seems fenced and she the elusive guardian at the gate. She is loving, though, attentive; no one else listens to his plans with such intensity or understands the demands on him so well. Her wisdom is astonishing. Her beauty takes his breath away, always. People turn to stare in corridors and down streets. It's difficult to let her go, difficult to get out of bed. They make love all night sometimes. He's never felt like this before; it frightens him. He'd marry her tomorrow but she needs more time, it's only been six months. He'll ask her in the spring, everything begins in the spring. His mother's emerald engagement ring is waiting at home in the silk-lined box he bought specially from Cartier's.

'Twenty minutes to go,' Owen warns, closing the door quietly behind him as he leaves to check the patient in the scan.

Ted paces up and down the small room, watching

the clock. The constant movement distracts Albie; it must disturb Jenny, though Owen has told him they live mostly apart. There have been rumours of a long-standing affair which ended after Albie arrived; a needy woman with a relentless streak, so the gossip went, though no one knew her name. None of this is his business, but he wonders, as Ted turns and turns again, how you can think yourself immune from discovery or punishment. Why risk the loss of wife and family, everything you treasure? Some men cheat all the time, perhaps they like the risk. Beth's body had been warm against his this morning; risking anything would be unthinkable.

'God, how I hate this,' Ted mutters as he walks back and forth, glancing at Albie.

'It'll be fine, Ted.'

'As I tell myself, but there could have been a blood vessel we didn't see. He could be haemorrhaging into his cerebrum right now.' Ted's hands ball in the pockets of the blue cotton trousers.

'You make decisions based on the evidence to hand. It's all anyone can ever do.'

Ted flashes him an exasperated look.

'There were no obvious vessels in the way,' Albie continues, smiling. 'There won't be a problem.' The electrode was perfectly placed, what follows has become a routine miracle. The patient's tremor will be abolished. He will be able to drink a cup of tea, walk across the room. Sleep.

'There's always the risk of the unexpected, don't forget that while you're quoting my words back at me.' But the pacing has slowed, the hands unclench. Ted grins back. 'Sit down, Albie, you look exhausted.' He indicates the small red sofa. The base sags, sacking hangs down to the floor and the cushions are thin, but Albie sits with a little groan of relief, his back aching after hours of assisting Ted, who seems tireless.

'I'm leaving for the States shortly so I need to tell you about Viromex Pharmaceuticals, the US company.' Ted draws up a chair and sits facing him. 'It's been a few months since I submitted our varicella virus patent to the patent agent.' Ted runs his hand over his hair. Albie stares. *Our* patent? 'My name was on the application along with yours, as co-inventor,' Ted continues smoothly. 'The patent itself is owned by the university, but I think you knew this already.'

He nods, hiding surprise. He didn't realise Ted would claim to be co-inventor. Ted knows that he, Albie, is entitled to sole ownership of the patent. He modified the virus, after all. A few seconds tick by; his mind flicks back to the pituitary tumour operation, the cut artery, the spiralling guilt, the way he was saved. He can trust Ted. He waits.

'The patent agent has done a search; there's nothing as specific out there which also stimulates an immune response.' Ted leans forward. 'The university has pitched the concept to Viromex. We'll get a deal, a bloody good one.' He pauses, a punchline is coming. 'They say they'll give us an upfront payout of two hundred and fifty thousand; quarter goes to the university; we receive the rest. I get sixty per cent, you have forty.' He smiles, a disarming flash of blue eyes and white teeth.

Albie calculates swiftly: his share will amount to seventy-five thousand pounds: more money in one lump sum than he's ever dreamt of possessing. This will have been the best deal Ted could obtain on his behalf; it doesn't matter if they receive different sums, not really. He's grateful, of course he is. A cure is in sight which will now reach thousands; to be an author of that, so early in his career, would be extraordinary.

'Fantastic news, Ted.'

'We're at an early stage. Viromex haven't signed the contract yet.' Ted's tone has become businesslike. 'We'll need to run dosing studies to find the best concentration of virus for tumour shrinkage. Bruce can do those now you're back on the wards. Once Viromex sign, the money is released to us when we hand over results of those studies, and the patent, of course. They'll run their own checks after that, then the trial in children will start, probably in Boston Children's Hospital.' He leans back, grinning. 'This will be huge, Albie. There is no known cure for this bloody disease, no prospect of survival for the affected children beyond seven months. It will be taken up in a flash.'

Albie pictures the little girl he saw on the ward round earlier today, the lovely child he had first met in Ted's clinic three months ago, with her fairy wings and missing tooth. Her mother had been hunched over the bed this morning, her father standing against the wall, weeping. The sheet was barely tented over her body, her skin was yellow, her breathing shallow. She was dying. Cured of her brainstem tumour, that little girl would gain weight and sit up; in time she would get out of bed and walk from the ward, holding her parents' hands.

'Looking ahead, the royalties could be impressive too.' Ted glances round the room, checking they are still alone. 'Each treatment will cost twenty-five thousand pounds; let's say there are a thousand cases a year, that's a potential income for Viromex of twenty-five million.'

Albie tries to keep the shock from his face. It seems obscene, though he's not sure quite why. Drug companies need profits – it's a job, after all, a business.

'The university take their share of the royalty; we divide the rest,' Ted continues. 'Your portion of our share will be around seven hundred and fifty thousand every year.'

The money seems unreal; far more than he would earn in a year, even at the height of his career. He tries to visualise it as notes on the table in front of him, set out in straight-edged towers, like those stacked by criminals in gangster movies, but all he can see is the little girl turning to wave goodbye at the door of the ward. Other children will follow her; children who now face certain death will survive because of his work.

Ted takes a sip of coffee, 'I've been appointed to Viromex's scientific advisory board for the purposes of the viral trial,' he says, watching him over the rim of his cup.

The swift dart of jealousy surprises Albie; he would have relished that role. Beth will tell him it could have helped his career. He takes a mouthful of tepid tea and swallows it down. He'll have to explain that he owes Ted the chance of research in his lab, and for the locum that's about to start; he'll tell her if it wasn't for him he'd be in hospital management now. He owes Ted everything.

'. . . plenty more viruses for the lab to try out.' Ted is nodding encouragingly. 'You're good at developing ideas, Albie; the pharmacology world is keen to buy them.'

Ideas bought and sold, like tea or coffee. It never occurred to him that his thoughts would have a monetary value. He is used to the performance of being a doctor, of being rewarded for all the exhausting ways in which his energy and stamina are used; to be paid for ideas seems too easy, like cheating.

'We could be rich, given time, very rich,' Ted says quietly, so quietly he could be talking to himself. Then he smiles. 'First things first. We'll have to wait for Viromex's signature on the contract and those dosing studies. It could take a year before payout, but don't worry—'

Ted's phone rings and he turns away, mobile to his ear. Albie looks out of the small window which gives a view of the back wall of the hospital kitchens, lined with great waste bins, boxes and crates of rubbish. Complex systems of chimneys and pipes run against the walls; prefab units are jammed among Victorian brickwork. The intricate working parts of the system, hidden from sight and dark with grime.

Rich: the word has a glow to it, like a bar of gold. Ted has always been astute. He put a bungalow in the garden of his Bristol house and sold both when he moved to London. Owen confided that the sum had been eye-watering. Ted mostly lives in the Chelsea penthouse and holidays in Greece; Jenny stays at the cottage in Dorset. They have found what works for them. Albie stares down at his hands, remembering the silky feel of Beth's skin this morning, wondering how it's possible to live apart from the woman you love. He never aimed for wealth but all the same, the bar of gold wedges open a door in his mind through which the future glitters. One day he could pay for a laboratory and then what he invents will belong to him. It doesn't matter if Ted gets more now, his turn will come. He learnt that as a child; the slow crawl on his belly over heather during the stalking season, the hours of watching for an opportunity, the way time is defeated by patience.

Ted has finished his phone call. 'I'll get Bruce to start the dosing studies; he'll need to order the delivery of rats and obtain more viral supplies.'

Albie opens his eyes and smiles, scarcely hearing. Dunbar will be safe now; he can restore the Hampstead house too, recreate a home for a family as it was in his grandparents' time. Through the door of the future, Beth is picking roses in a garden, his children fly kites on the Heath.

'So what do I need to do?' he asks Ted.

'All fine,' Owen sings from the door, 'We're good to go, folks.'

Ted gets up; Albie rises too. Ted takes a fraction longer to straighten his spine. He is taller by half a head but Albie has the width, his hands are bigger.

The men look at each other, Ted smiles. 'I'll organise everything. Trust me.'

6

London. Spring 2016

A web is stretched across the footlights, intricate, shimmering.

What's it supposed to be? The worldwide web? The deep one? The dark one?

Arachne and Anansi gossip in the wings, old friends. The orchestra tunes up.

Shelob and Aragog come on dancing; the audience roar.

Three hooded figures in black enter and walk from side to side, unfurling skeins of silky stuff.

Oh for God's sake, the audience murmurs. We want dialogue, costumes. A script. We want to know where we are.

It's late by the time Albie finishes his operating list. Three months into the locum and he is still going carefully, meticulous with every stitch, noting down operations in his leather book, an aide-memoire for the future. Tonight he's meeting Beth at Quaglino's; the box with the ring is in his jacket pocket. Her text comes through as he is hurrying down the hospital steps, struggling into his jacket and still clutching his book. She's been asked to cover the night shift; they will have to meet tomorrow instead. She's sorry and sends love but the disappointment is sharp, like a slap. He pushes the ring further down in his pocket; tomorrow then, he'll ask her tomorrow. He texts a cancellation for the dinner but as he walks slowly past the Institute, he hesitates. Bruce will be in the lab, amusing if irritating, and full of the latest gossip, but up on level ten the labs are empty. Bruce has gone home and isn't answering his mobile. Albie turns to go, catching a flicker of movement round the corner of the corridor. His pulse quickens: intruders. Porters man the desk at the entrance but someone could have slipped through. The door to the animal room is ajar. He tiptoes to the lab, glancing at the walls and ceilings – no CCTV – Bridget and her economies. At the door he pauses, heart thumping. Animal rights protesters can be violent; he takes out his phone ready to take photographs or call the police, then peers cautiously into the room.

'Skuld!'

She is bending over a cage and lifts her head unsmiling, unsurprised. She looks different from her daytime self; her hair is loose around her face, she's wearing a short dress in some semi-transparent material. A brown satchel is slung across her chest and a jacket over her arm.

'When I got home, I couldn't remember if I'd fastened the cage properly.' Her voice is as calm and lilting as he remembers. 'I had, though.' There is a faint bloom of pink along her pale cheeks but she regards him steadily.

'You could have phoned the porter and saved yourself a journey.' His heart slows and he puts his phone back in his pocket.

'It was my fault,' she says simply. 'I had to deal with it.'

Not every lab assistant would have bothered. He smiles at her; she looks vulnerable in that flimsy dress, one small hand on the metal bars of the cage. It occurs to him he has never yet thanked her, the harbinger of his good fortune.

'I wonder – I mean, if you've got nothing better to do, perhaps you'd let me take you for a drink?'

'I'm meeting my sisters in the pub over the way.' A smile flickers over her face; she adjusts the strap of her satchel and pulls on her jacket. 'Come if you like.'

The Queen's Larder is hot. She slips her jacket off again as she sits; her bare arms gleam amid the pressing crowds. He puts his coat on the chair and notebook on the table while he orders cider at the bar for her, beer for himself. Her sisters haven't arrived yet.

'I owe you thanks.' He hands her the cider and sits opposite. 'You told me what was said at that consultant meeting; you were spot on, as it happens. The Prof repeated everything you overheard, word for word. I'm doing his locum now, which I take as a good omen.' He smiles at her across the table, feeling relaxed for the first time that day. He'd forgotten her air of stillness, the sense of calm she projects. 'So how's life in the lab?'

'Okay. The people are nice.'

He probes gently. He discovers she lives in Finsbury Park and swims most weekends in the ladies' pond on Hampstead Heath with her sisters, even in winter. They own a menagerie of animals; it started with the school rats she brought home in the holidays. They have something in common then, he tells her. He looked after the rats at school too, medical school in Glasgow. He spent a year monitoring their stress for a project. She smiles when he describes the lab manager, a tough cookie called Hilary, as unrelenting to him as she was to her three little girls, who clustered round his desk to watch him work while they waited for their father to take them home.

'Well, well, well.'

He spins round, meeting the sardonic expression of a tall woman with thick grey hair piled high in a loose knot. Her lean face seems familiar. As she bends to kiss Skuld he remembers why: she was one of the waitresses serving food at Ted's party.

'Verdandi,' murmurs Skuld, sipping her cider.

He pulls a chair out for her and introduces himself. Verdandi nods coolly. 'I know who you are.'

He returns to the bar to buy her a cider as well,

watching as a third woman joins the group, small, plump and laughing, shedding scarves and jangling bracelets. The three heads move close together, lemon blond, pale grey and now fiery red. He orders another cider.

'Sorry for crashing your party. I'm Albie.' He distributes the drinks, then leans to shake the redhead's hand. She stares. 'Gosh, do people really still do that?'

He withdraws his hand and sits down, discomforted.

'I'm Urth.' The brown eyes mock him. 'Pronounced earth, as in salt of the. I saw you at that party.' As she reaches for her glass, her bracelets slide back and reveal a little mouse, inked in red on the base of her thumb.

'Ah. The mark of the sisterhood.' He smiles.

She ignores him, lifting her glass. 'To freedom.' A few heads turn but the sisters seem unaware; they are focused on each other as they clink glasses. Perhaps they do this every evening, celebrating the moment of release at the end of the day. That sense of freedom hardly registers with him nowadays as he hurries down the streets into the underground, heading home to write up his PhD until the early hours.

'What's this then?' Urth spots his notebook and begins to turn the pages with stubby fingers; her tone is amused but her cat-like eyes are avid.

'Oh, records and plans, that sort of thing. Boring

stuff, really.' His face burns as he reaches for the book and slips it on his lap. He doesn't want her making fun of his drawings. 'So Skuld told me one of you works with animals and one of you in the kitchen—'

'I'm the cook.' Urth opens her coat to reveal a striped apron underneath. She laughs, a sexy, low-pitched chuckle. 'Very scientific.'

'So . . . you both work in the lab?'

She shakes her head, grinning at his confusion. 'No, that's Verdandi. I work in the kitchen, producing food for the consultants' meetings and their personal events. And I run a little cake-making company on the side. We deliver, since you ask.'

'All this on your own?' he asks, surprised out of his awkwardness.

'My sisters help when they can. Mum chips in. Chips – that's a joke.' Her sisters smile too, watching him.

Is it all a joke? 'Sorry, I thought Skuld said your mother—'

'Works with animals?' Verdandi interrupts. 'She does. A woman of many talents, our mother. Baking's her hobby; what do you do for fun?'

He hasn't thought of fun for a while. It was his brother's word, not his; it belongs back in childhood and disappeared when Jamie left, along with surfboards and music, outrageous clothes and crowds of people. *Fun* recalls the fairs their mother took them to as little boys; it has a taste as sweet and brief as candyfloss.

'I play squash.' Though not now that Ted's away. He won't mention Beth either; they'll turn that into a joke. It's hard to think of anything unconnected to work. 'I go for runs. I went to the theatre a few months back, but most nights I'm on the wards or writing up my research . . .' His voice trails off. They are looking at him with pity.

'Make cakes,' Urth says. 'More fun.' She moves closer until their shoulders touch. When she opens her mouth he can see the glint of a piercing through the point of her tongue. 'We're going out for some fun now, come with us.'

He could swear there is a feather-light touch on his leg, like the brush of a small foot. Around him the noise in the pub coalesces in an unpleasant roar of sound. Something dark seems to hover in the air. People look round at the scrape of the chair as he stands. The sisters stare up at him as if he were an amusing spectacle at the zoo, and no doubt he is being ridiculous.

'Past your bedtime?' Verandi's eyebrows rise on her forehead; they are thin and grey like the tails of tiny animals.

'Forgive me.' He blushes. 'I've just clocked the time. I'm meeting a friend . . . supper . . .' His lies stumble on. 'We must do this again.'

He walks to the door with his book, conscious that their heads are close together again; he hears laughter. The cold air calms him. How stupid he's been. He's dog-tired; the day has been exhausting – a pint of beer and he feels threatened by a bunch of girls. All the same, as he hurries down the road, he is conscious of a sense of danger looming somewhere just out of sight. In the station, the sleepy pigeons flutter from his feet and swoop low over the track. The birds in Jura come to mind, the sea eagles that fly over the waves looking for prey, their great wings casting wide shadows on the water as they skim the surface.

7

Jura. Late Spring 2016

A mass of black hair moves sluggishly in the water, the strands separate as the waves bring it forward and close together when tugged back. Beth dips her fingers in the icy foam. The strands are slimy, fibroid. Seaweed, not hair. The ring on her finger flashes, a fragment of green ice refracted in underwater sunshine; the gold band above it sparkles. She wipes her hands on her shorts and shoves them deep in the pockets. She won't tell Albie. He would smile and ask how human hair could possibly come to be floating in the tide at her feet. She kicks the dark hank aside, disliking the way it clings round her legs. A couple of dead fish lie at the edge of the water; the eyes have gone and nests of flies are busy in the sockets. Albie is further down the beach, stretched out on a ledge of rock in the heat. He hasn't moved for ten minutes; one arm is over his eyes, the elbow pointing skywards. He looks at home, moulded to the landscape.

Harris noses at dried seaweed and coils of rope at the back of the beach; behind him the jagged rocks rise to an overhang of grass and heather. A bright strip of gorse straggles near the edge where a tree clings to the top of the cliff, bent by the wind, the trunk soft and green with lichen. The Paps, Jura's central mountains, loom distantly. Her face had been wet with sweat when they climbed them yesterday, her feet sliding on scree, but Albie had pulled her on. At the top he showed her the empty moorland stretching to the sea, the small white crofts dotted along the shore and clustered around inlets, with Dunbar further up the coast on its own. The land rose and fell, patterned with shadow and pocked by inland lochs; uninhabited islands were scattered off the coast and across the sea, the mountains on the mainland were faintly visible, purpled by distance. A vast landscape inside which her world had narrowed to the hot clasp of his hand.

A curlew treads at the foamy edge, one curled foot held high as the downward-sloping beak probes the sand. The warm air carries its watery cry above the thud and suck of the ocean. A tern swoops low, wheels, then comes back at her fast, the wings beating close to her face. She holds herself very still. The cold surf swirls over her feet, as lacy as a wedding dress, though hers had been quite plain, a sleeveless white shift bought in a hurry online. Albie had been in a rush, keen to take her to his island home as his wife. Their home, he had corrected himself, a place where they could escape. A place for children. They had known each other for six months and been engaged for one – why wait any longer?

Children. Her heart had swollen with hope but a shiver ran over her skin, like the tremor of water in a passing wind; could she risk loss another time? She smiled and agreed to everything. This was a time for happiness; nothing must get in the way.

They were married a month later, Owen and his wife Elsa came as witnesses. Owen's beard tickled as he kissed her; the beads strung into Elsa's blond locks clicked and swung merrily when she hugged Beth, but Gus, their two-year-old, cried loudly throughout the service. Owen threw rose petals over them on the steps of the registry office afterwards, but it was raining and the petals melted to brown scraps underfoot. The weather was cold for late May, her sleeveless dress had been a mistake. People stared. The rain, like the child's incessant sobbing, seemed unlucky, a bad omen, though Albie smiled all day, gripping her hand like a prize he'd just won and didn't dare relinquish. They took the train to Glasgow then drove to Kennacraig, caught the ferry to Islay and another to Jura, the skies clearing as they arrived. A good omen at last to set against the bad. Dunbar was waiting, the white walls bright in the sun. She stumbled from the car into warm air scented with grass and salt; he led her across the lawn and through a gate where a path wound steeply downwards to the beach, narrow between high banks, quiet and shaded with ferns. When they emerged on to shingle with the seabirds wheeling above, it was as though they had entered a cathedral of light and song. He spun her round until she was giddy. A sense of happiness and luck enveloped her; she felt married then.

The tern moves away, hovers over the breakers and dives, hovers again. When she reaches Albie, she lies down next to him, sliding her hand under his, settling her face against the rough linen of his shirt. He wakes and grips her hand, holding it against his heart.

'I dreamt about you.' He tucks his chin down, staring at her.

'What was I doing?'

He doesn't answer but kisses her fingertips, one by one.

'What was I doing?' She slips her free hand under his shirt, and watches his pupils dilate in her shadow.

'You were in the sea a long way out, struggling on your own.' His voice is strained. 'It seemed real. Promise me you'll never swim by yourself.'

If it was real, he must have glimpsed her past and not the future; as a child she had wandered into the surf on her own, while her parents lay sleeping on the sand, their empty bottles strewn around them. She was up to her neck by the time a passing stranger hauled her out.

'It's hot. I want to swim now.' She frees her hand, takes off her shirt and lies back to push down her shorts. She is wearing nothing underneath her clothes; he stares down at her, surprise and desire flitting over his face. She smiles. 'If you're worried by your dream, you'll have to come with me.'

He sits up to take off his shirt and bends to kiss her right breast, taking her nipple gently in his mouth. His tongue is warm. He lifts her from the rocks to the sand and carries her into the sea till they are waist deep, then sets her down gently as if she were a bottle of wine that he doesn't want to spill. The water is shockingly cold. They swim the length of the beach diving under the waves, the noise thundering in her ears. Seals bob up to watch, disappear then resurface metres away, their dog-like faces placid. After a while the chill seems to enter her bones and she comes out, struggling to find her feet in the surf. She sits on the pebbles wrapped in a towel; Harris pushes his sandy body against her and the shuddering gradually slows. Albie stays in the water for another hour.

Later they drive to the hotel in Craighouse for lunch, leaving Harris at home. The hotel faces the shore, next to the distillery. The air smells of peaty alcohol, as if the molecules themselves were saturated in whisky. Stone bungalows line the road facing the sea. A couple of freckled little boys lean against the village store, balancing on bikes; their fair hair shines in the sun as they suck ice lollies and stare at Beth. Three men in overalls stroll to the quayside from the shop, sandwiches in hand, while a group of tourists in bright anoraks troop into the distillery. She watches them disappear into darkness, glad that she isn't one of them. She has a home on the island, she belongs here now, an insider.

In the hotel reception a round-faced woman with a

wide frizz of grey hair is writing in a red file; she looks up when they come in, her eyes widen comically, then, whipping off half-moon glasses, she comes forward to grasp Albie's hands. 'Well now, I heard you were here.' She stands on tiptoe to kiss him and steps back, eyebrows raised, smiling at Beth.

'Iona, this is Beth, my wife. Darling, Iona. She keeps an eye on Dunbar when we're away; she's in charge of pretty much everything on the island.'

Iona laughs, shaking her head. 'Welcome to Jura, Beth.' The hug is scented with jasmine. 'Congratulations.' She turns to Albie. 'Your father would have been so happy. Dunbar has been empty for too long; people have been enquiring if it's for sale—'

'It isn't; I thought you knew that.' There is an unfamiliar edge to Albie's voice.

'Of course I know that, dear, but it could do with a bit of money spending on it. There are gaps in the roof where the tiles have been blown off. The window sills are rotting. I can see why people think it's been abandoned. Now, what do you think, Albie?'

'What do I think?' Albie's eyebrows descend, his lips tighten. 'I think we'd be extraordinarily lucky if there was any money at all to spare for repairs.'

'Well, we're lucky with the weather.' Beth slips her hand into Albie's. 'We went swimming by the house this morning.'

'You'll be hungry then.' Iona nods, her eyes meeting Beth's with the ghost of a wink. 'Follow me.'

It's early in the season; she leads them through a forest of empty tables to a place by the window. Beth leans her head against the glass; while they were talking to Iona a summer squall has blown up. The sun is still strong but rain is pattering against her cheek the other side of the pane. The fronds of the palm tree outside are moving in the wind and the wire is slapping against the flagpole on the lawn. A large boat stirs at anchor by the end of a stone pier over to the right. Men load casks on to a crane that lifts the heavy barrels on deck; they work stolidly on in the rain. The wet air is luminous. A rainbow stretches across the sky. Albie hasn't noticed. He's studying the menu, deep lines between his eyebrows. The exchange with Iona has worried him. Some deal Ted arranged with a drug company to buy Albie's virus patent seems to have come to nothing – like all Ted's promises, though Albie doesn't know that yet. Beth reaches to touch his hand across the table. Albie looks up and smiles, covering her hand with his.

'Have the fish. It's simple and good, like everything Iona does. People come back, the walkers and birdwatchers, year after year.' He looks around the room at the modest furniture, the jars of spring flowers and the sepia photos on the wall of the island a hundred years ago. 'Jamie overreached himself with his grand schemes. The jet set didn't like the island, they didn't understand it. It's true the magic doesn't reveal itself easily; it creeps under your skin gradually, if you let it.'

After lunch, Albie settles the bill and chats to Iona while she wanders down the village street on her own. The rain has stopped, a hard light glints off the sea facing the bungalows. It would be easy to feel trapped here; the view from those windows would be full of ocean day after day after day. The dancing light and endless waves could drive you mad. She understands those rich guests of Jamie's who never came back; the magic is hidden from her too. The sea seems to glimmer with menace. In the distance, a boat struggles against the wind, the sail blown full, listing to one side. Just then Albie comes out of the hotel, waves cheerfully to her and walks to the shop. She hurries after him. Inside the door, postcards in a rack show the hotel, the ferry and deer on a beach. She picks the deer card for Gus while the hard-eyed blonde in tight overalls watches her closely from the till.

'Why is she looking at me?' she whispers to Albie, half amused, half irritated. 'Does she think I'm going to steal her cards?'

Albie reaches for coffee on a shelf. 'She probably thinks you're a film star.' He kisses her. 'I'm surprised you're not used to it.' He puts the jar in the basket and, humming, bends to examine wine in a rack on the floor. She is used to it. Glances, smiles and whistles have been a backdrop to life since she was thirteen, but this woman seems hostile, as though Beth is an imposter who doesn't belong here. She drops the card into the basket and takes Albie's arm.

On the return drive, Albie points out a wide scoop of sandy beach where the island's young men embarked for America a century before. Some were boys, little boys. Times were hard, their mothers knew they'd never come back. On dark nights, he tells her, the islanders hear the sound of sobbing, dead mothers crying for the children they'd lost. He is intent on the story and doesn't notice she's stopped talking. He brakes and suggests a walk on the beach but his phone rings so she clambers alone across the rocky foreshore, removing her shoes on the sand. He stays in the car; when she looks back he waves, phone to his ear.

The sun is lower in the sky now; the feathered clouds are underlit with crimson like the ragged edge of a bruise. The wet sand is cold under her feet. It's safe to let tears come. It would have been better if she could have cried at the moment of loss, like the island mothers. It might have made it more real. The bleeding was real and the pain, but not the small body on the sheets, the translucent fingers moving as though in a slight wind. A tiny daughter, born too early; alive then not alive, slipping invisibly between worlds. She'd wrapped her in white for the funeral. Two years ago; the wicker coffin would have rotted now, along with the transparent skin and delicate bones. The only place her baby exists is in a space in her mind. Beth wipes her cheeks; she must pull herself together, the suffering is done. She must push the past down, nail boards on top, walk away. Up ahead Albie has finished his phone call and is coming to meet her; even from here she can see he is smiling. She begins to run across the sand towards him and as they collide he wraps his arms round her. She presses her cold face into his neck. She will be happy; they will be happy. They'll make another child, her heart will heal. They walk back to the car entwined.

Albie starts the engine and, taking her hand, begins to whistle. He drives fast and seems excited, glancing at her and smiling as he drives. She lifts his hand to her lips. It's too late to share her secrets now, far too dangerous. Outside tussocks of grass and darker clumps of heather line the road, beyond them stretch the hills and valleys; the flat surfaces of ponds and lochs are revealed then left behind as the car passes. The colours are clear after the rain. The past slips underwater again.

The road ends and they bump forward on the stony track to the north, lurching from side to side until Dunbar comes into view, glowing white through the dusk. Harris, let out, disappears around the back, barking loudly. A moment later a couple of deer bound from behind the house, float over the fence and run across the track and the field beyond to the trees. They are followed a second later by a large stag. He moves more slowly, jumps with ease, then stops on the track to look back at her. The deep gaze is neither hostile nor interested; he seems simply to be absorbing her image. His antlers tilt against the sky, he turns and trots after his does.

'I was beginning to think there were no deer here,' she whispers, elated.

'They outnumber us by thousands but they're clever at hiding.' Albie stares at the woods where the deer have vanished. 'My father came here with his stalkers, hunting them down.'

The wind has freshened and the pines behind the house are bending and swaying in the dusk; the sea crashes against the cliffs beyond the garden. Her bare arms are covered in goosebumps. Albie puts his jacket round her and leads her inside.

He kneels to light the kindling in the grate in the little sitting room off the kitchen, the dry tinder crackling as it catches. As she draws the curtains against the gathering shadows, the room springs into warm focus. There are two deep armchairs in front of the fire and a sofa in faded blue linen. An old axe with a worn handle leans against a pile of logs in a basket next to the fireplace. Wooden deer decorate the mantelpiece. The light from the leaping flames gilds the spines of the books packed into alcoves either side of the grate: a tattered set of children's encyclopaedias, manuals on fishing, a hardback of *Legends of the Western Isles*, a dog-eared Raymond Chandler. She draws out *Treasure Island* in its torn orange jacket, blows the dust from the top and settles in the armchair to read by the fire, quickly immersed in the familiar story.

'What do you think about us coming here whenever we feel like it?'

'Jamie comes here too, doesn't he?' she murmurs, reading.

'We could buy him out.'

'Maybe. One day, if we can afford it.' She glances up reluctantly, her finger keeping her place on the page.

He gets to his feet, brushing splinters from his trousers. He is smiling. 'It was Ted on the phone earlier.'

'He couldn't leave us alone on our honeymoon?' She swallows anger. Ted has Albie on a piece of string which he can twitch whenever he wants.

'He was keen we should know the good news.' His voice trembles with excitement. 'The contract has been signed off between Viromex and the university today.'

'What does that actually mean, Albie?'

'Viromex are now committed to buying the patent for my virus.' The smiles broadens. 'Our money could arrive soon, seventy-five thousand pounds!'

'I think he's teasing you.' Cruel of Ted to dangle money in front of Albie, a promise made to be broken. Albie doesn't know that Ted breaks his promises.

'Ted doesn't tease. He believes in me; he extended my locum by another five months today. You don't know him like I do, sweetheart.'

The logs spit, the flames leap high in the grate. She sees Ted in her flat, in her bed, talking to Jenny on the phone, lying again and again. The day he left for the last time, he promised to return even as he hurried away. Perhaps Albie is right and she doesn't know him, never really knew him; perhaps such knowledge between people is a fantasy. No one gives every secret away – she glances at Albie's radiant face – not even to the people you love, especially not them.

'Look. He sent the contract through, it's on my phone.' Albie bends to show her the document from the CEO of Viromex on his iPhone. The offer is headed and couched in official language, signed and stamped.

'What happens next?'

'Bruce has to complete some dosing studies, then Viromex take it over and give us that first payment.' He paces about the room, his eyes shining. 'When the treatment becomes available, my share of the royalty could be seven hundred and fifty thousand, every year.'

'It seems unreal.' She is wary rather than glad, still suspicious. 'It's so much to take in all at once.'

'Isn't it great? When Ted confirmed it today, I knew I had to tell you here, in this house, with champagne. That's why I drove back like a maniac.'

He goes into the kitchen whistling; she hears the clink of glasses, the sucking pop of a cork being pulled. 'I'll arrange for the repairs to be done here first,' he calls out joyfully, 'then book the builders in to turn the Hampstead house back into a proper home.'

The stone floor, the bookshelves, the splintery pile

of logs next to the armchair are as they were a few minutes ago but something else has entered the room with them, like a sail blown tight, bulging in her face. The world lists. What have Ted's words set in motion? Everything could be at risk. Albie comes back and hands her a foaming glass.

'Can we afford the conversions in London, Albie, as well as repairs here? The money might not cover everything.'

'We'll only be converting the London house back to what it was, it won't be that expensive. I'll take out a mortgage until the first payment comes through.' He sips his champagne. 'Ted's flat is amazing; I'd love you to see it. He won't mind if we copy his ideas.'

She would, though. Ted's flat is like a stage set filled with costly furniture; no one sits on the large sofas or plays the grand piano, there is expensive art on the walls but no photos. The kitchen is like an operating theatre.

'. . . the rest of the house can be bedrooms. Enough for a whole family of children.'

She stands to take one of the carved deer from the mantelpiece, touching the wooden head for luck. 'What if the lump sum doesn't come through, Albie?'

'You saw the contract. Of course it'll come through. The mortgage will tide us over until then. Ted will retire eventually; once I land his job, my salary will increase.'

'You seem very certain of his job.'

'This locum makes me the obvious candidate, especially now it's been extended.'

She replaces the stag. 'You work hard, Albie, you're a good surgeon; that's why you got the locum and why he wants you to stay on. The consultant job is different. It's not his to bequeath even if he wanted to.'

'I was discussed as his replacement at that consultants' meeting, remember?' He takes her hand. 'And then I'm lucky.' He kisses her palm. 'The luckiest guy in the world.'

'You aren't listening.' She pulls her hand away. 'You have to be careful, we need to be safe.'

'The value of the house will increase when we upgrade, there's no risk. You mustn't worry, darling. I know how to be careful, unlike Jamie.'

That wasn't the kind of careful she meant; she didn't just mean money. Life takes things away from you, the most important things. It took her child. Albie has no idea how careful he needs to be.

After supper he banks the stove and they go to bed. The memory of the sea and the struggle to find her feet threads through her dreams; she sleeps badly. Gradually the room lightens and the shadows disappear; when the birds start singing she gets up, relieved the night is over. The stove is still hot. She puts in more wood and sets a pot of water to heat on top. Outside the air is fresh; she walks down the garden searching for deer spoor, her own footprints leaving a dark trail in the wet grass behind her. The wind has calmed and the waves breathe peacefully as though the sea is still asleep. She feels stronger in the daylight, more certain of her ground. Albie can believe what he wants, she'll keep watch for them both. She learnt vigilance as a child; survival is second nature. At the bottom of the garden, the delicate tips of a little stand of trees by the fence are shining green-gold in the rising sun. Their pale trunks, coiffed in coils of papery white, stand in circles of freshly dug earth.

'Those are for you.' Albie's whisper jolts her. 'I asked Iona to organise it with the hotel gardeners before we came. Your wedding present.'

Trees of her own; she puts her arms around him. 'I can't think of a lovelier gift.'

'Silver birches symbolise happiness and safety, I looked it up.'

The young trees already lean to one side in the direction of the wind. She puts her hand on a slim trunk. The trees remind her of herself as a young girl, one in a line of white-faced teenagers in school assemblies, depleted by periods and dieting. Happiness and safety. 'That's quite a lot for a little tree to symbolise.'

'They ward off evil too.' He takes her hand.

Above their heads the leaves turn and spin in the light breeze, catching the sun, fluttering and fragile, like so much tissue paper.

8

London. Summer 2016

The child is unconscious. His heart rate and breathing remain steady thanks to Owen's skill; Albie pushes the heavy steel pins through the dark eyebrows, penetrating the soft skin down to bone. Two more pins are inserted through the scalp at the back, careful wounds inflicted with precision; the scars won't show in these places. No one will notice – not the parents, not Karim when he grows up; God willing he does grow up.

Albie met the family a week ago, in Great Ormond Street Hospital outpatient clinic, round the corner from the National Hospital, conveniently placed, time being pressing, time always being pressing. He is busier than ever, juggling commitments, hurrying from ward to ward. Bridget, running the lab in Ted's absence, is often on the phone with problems since he left: rat numbers are down and Bruce, occupied with his PhD, has hardly started the viral dosing studies Ted requested. 'Oh and Albie, the waste-paper bin in Bruce's room caught fire yesterday. We spotted it in time so no harm done, but he should stop smoking. Could you have a word? He doesn't listen to me.'

The worries mount. Dunbar's repairs were more expensive than he'd thought; the conversion in Hampstead has been phased to run over two years now. Money will be short until the payout and now Bruce is holding things up. Albie is ashamed of his anxiety, as nothing compares to the worry Karim's parents must endure. At first they were silent when he met them in clinic, like refugees beached in an unknown country, uncertain of their safety. The father held a folder of notes with X-rays and scans that spilled out repeatedly, while his wife pushed at her hair with thin hands. There was another child, a girl, dressed as for a party in tutu and pumps. She had flattened herself into her mother's skirt, her stare travelling around the walls. Remembering her, as he positions the head frame on her brother's head, he is pierced with longing for a daughter, a girl like her, dark like Beth. He sees so many families now, he allows himself to imagine his own. A girl first, maybe. He'll take her to Jura, give her sandcastles and swimming lessons, bedtime stories under the stars. He has shared these thoughts with no one, not even Beth.

Albie had put the scans on the light box and traced the tumour out for Karim's parents, an egg-shaped area of different intensity seeming to take up all the space in the brainstem. The parents had fallen silent. It was a death sentence and they knew it; there was no treatment of any kind in Iraq, the father explained. Hospitals had been destroyed. Albie told them that there was an experimental treatment he could offer which had shrunk the tumour in animal models. It would involve an operation, threading thin tubes into the child's brain to infuse chemotherapy directly into the tumour. It might not be a cure but it would buy them time. He didn't tell them about the viral therapy; it was too soon, the trials in Boston still a long way off. He had looked down at his hands as he waited for their decision; the father glanced at them too as if assessing their capability, though it was doubtful he saw them drilling holes in his son's head. When he looked up, the parents were staring at Karim with dread and hope. Later, by the bedside, he had gone through the risks with a translator.

The porter and Owen wheel the unconscious boy to the MRI scanner; Albie selects targets within the grainy images, planning the trajectory the catheter will take through the brain to avoid the white tracery of blood vessels. Karim is returned to theatre and Owen transfers him to the table with infinite care. Albie positions the small, dark head, locking the head frame on to the robot stand; the jointed arms of white steel look enormous near the body of the child. He fixes the laser on to an arm of the robot; pressing a button causes the arm to move, carrying the laser into the correct position, just above the skull. Karim's father had explained before surgery that they wouldn't be going home to their country; their house and city had been bombed. At this very moment across the globe in Karim's country, trajectories are being double-checked, remote controlled buttons pressed, machines slid into place before missiles are fired. Death, not life. At the touch of another button, the robot directs the sharp laser beam on to the scalp and Albie marks the point with ink; the process repeats three times.

While the alcoholic skin prep is evaporating, Albie drapes Karim's head with blue paper towels. He incises the scalp, mills out a cylinder of bone beneath and drills to penetrate the skull. Using a sharp-tipped probe within a guide tube, he penetrates slowly through brain to the tumour, conscious, as he advances the guide, that he is traversing tissue that holds thought, emotion and memory. Everything that makes this little boy human. His back is wet with sweat; along with the fear of causing a haemorrhage, the very stuff of consciousness is at risk. This is the trade-off he warned the parents about, but parents with a dying child agree to anything and they had agreed to the operation. Albie had felt a queasy mix of relief and guilt; they'd had no alternative; if you are about to lose your child, choice becomes a luxury. He reaches the tumour, removes the probe and slides the catheter down the guide tube, leaving both in place. He has hardly taken a breath during the insertion; now he inhales the dull iron tang of blood and the cooked smell of vessels. He reassures himself that whatever damage he is causing, the tumour would cause the greater harm; it's a question of balancing risk. He repeats the procedure three times at different points on the skull. Behind him the staff are murmuring but the world has faded; as Ted taught him, his focus is absolute. Nothing exists except the small brain under his hands, the careful placing of the catheters, the avoidance of blood vessels. After he has sewn up the scalp around the catheters, he gently washes the blood-stiffened hair. The child will look strange enough, a fugitive from a science-fiction film, with four fine tubes emerging from his head, each attached to a syringe driver; he can at least spare the parents the sight of blood in their son's hair. Owen wheels Karim to the recovery room. The mother comes in silently and, taking her child's limp hand, covers it with kisses. The father stands behind her; he stares fixedly at Karim's sleeping face, as if his son's life depends on him keeping watch. Albie tells them that the operation has gone smoothly, that the child may take a while to wake. He shows them the tubes, and explains that the infusion of chemotherapy starts the next day. Karim may be made worse for a few days because of local swelling. He will become clumsier, there will be slurring of speech and difficulty in swallowing until it subsides. By six weeks, though, he ought to feel better, the cancer should be shrinking. The mother folds her arms around her husband, she is smiling and smiling; he takes Albie's hand, pumping it up and down, crushing the fingers, tears pouring down his face.

In the changing room Albie makes a few rapid

sketches in his notebook to record his approach to the tumour. He chats through the operation with Owen as they strip off their blue cotton togs and dump them in the laundry bin, both relieved. The operation went well, Karim and his family have been bought a reprieve. Owen dresses swiftly then leaves to check the boy on the ward, raising his hand in a laconic gesture of congratulation at the door. Albie grins back, though his mouth is dry with thirst and his head throbs painfully. In the shower, the water hammers down on his skull, millimetres away from his own grey matter, whose glistening health he takes for granted but which is no more immune from catastrophe than the patients he sees daily. Afterwards he rubs his scalp vigorously with the towel as if trying to rub away the thudding headache. It is possible that within his own skull the seed of some deep-seated monster is growing; a hidden malignancy swelling in the dark folds of his brain, waiting to overwhelm his life. He dresses; dehydration, he tells himself, is far more likely. He collects his notebook and walks slowly from theatres to the ward, head lowered to minimise the pain, eyes half closed against the light. He collides into a ledge at hip height; there's a sharp rattle of crockery and a suppressed gasp. He looks up to see Skuld behind a trolley which is laden with used cups, plates with dark cake crumbs and half-finished jugs of juice.

'So we bump into each other again.' He smiles.

'Shouldn't you be in the lab or do you only visit secretly at night?'

It was meant as a joke but her face burns. 'I was in the lab early today to make up my hours.'

He glances at the remains of the orange juice on her trolley. 'I won't tell if I can steal a drink.'

He watches her pour out a glass of orange juice. 'One of Urth's personal events, I suppose?'

She hands him the glass, shaking her head. 'Not exactly. The consultants' special planning meeting. I help every time now.' Her glance slides to his face. 'It's only once a month; she says I make all the difference.'

'You're lucky. I'm still waiting for my invitation.' He drinks rapidly; the liquid seems to seep into his very bones. Sighing with relief, he holds the glass out for a refill. 'But then I'm only a locum consultant.'

Her mouth twitches. 'It's very boring.' She empties the jug into his glass. 'They were arguing about employing more nurses. They always argue.'

'I bet they do.' He laughs but takes note; a little spy in that camp could be useful when it comes to future appointments. Skuld would make a perfect spy; her English has already improved. He drains the juice; the headache is receding. 'Thanks.' He gives her back the glass. 'You saved my life.'

'You still have that book with you.' She nods towards his notebook.

'My whole life is in there,' he says jokingly, though

his reply is near the truth. His entire working life is mapped in those pages, recorded in sketches and charts, operation notes and plans for future research. She returns his smile with a fleeting one of her own and replaces the glass, pushing the trolley past him without saying goodbye, as though he had become suddenly invisible. He watches her dipping gait until she is out of sight. Her sisters make him feel awkward but he relaxes with Skuld. He has never met a girl with so little need for pretence; it's as though she has known him for years.

He hurries on down the corridor. One day he will be at the meeting himself, maybe even chairing it. He'll wait as long as it takes; it's a matter of work and time, that's all.

9

London. Early Summer 2017

The stage is empty now except for the hooded ones, their weaving finished. They point into the shadows at the back; their voices hiss.

'Here he comes, the man with red hair. Red for danger. Red for blood and lust and fire.'

He's out of breath, late but not too late, naïve but not innocent, impatient but not desperate. Dangerous but not yet.

The chant begins: 'DNA, Destiny. Destiny, DNA.'

Of all people, he should know that they are, more or less, exactly the same.

By the morning of the seventh consecutive day of unseasonable heat, London feels like a city further south, habituated to sun. Sleeveless women in sunglasses stroll on the pavements, awnings are up outside cafés, people spill into the roads with their drinks. The atmosphere is celebratory. Men in suits eat ice creams. The streets are hot, as though the air itself might ignite.

The taxi is caught in traffic as it approaches the hospital. Albie is on his way to Ted's lecture. Ted has flown back from California specially to present research at the conference. Albie will reveal his viral work at another meeting, once Ted has returned his PhD with amendments. The locum ends next month; he hopes to discuss the timings today.

The morning has been marked as study leave; there is a spacious feel to the day, like the start of a holiday. Beth was half asleep when he left, her skin luminous, the nipples darker. She could be pregnant; it's been a year. Their first wedding anniversary was last week, Istanbul for a snatched weekend: a dizzying round of mosques and minarets. In bed this morning her face reminded him of Mary's in a Byzantine fresco in Hagia Sophia, as mysterious and peaceful. He couldn't bring himself to ask.

The taxi driver swears under his breath; the traffic is at a standstill. A large crowd has gathered outside the hospital, blocking the road. Albie gets out and is confronted by placards displaying posters of blood-stained mice and chimps behind bars. There are no photos of unkempt rats grown thin with tumours, but all the same, as he pushes his way through the crowd, it's as though he is pushing through tangled threads of guilt meshed across the road – his guilt. If these protesters knew about his research they would probably turn on him. As if on cue, a muscled young man in an orange tee shirt approaches and begins to shout in his face, clenching a meaty fist; a punch is imminent. A policeman steps swiftly between them allowing Albie to pass through the entrance of the hospital; once inside, he removes his jacket with trembling hands. The wide entrance hall is empty; the talks must have started. He hurries through deserted corridors to the Wolfson lecture theatre and collects a pack of research papers and a timetable from a desk by the door. He tiptoes in and eases into an end-of-aisle seat, struggling to breathe quietly. The attendees around him are focused on the stage where he sees Ted pointing out slides on the giant screen, he hears the familiar voice ring round the theatre. He leans forward eagerly, smiling to himself. He's missed Ted, he's missed that voice. As he listens, the demonstration outside recedes from his mind.

It takes a while to realise that the mauve and pink stained slides of rat brain are those he sent to Ted for approval. The images are impressive but they are his images, his rats. The people next to him are leaning forward as they absorb the evidence of tumour shrinkage with viral infusions, the work which he was due to present; his own work. The words he wrote, rebranded in multi-coloured bullet points, flash on the screen in front of him. Ted is walking back and forth, his head held high as he points to the slides, all taken from Albie's PhD.

He lowers his head; his face hurts as though he's been punched after all. There is a loud drumming in his ears. It happens, he knows this; the head of a research laboratory often presents the work done in that lab – why should it be any different for him? He breathes deeply and slowly, containing the hurt. It shouldn't be a surprise. He is too close to it, probably, all those long days and late nights in the quiet lab, an enclosed world that he'd thought belonged to him. That was an illusion. The discoveries he made aren't his property, nor are they his to present. The information needs to be out there; the results belong to the world. Nevertheless, when the clapping starts he walks out. He feels light-headed, not yet ready to meet Ted.

A voice by his side penetrates; a short man is standing at his elbow. The round face, soft as a bun, is marked by trickles of sweat. He jerks his head towards the door.

'I said, are they finished already?'

Albie nods. The man's voice seems to come from very far away; the shock has distanced the world. There is a drumming noise in his head. He needs coffee and something to eat. He begins to walk down the corridor but the man follows, his breath rasping as he unfolds a map of the hospital interior, the kind given to patients when they arrive.

'I came a long way for this.' The crumpled sheet is thrust into Albie's hands; it shows a circle around a room beyond outpatients. 'There's a lecture going on somewhere else, it's only just started. Do you know where this is?' The man jabs at the circle. His accent is reminiscent of Amil's; he looks about to cry. Albie relents.

'Follow me.'

He leads the way past outpatients, turning right by a reception desk, then up a few steps to the function suite. The man keeps pace, wheezing noisily. A faint voice comes from a door to the left, Albie pushes it open and they enter a small lecture theatre. His companion dives for a seat while Albie stands with his back against the wall, catching his breath. A tall woman with a soft Canadian accent is talking in front of a screen. The room is cool and dark, the voice is soothing. The drumming noise in Albie's head begins to lessen.

'We can see that the amygdala of the rats in Group A, the animals exposed to stress in early life, look different from those that were protected.' The lecturer uses a long pole to tap the screen where a lit diagram of the brain glows in the dark. Albie picks up a flyer on the seat in front of him: *The Neurobiology of Evil.* He sits down next to the man who followed him here.

'It was this group who were most aggressive to intruder rats. As with rats . . .' She clicks to the next slide; he sees the familiar curving shape of the human limbic system on the screen, lit up in red. 'So in humans: here we have the amygdala again.' The pole taps insistently against a circled density in darker red on the screen. 'Murderers and other criminals have amygdalae that are smaller than average.'

Albie stares at the slide, imagining his own limbic

system lit up in crimson, pulsing with blood as it processes what just happened. He closes his eyes and Ted's face slides into his mind, all the faces of Ted, serious in the operating theatre, alight with good news or calmly assured as in the auditorium just now, a face he thought he knew better than his own.

'Our newest research in the university of San Francisco has sought out specific genes that predispose people towards antisocial behaviour. Seven have been identified; these are the suspects for neuroscientists looking beyond brain anatomy to the genetic origins of evil.'

The silence in the theatre seems to deepen. Evil. The word conjures images of towns in flames, of men in orange forced to kneel in the dust with a butcher's knife at their throats. The savagery of war. A medieval word that jars in a medical lecture in a hospital in London; he's not even sure what it means.

The tall lecturer turns away from the screen to address the audience. 'In summary, we think early adverse environmental influences alter genetic expression, triggering changes in the amygdala that lead to criminal behaviour.' She puts down her pointer. The lights spring on and she gazes around, smiling expectantly, 'Any questions?'

Albie's phone vibrates. A text from Owen: they need to discuss the patients for theatre tomorrow. When he sees Albie get up from his seat, the man who came in with him stands too.

'She hasn't addressed the main problem,' he whispers as he accompanies Albie through the door; he trails him down the corridor. 'Are some genes more vulnerable to the environment than others, or would everyone become a criminal given the right amount of stress?'

They are back in the entrance hall now. There is a table in the corner surrounded by a jostling mass of attendees; he glimpses a white fall of tablecloth and inhales the scent of coffee. The crowd shifts; a woman with curly red hair is handing out cups. Urth – maybe she has brought her cakes along. He starts towards the table but the man bars his way again.

'She talks of murderers but is all killing evil? Killing of animals, even?' He gestures to the protesters outside still waving their placards. Albie gazes down at the sweating face. It depends, he wants to say. It's complicated, and who is he to pronounce about the killing of animals? He shakes his head and steps to one side.

'No, please.' The man plucks at his sleeve. 'I have one more question, it's important. If you kill in the name of your tribe or of your God, are you evil or simply being obedient?' His voice has risen to a shout, there are beads of spit in the corners of his mouth. This is personal.

'If you go back and ask the lecturer, she might be able to answer your questions.' He should seek out the victims of war; they would have all the definitions of evil close to hand. At a guess he's from the Middle East. Syria or Iraq. Amil's territory, Karim's too; he could be a victim himself. Albie nods as he edges away uneasily. The man in front of him might tell him that edging away from questions of evil amounts to encouraging it, and perhaps that's true. Nevertheless, he decides to forego coffee and turns to the door.

'Hello there!' Ted's voice behind him is cheery. Has he been lying in wait? 'Thanks for dropping in. How's married life treating you?' He doesn't wait for an answer. 'It's a pity you had to leave early; you missed the slide at the very end, the one that gave you credit for your work.' The smile dazzles against the tan. 'I hoped to catch you.' He puts a hand on Albie's arm. 'It's getting hard for me to manage the lab from the US. There's a few problems, Bruce being the main one. I gather he caused a fire the other day. It's not clear to me where he is with our dosing studies, either.' He sighs, shaking his head, 'Well, Bridget does her best as laboratory manager but I'd prefer a clinician at the helm. You have the context; I'd like you to head up the laboratory going forward, starting now. Get Bruce to complete those studies; Viromex are waiting on the data. It's been a year since the contract was signed. You'll be in charge of research; I'll be in the background. What do you say?'

How like Ted: at a moment of taking, another gift arrives and the landscape shifts. It happened with the Viromex deal. Taking and giving. Whether or not there had really been a slide bearing Albie's name which he missed, Ted is trying to make amends. If Ted feels guilty, this is his way of saying sorry.

'That sounds brilliant, Ted. The locum ends in a month,' – the consultant locum and the lab together might be tricky, and he needs to do his best if he's to make a good impression – ' so if I can delay starting in the lab till then—'

'I managed both.' Ted grins. 'I need you to start right now. We should talk about that locum too. I've been offered the chance to extend my time in the US for an additional year's sabbatical, teaching and operating. The hospital management at the National has agreed to extend your locum for another year.' He looks thoughtfully at the floor, nodding as he speaks. 'If you take over the running of the lab as well, I may not need to return before I retire from the NHS, which is when the two roles will be up for grabs . . .'

Here it is, already. The future. Albie's heart begins to race; the consultancy and the lab are coming his way far sooner then he'd thought. *They want to hire someone ahead of the Professor retiring to take over his jobs when he goes* . . . Eighteen months ago, Skuld overheard the departmental plan; it seems he is being prepared for the final stages already. He smiles at Ted, thinking fast. He'll be able to protect his own work when he's in charge of the lab, no one will use his research then. He'll sign his own contracts as well. In addition, his salary will increase.

'I'll start straightaway then, and give it my very best shot,' he replies quickly. 'Thanks, Ted.'

'Good man. We have to leave the current contract with Viromex as it is for the moment.' The blue eyes follow his. 'But there'll be other trials based on other viruses. When your future patents are sold, your name will be on the contract, not mine. To be acting head of the lab is a huge opportunity for you, Albie.'

So they are keeping track, the pupil watching the teacher who is watching him back, shadowing each other's very thoughts. It's as if Ted can read his mind. Should he be more on his guard?

'Thanks, Ted,' he repeats more slowly. 'It's an honour, I'm sure I'll cope.'

'You'll cope all right, you always do.' Ted laughs, aiming a mock punch at Albie's shoulder. 'I want you to assume leadership as soon as possible; Beth won't mind you working late.' He glances at a group of Malaysian attendees who are hovering near. 'I'm heading back to California tomorrow, but Jenny will send you an invite to our party – Ed's engagement to Sophie. Early autumn. Everyone will be there; I'll formally announce the transfer of the lab that evening. I'll get my secretary to set up the official contract to take effect from that date and in the meantime pay you out of research funds. Between us, it's all yours from now on. I'll be in touch.' Then he's gone, striding down the corridor, the Malaysian doctors running alongside. Others fall in behind them and the blond head disappears, borne away by the river of people. Albie stares after him, feeling the tug of a current flowing between them, connecting them even as Ted vanishes from sight.

Outside colours seem fiercer, the heat more intense. He feels dizzy with excitement; he wasn't expecting this just yet. He texts Beth the news but a faint ringing noise starts up, like a car alarm that's so far away it might not even be real. How could Ted have known Beth wouldn't mind if he worked late? He deletes the text. He can tell her the news later, in person.

Chains of policemen have corralled the group of protesters on the opposite pavement; the shouts are quieter. Albie walks over. The crowd has been in the sun for hours, people are sitting on the ground. A neatly dressed woman stares at him, her mouth turned down as though repulsed. The man in the orange tee shirt gets to his feet. He is larger than Albie and looks much fitter. He slips around the line of policemen and moves close. Albie holds his ground. On the operating table, the belligerent face would relax; that broad chest would inflate with anaesthetic gas and oxygen. The man would be vulnerable, like all patients. Albie wants to tell him about Karim. He has the scans on his phone, before and after treatment, showing the way the tumour has begun to shrink, more quickly than predicted. He'd like to ask him how he'd feel if Karim was his own son. His phone bleeps the arrival of a text. Owen again. The man is very close now.

Albie can read the exhaustion in his eyes. Albie raises the hand holding the phone in a gesture of apology and recognition, and then walks rapidly away.

'I'll manage.' Beth looks away from him into the garden. Ted was right, she doesn't mind. The remains of supper and a bottle of wine are on the table between them. Night insects hover at the thick candle she has set between the plates; a speckled moth seems to be sipping from the little pool of melted wax under the flame.

A hose spins backwards and forwards in the dark garden, the roses Beth planted are soaked; their Turkish delight scent mixes with the woody smell of wet earth. The water pulses in the silence, darkening the dry stone of the walls. Yesterday a junior accidentally opened the carotid artery; the blood had sprayed on the walls, spattering everyone.

'You have to do this.' Beth turns back to him, her eyes shadowed. The builders are converting the top flat now and taking their time; the noise must be wearying. 'Whatever it takes. As head of the lab, you'll be free of Ted.' Her voice is bitter.

'Ted was within his rights to present my research, sweetheart; he's been very generous to me.' He leans to take her hand. 'He's on our side, you must see that. My main concern is that you'll be alone far more; I'll be working longer hours.'

'You will be doing this for us,' she replies, lowering her cheek to his palm. Her skin feels very soft. 'It makes us safe.'

He nods eagerly. 'We can pay off the mortgage with the extra salary, and crack on with the conversion project.' He hesitates, then leans forward, speaking softly. 'There's another advantage to putting in the hours now. I should be able to take time off in the future, if a baby arrives, I mean.'

She is silent, her eyes move back and forth, following the undulating water.

He squeezes her hand. 'So . . . ?'

She turns her face away. 'I'm not pregnant, Albie.'

'Perhaps I'll get myself checked out.'

'It's only been a year, surely—'

'David Smith is the man. He specialises in conception. If I'm okay, he'll look at you.'

She releases her hand and rises without answering.

'Beth?'

'I'm tired. I'm going to bed.' She stoops to kiss him.

The disappointment settles in the pit of his stomach, a background ache. It was foolish to allow hope to grow. He gets up, turns off the water and bends to blow out the candle on the table. The speckled moth is lying at its base, the wings still. Attracted to the flame it has paid a heavy price. The bulging eyes on the tiny head are thickly coated with wax.

10

London. Late Summer 2017

A video is projected on to the back wall.

A man genuflects on a hill. The shot is grainy, unsettling, a rite of some kind – religious, maybe, a sacrifice perhaps. The audience sit up but the commentary is calm, the voice female.

'He has come to worship his gods in the open, high up, as his ancestors did. They prayed for success, to defeat the enemy in battle, for children to continue the line.'

This man wouldn't call his prayers, prayers. They are thoughts, wishes, desires. Ambitions. It's all the same to the gods; he'll do as his ancestors did. He'll cheat, lie, steal. He'll kill, given time. There will be a sacrifice, though not yet.

Albie gets up at five thirty each Sunday. The weekly routine involves prolonged immobility. In theatre his movements are meticulous, minute. By the weekends he is restless, like a horse that's been kept in the stables too long. He pulls on his running shorts and an old tee shirt. Beth is still sleeping, her bare arm on the sheet as cool and smooth as the metal arms of the mother in Queen Square, the bronze woman who holds a child. He can never decide if she is meant to represent the Madonna or any mother cradling her child; to him, she is Beth with her flawless face and lowered eyelids. Beth with a child.

He jogs down the quiet crescent. The mansions are curtained at this hour. The flowers in the gardens are radiant in the early light, roses spill over the walls. Some are dying, others are tight buds. Close up, they must be swarming with greenfly. Beth removes the insects from their own roses and crushes them to slime between her fingertips.

He increases his speed on the Heath, running past the duck ponds and willows then up the path that winds through leaning trees to the steep slope of Parliament Hill, the sky opening around him as he ascends, lungs beginning to burn. He rests at the top. Ahead is the familiar rosary of buildings: St Paul's, Canary Wharf, the Shard, now tipped with gold by the rising sun. He knows the view by heart. He reaches high then bends from the waist to touch the ground. The week went well; he'd pushed Bruce on as Ted had asked and the data from the dosing studies was sent off to Viromex a few days ago. Viromex now own the patent. The payout should arrive in a week. There are children waiting all over the world; success will be swift once the Boston children's trials are done. He stretches as high as he can, his hands against the sky as if reaching into infinity.

He sets off again, sprinting downhill to the tarmac path between lakes of water either side, left by the women's pond, back past the gates of Kenwood House. He is slowing so he imagines Ted and Owen alongside, pacing him. Running together on Sunday mornings used to be their weekly ritual. They took it in turns to decide where to meet. Ted would choose Hyde Park, Albie the Heath and Owen always took them round Brockwell Park. Back then Ted came to them, picking them up in his car, never the other way round. He must have been hiding the girlfriend in his flat, probably still in bed. Albie imagines a soft-faced young girl, pliant and pretty – perhaps still around; Ted inspires devotion. With a renewed burst of energy, he swings down hard through the trees. There are more people about now, dog walkers and runners, the day is heating up. Half blinded with sweat, he is crowded off the path by three women runners and their panting dogs, he almost falls. He turns in time to glimpse three ponytails swinging in unison as they disappear into the trees. Grey, red, blonde. He walks to the shops, determined not to feel disconcerted. It's unlikely to have been the sisters, they don't seem the type. Then he remembers the swimming. He picks up a weighty pack of Sunday papers from the newsagent's. They can't have seen him with all those dogs in the way, they would have been unaware of causing him to stumble.

Once home, he shucks off his trainers and socks with relief. He takes three perfect oranges and slices them as cleanly as if he were operating and the peel was skin, the orange flesh subcutaneous fat, shining in tiny packets. He juices them and, gripped by thirst, drinks straight from the bowl before juicing three more for Beth. He starts the coffee machine and then walks barefoot into the sitting room, circumnavigating packed boxes. Beth has been storing photos and books ahead of the builders moving downstairs. He squares up to the papers on his desk, a weekly task. He files bills and discards junk, scarcely attending to the contents. At the bottom of the pile is an unfamiliar bundle. He pauses to flick through. The sheets are headed with the National's blue and white logo – the papers he'd picked up at the conference a couple of months ago and overlooked till now; copies of research projects from the different speakers. As he folds them a title catches his eye: 'Immunotherapy: a warning note'.

He unfolds them again and walks back into the kitchen. The coffee is ready, and he sips as he reads. The research has similarities to his own. The study in New Zealand was small, but involved cancer patients. Varicella virus was used to switch on immunity . . . in ten cases of malignant melanoma the tumours decreased in size . . . two patients had a severe adverse reaction which was fatal. Fatal? His eyes flick back; he reads more slowly. A sample of twenty adults was infused with varicella virus through a drip into the arm. Improvements were noted in all but two individuals who experienced a severe asthmatic response followed by catastrophic liver and kidney failure resulting in death. Trial withdrawn forthwith. Post-mortem histology showed an inflammatory reaction indicating an aggravated immune response, presumably in individuals who had been infected with the virus before by chance. A red flag warning advised the withdrawal of similar trials of treatment pending the results of further investigation.

Albie slowly sits down on a cardboard box; he stares ahead, unseeing as if at the wreckage of his dreams. Empty minutes tick by before he stands, wiping his face with the edge of his tee shirt, and pulls his laptop from the case. He brings up the paper after searching the archives and scrolls down for detailed analysis and editorial comment. As he reads, he begins to relax. The trial was heavily criticised by the editor: a fixed dose had been given to all patients irrespective of their size, resulting in overdose in the two individuals who died. Albie's heart slows, he exhales a long, slow sigh of relief. It is unsurprising he missed the report: because of the faulty set-up, it never reached the wider scientific press.

The time is eight a.m., midnight in California. Ted's hour for reading emails. The phone is answered on the second ring. Ted listens and when he speaks his voice is very quiet. 'So there was a secondary immune response in two individuals, severe enough to be fatal?'

'The implication is that those patients with a catastrophic reaction were given too much virus for their size. They might also have been infected with varicella virus before, so yes, an immune response gone wrong.'

'Why doesn't this happen more often? After all, most people get reinfected with virus, they don't develop a deadly inflammatory response.' Ted is angry, as though this problem was directed at him personally.

'It's idiosyncratic, the risk is very small. I admit there's a theoretical concern, but in our trial the virus is delivered straight into the brain. It can't even cross over the blood-brain barrier, so the body wouldn't generate an immune response, only the brain. There's a vanishingly small chance of a similar catastrophe—'

'A theoretical concern?' Ted explodes. 'You may be in charge for the moment, Albie, but this research was done in my laboratory. Any risk is unacceptable. We must inform Viromex they'll have to wait for us to carry out further tests before proceeding. We'll need a new cohort of rats; each animal should be given two separate exposures to the virus. If any die on the second exposure, we'll have to scrap everything and start again.' A harsh sigh down the phone. 'This is a bloody nuisance; we were just about to receive that payout. Home Office permission for a double procedure will take a long time; the delay could be considerable. I rely on you, Albie, I can't think how you missed that research.'

'Sorry, Ted.' Best to keep it simple. The truth is he's busy, with Ted's patients, ward rounds, clinics and operations. Private lists. Meetings and appraisals, GPs' letters and phone calls; fifty emails a day to respond to. There's research to plan and coordinate, review meetings with Bridget, Bruce to keep in line. He doesn't say any of this. If he does, Ted will return and might reclaim the lab. Albie's future could be jeopardised.

'I'll have to come back and help you,' Ted says. Albie forgot Ted can read his mind. There is the sound of rapid footsteps, Ted is pacing as he thinks.

'I'll organise everything,' Albie rejoins swiftly, walking to the end of the sitting room and back again, phone tight against his ear. 'I'm in charge, remember; leave it to me.'

'If there is any perceived danger, it will kill the Viromex deal.' Ted isn't listening to him; his voice rings with anxiety. 'No one would run a trial in children with a risk like that, we'll lose everything.'

'Leave it to me,' Albie repeats, raising his voice, 'I'll contact Viromex tomorrow and inform them there'll be a delay for a few months while we run a two-stage trial.'

There is silence at the other end of the phone; Ted is listening at last.

'Bruce can order in more rats and organise the infusions,' Albie continues quickly. 'Bridget will buy in the virus and apply for approval. I'll copy you in at each stage.'

'Are you sure you can handle it all?' Ted is wavering. 'We can't afford to cut corners.'

'I know that, Ted. Trust me.'

'Good man.' The relief is audible. 'I'm back in a couple of months for Ed's party, you can fill me in then.'

The conversation is over. Albie leans against the counter; the glow has gone from the morning. He makes coffee for Beth and puts it on a tray with the juice and the paper. Beth is still in bed; she glances up from her book. He'll tell her about the phone call next week after her test at the clinic; no point in worrying her now. He sets the tray down on the table, puts the paper on the bed and hands her the cup of coffee.

'You were pacing downstairs.' She sips the coffee. 'Back and forth, like a caged animal.'

'Was I?' He sits on the edge of the bed. 'I didn't realise. I was on the phone to Ted.'

'Bet he was pacing too.' A smile flickers across her face.

'What makes you think that?'

Her eyes are lowered to her cup. The window is open, but there is little traffic on a Sunday down their road, it's completely quiet, as though she were holding her breath.

She looks up, still smiling, 'You've told me enough times.' She replaces the cup on the tray. 'You always say how much it annoys you and now you're doing exactly the same.'

He'd forgotten. He forgets everything these days, though a memory gleams out from the past at her words, of stags pacing each other up and down on the hill behind the house, as they assessed their rival's strengths before the rut. There hasn't been time to go to Jura this summer. He stares outside at the sky circumscribed by roofs and the parked cars glittering in the sun. In Jura the sky is untrammelled, the sun lies on wide expanses of grass where the deer run wild. Next year.

'Albie, look.' Beth's voice pulls him back. She is pointing to a column at the front of the paper. 'I've seen this guy before.'

He leans to read the headline. 'Man accused of Greenwich Murders, released after a ten-year campaign led by Jake Valance.' A haggard face stares from the page. The man looks ill, as though freedom came too late to make up for ten stolen years. 'Poor guy. How on earth do you know him?'

'Not him, sweetheart, the journalist, Jake Valance.' Beth indicates a small picture by the side of the piece above the byline. The reporter has a shock of hair, an intense stare. 'I remember the name. He was at that party where we met. He was with Ed. I happened to be standing near, I heard them talking. He looked just like a fox, he still does.'

'I'm surprised you remember so much detail; it was a long time ago now.'

'I can't think why you're surprised.' She smiles up at him. 'I remember everything about that party.' She slips her arms round his neck. 'It was the most important night of my life.'

He smiles as he bends to kiss her. 'Now why would that be, I wonder?'

'I met this incredible man,' she murmurs into his ear. 'He was exactly the kind of guy I'd been waiting for.'

Later, while Beth is showering, he takes the paper and breakfast things downstairs, then retrieves his notebook from its shelf on the dresser. He has to plan the new two-stage trial now. He begins to draw up a list of what he will need: three rats in each dose group, and three in each control. Separate quantities of virus for abdominal and intracerebral delivery. He pauses, pencil in hand, to glance over at the newspaper left on the dresser, neatly folded. The photo of the young journalist is uppermost. Unlike Beth, Albie hadn't noticed Jake Valance at all. He can't remember anyone that night apart from her. He hadn't been waiting, though; she'd arrived in front of him like a gift from the gods, all the more thrilling for being completely unexpected. It was just a turn of phrase, but it's strange to think it might have been quite different for her and that she had been waiting, as she said, for a guy just like him, all along.

11

London. Autumn 2017

It was a mistake to have lied; biological evidence always trumps a lie.

Two weeks ago they had been sitting opposite David Smith in the slippery leather chairs of his fertility clinic in Harley Street. The appointment had come through in a month, but Albie had to change it twice because of emergency operations. Beth had been glad of the delays; she hadn't wanted to go at all, frightened that the past might emerge from the shadows, but she was unable to think of an excuse. They finally met him, pink-cheeked and white-haired, apparently genial though the small eyes had moved back and forth rapidly as though this was a game of piggy in the middle and he was trying to catch what was passing between them. He told them Albie's tests were fine and then took Beth's medical history; he didn't have it to hand, he explained, because hospital and private notes were held separately. No GP's letter either, this being a favour for Albie, a colleague; so when he asked her if she had ever been pregnant, she lied.

David had examined her behind the screen, his gloved fingers probing painfully, but he informed them afterwards that he'd found nothing amiss. Albie had squeezed her hand and she was unable to speak, she hadn't allowed herself to hope. Her blood tests were normal too, but David advised a hysterosalpingogram to outline her uterus and fallopian tubes with dye, just to be sure. He shook Albie's hand. She took the leaflet the receptionist gave her and on the pavement outside began to weep. Albie hugged her. Clasped and stumbling they made their way to an Italian restaurant on the corner where they drank a toast to the future and Albie wrote lists of baby names on a napkin.

Albie phoned from the hospital on the day of her test. 'I'm so sorry, darling, it seems I can't join you after all, but you should go ahead. We've waited a long time for this. Forgive me. There's a neck to stabilise. An alcoholic; she smashed up her car and in the process—'

'It's okay, Albie.' She didn't want the details, she could imagine them: the smell of alcohol, broken glass in tangled hair, pools of blood on the tarmac, images that had haunted her for years. It would be better to be alone anyway, easier. Something could yet be revealed, a minor legacy of the pregnancy, enough to give her away. She was careful not to sound relieved.

The nurse draped towels over her bent knees to cover her pelvis and explained what would be done in a breathy whisper that smelt of coffee and biscuits. A series of increasingly thick probes would be inserted to stretch the cervix before a catheter was introduced, down which the radiopaque dye would be injected to outline the uterus and fallopian tubes along their length. David stood by silently during the explanation; he was offhand today as though without her husband she was less worthy of attention. She tightened her fists under the sheet. This would be over soon. In just a few minutes she would be able to leave, phone Albie; the future would begin.

The metal probe is cold; it slips easily, too easily, through the opening of the cervix. A stretched cervix means childbirth, biological evidence, the lie revealed. She hasn't thought this through; David might inform Albie. Sweat gathers along her neck as she watches the radiopaque dye flow into the pear-shaped uterus on the screen by her side. David smiles down at her, a professional smile that doesn't reach his eyes. 'The uterine cavity looks fine, Beth. No suggestion of fibroids or any other obstruction.'

He tilts the screen further towards her so she can see the smooth outline of dye filling her womb while he makes measurements of the lining and thickness of the wall.

'All completely normal so far.' Relieved, she raises her head to look more closely. 'Keep still, please,' he tells her sharply. 'There may be a little discomfort as the dye spills out into the pelvic cavity.'

The nurse moves around the room behind her then settles her bulky frame on the seat close to Beth's face; it's as though Beth's head and pelvis have become disconnected, each being separately attended to. David is talking about his summer holidays in Cornwall next week, but his words peter into silence. She waits for the discomfort; the dye is taking a while to spill out. After a few minutes, David leans forward abruptly. She cranes to see past his shoulders to the screen where the lines of dye stop abruptly a few millimetres out from the uterus. The image is different from the picture on the leaflet where delicate white arms had stretched out on either side of the womb; at their far ends the pale radiopaque liquid had feathered out into the darkness of the pelvis. Instead of fine limbs, the screen reveals balloons of distended tissue, the trapped dye inflating the truncated tubes.

The room is very quiet; the pain turns out not to be in her pelvis but in the centre of her chest, as if the fibres of her heart were breaking apart. The nurse puts a pudgy hand on Beth's knee, but Beth moves her leg away sharply. David looks down at her, his face impassive.

'When you are ready, come into my office on the third floor.'

She dresses in haste, pushing her feet clumsily into shoes and bundling her jacket under an arm. When she enters his office, David is leaning against the side of his desk staring at his shoes; brogues, the shiny leather laced so tightly that his pink socks bulge where the leather cuts into his flesh. His expression is impersonal, though moments earlier she had been half naked in front of him. She sits down, smoothing her skirt over her knees, and waits.

'I'm sorry to report that the dye failed to penetrate the length of the fallopian tubes.' He pauses to let her absorb what he is saying, but she knows already and she knows what it means; she knew the instant she saw the images on the screen.

'The tubes are damaged, rather badly as it happens.' His tone is bland; he could be discussing the weather. 'Eggs can't therefore pass from the ovaries down the tubes to the uterus and it follows they will be unavailable for fertilisation.' He pauses again. He must have been taught to give the patient time but she wants this to end quickly. She keeps her face quite still. Doctors get the bad news out of the way first. She sits motionless; in a minute he will say that nevertheless a child is still possible by some new technique he is developing. She digs her fingers into her palms; she must wait for those words.

'The usual cause of a blockage is previous infection leading to scarring.' Another long pause. His cheeks are shiny and smoothly puffed, incongruous considering the white hair; perhaps he has had plastic surgery, done cheaply as a favour by a colleague. If she threw something at him, a cupful of dye for instance, it would slide off that stretched surface without leaving a mark. She closes her eyes.

She never knew what the nurses called her; a baby or a moving foetus. She had asked to be left alone. She held her nipple against the tiny mouth that seemed to open as if trying to suckle, but then, nothing. The mouth closed, she stopped moving after ten minutes. The colour changed, pink to blue. Afterwards Beth couldn't remember how long they'd had together, half an hour, maybe less. When they took her baby away she dressed and walked out; she wasn't supposed to go before being checked but she left anyway. The pain and temperature built over days. She made it to the funeral, just her and a priest, rain falling from a dark grey sky. She put snowdrops on the tiny coffin. A day later a fetid discharge developed, later still she crawled to the GP for antibiotics. She went back to work after two weeks, needing the money for rent. Sorrow sank below anger; she never contacted Ted again. Some months later he began to phone and when she didn't answer he tracked her down and came knocking. She hid in the dark till he gave up; it was too late. The damage was done, though she had no idea then how much. She moved from neurosurgery theatres to orthopaedics. When she saw Ted in the distance down a corridor she chose another route. A year went by before she heard about the party.

'. . . unlikely to yield a positive result. In my opinion, the scarring is too widespread for surgery; the infection must have persisted a while, the damage would be extensive.'

There will be no other child then, no other daughter. On David's desk a great bunch of lilies are jammed into a glass vase; the heavy scent fills the room, obscenely sweet. The snowdrops had smelt simply of earth. She stares at the thick white petals as she holds back tears, wanting to smash the vase, trample the flowers into a juicy pulp on the carpet; the damage would be extensive.

'. . . IVF, of course, with a thirty-two per cent chance of a viable pregnancy.'

David smiles. She doesn't understand why; that percentage, far less than half, appals her. She doesn't smile back. He walks around the desk, sits in the wide chair, wriggling a little to make himself comfortable. 'You will want to discuss this with Albie, and then we should meet, all three of us, to work out the way forward.' His plump hands pat the table gently.

Albie is happy, they both are. If she tells him the truth, his happiness will turn to anguish. He will blame her, though he wouldn't admit that; he might turn away from her at meals, in the house, in bed. Silence would grow between them in the place where a child might have been. She links her hands tightly across her pelvis. She could undergo IVF in secret maybe, but the odds against success are too high, failure would be unendurable. It would be like losing her baby all over again. If she tells Albie, he might want to try many times and the strain of that would pull their marriage apart. If she stays silent they still have a future, they have each other.

She stands. 'This information is to be kept between us. If my husband ever hears about this, I will know where it has come from and I will sue you for breach of confidentiality.'

David's pink face becomes deep red. For the first time he seems to be registering emotion, but whether anger or fear is hard to tell. He leans forward and clears his throat, but before he can say anything she walks out of the room.

'That's wonderful news; what a relief!' Albie throws his bag in the corner of the bedroom and hugs her, wrapped as she is in a towel, still wet from her shower. 'I knew it. It's just a matter of focus and time, like everything else. God, how marvellous.'

'I can't breathe, Albie.'

'Sorry.' He unlocks his hold, still smiling. 'So when are we seeing him again?'

She walks into the bathroom and presses a flannel to her eyes. After a while she calls out, 'We're not.'

'It's usual to have a follow-up.' Albie's puzzled voice floats through to her.

'No point.' She dumps the flannel in the laundry basket, turns on the bath taps and walks back into the bedroom. 'There's nothing more to do. I told him how busy you are.' It's not a lie. There is nothing more to do, or at least, nothing more she will agree to do.

'If you're sure.' He watches her drop the towel, hook on her bra, slip on pants.

'Hurry.' She gives him a little push. 'Ed's party. Your bath is running. I'll come and talk to you.'

'Are you still up to going?'

'This is the night Ted officially gives you the lab; of course I'm up to going.'

She sits on the side of the bath, looks down at him. The shining planes of his body are half submerged, the wide chest, flat stomach, broad shoulders. His large hands. The tired eyes. The whole of him, everything she has.

'Thank God the tests worked out. Things are getting complicated with that Viromex deal.' He slides under the surface of the water and re-emerges, his hair matted and streaming. She rubs shampoo into his scalp; he sighs and closes his eyes. 'I didn't want to tell you while you were waiting for the test, but there's been a hold-up; the payout will be delayed. Money could be tight for a while yet.'

'A hold-up?'

'More work is needed, there have been problems. Viromex won't pay us till we're finished.'

'What kind of problems?'

'There's some research out there, poor quality, admittedly, but the premise is similar to ours. Patients with malignant melanoma were treated with intravenous varicella virus to switch on their immunity. Two had a fatal reaction.' He dips his head back under the water then pulls himself out of the bath; she hands him a towel and he wraps it round his waist. She takes another towel off the rack and he sits on the edge of the bath as she rubs his hair. 'It seems their immunity was primed by a previous infection with the same virus. The patients who died had organ failure.'

'Why wasn't everyone affected?'

He pulls his head free. 'Not everyone would have been infected previously; besides, these kind of reactions are very rare. Their research sounds faulty too; the patients who died received too much virus.' He walks through to the bedroom and sits heavily on the bed. 'In any case, Viromex would have repeated our studies on their own rats just to be sure. Drug companies don't like risk. All the same, Ted says we should start all over again.'

'Did any rats in your own experiments get an immune response when they were infused?'

He shakes his head. 'They'd been brought up in a sterile environment. They hadn't met the virus before, so there was no chance of a dangerous immune reaction.'

'What now?' She puts a hand on his knee; under the warm skin the bone feels wide and hard. Viking bone, fighting stock.

'More work. Bruce has been instructed to inject virus into the abdomens of a new cohort of rats, then he'll infuse their brains with the same virus after a couple of months.'

'And if they die?'

'Viromex would reject the deal.' He gets up and walks to the wardrobe, yanking it open so the hangers jump and jangle. 'The payout and the royalties would be cancelled. I'd have to start all over again.'

She moves to the window. Beyond their back garden she can see the rear of a Victorian house split into flats like theirs. A rectangle of light flares from the window of the top flat; a little boy in pyjamas runs into a bedroom and jumps on the bed. If Albie starts again, it will be a long time before children get the treatment. He could be in the lab for months, years maybe. Long hours and late nights. He could be tempted in ways that haven't yet occurred to her. It hadn't occurred to Jenny that her husband would be tempted, but if this is retribution, she has already paid her dues. It's Ted's turn now.

'Given Viromex run through the same process again, does your trial need to be done exactly as you describe? Who'd know if you didn't?'

He wrenches his shirt out of the wardrobe. 'Everyone in the lab, though the irritating thing is the chances of a reaction are minute.'

'What if there are no chances?'

'What do you mean?' He puts on the shirt and buttons it up. 'We can't eliminate the possibility of a reaction.'

She looks out of the window again. The child is still bouncing on the bed, his dark fringe rising and falling on his forehead; with each leap she winces as if he were jumping on her body.

The tubes are damaged, rather badly as it happens.

Her hand goes to her lower abdomen, fingers spread out. A tall woman enters the room opposite, hair scooped into a ponytail. She moves swiftly between Beth and the boy, the curtains are drawn, cutting her out. The child disappears from view.

Her new black dress is hanging on the door where she put it ready earlier; she slides it over her head and in that instant an idea develops fully, as if it has been hiding in the dark folds of silk. She pulls her head free and faces him across the room. 'What if the chances of a reaction could be eliminated?'

'Impossible. Bruce will follow the protocol, the vaccines have been ordered, it's all set to go.'

She comes close, whispering, as though someone else were in the room, listening. 'There might be things that can be altered . . .' Her voice trails off, she studies his face.

'You can't alter a trial.' He steps back. 'It would be unethical, far too risky. What if a child died?'

A child has died already because of Ted, her child. Ted had power over her once. He has Albie in his grasp, but power can be wrested away.

'Progress is always risky. People die in the process, but many, many more live.'

'We need to go,' he says, as if he hasn't heard her.

She sprays lavender scent on her neck and arms,

then switches off the light, turning to him as they leave the room. 'Hundreds of children could benefit from your treatment, Albie. Thousands. This trial needs to be successful if the treatment is to reach them.'

'The trial has to go ahead as planned,' he says quietly. 'But bless you for trying to help.'

She doesn't answer. In the car he shivers as if cold or sickening with a virus. She takes his hand. There are so many kinds of heat: heat of the moment, heat of battle, hot-blooded courage. As he manoeuvres the car through the streets, she imagines her heat creeping from her hand and into his skin, then travelling along the veins to his heart.

12

London. Autumn 2017

Intermission.

An old man steps out in front of the curtains. He is wearing a bow tie and a waistcoat under his white coat. His voice is reassuring; a doctor, obviously, the old-fashioned type.

'Surgeons know all about wounds.' He smiles around at the members of the audience; they stare back, startled, their mouths full of ice cream.

'We inflict them daily.' He produces a card from the pocket of his white coat with a flourish, then he gropes in his waistcoat for bifocals; thus equipped, he begins to read.

'A wound is an injury to living tissue, caused by a cut, blow or any other impact. To inflict a wound means to injure, hurt, damage, harm. Scathe. Cause a scar.' He twinkles round at the crowd. 'Wounds can be open or closed. Clean or dirty. Superficial or deep. They can be life-changing.'

*

At the party they separate as if the weight of what they discussed is too heavy to carry between them. He watches her weave into the crowd, then he picks up a drink. The room looks more glamorous than he remembers; an interior designer has been at work. The walls are dark grey silk now, there are more paintings, large ones arranged in heavy frames to ceiling height. Enormous red sofas are crammed full of people, talking and drinking. Other guests are outside on a balcony where flames in iron boxes leap high against the black sky. There are colleagues from the hospital and other, unfamiliar faces – possibly from a moneyed art world; he's heard Jenny is successful now. He tours the walls, sipping wine. He recognises her work: seascapes mostly, gunmetal waves and smoky skies, layered cliffs. A bleak sweep of grey pebbles, all the shades of grief. His mind touches on the lost daughter, the difficult teenager who didn't return. Ted doesn't speak of her; the tragedy is never discussed, but what compensations might it have allowed, still allow? Perhaps there's a girlfriend in this very room, hidden in the crowd of guests. He wouldn't put it past Ted.

A tray appears before him; he takes a little scone with a lick of green on top, looks up to thank the bearer, turns away, turns back. The grey hair is sleekly blow-dried, the thin face carefully made up. He remembers the unusual hair but the glamour takes him by surprise. She returns his gaze, a gleam in her dark eyes.

'Verdandi.' He smiles. 'I might have known you'd be helping.'

'No names.' Her lips twist, more of a grimace than a smile. 'I'm in disguise.'

He takes a bite of scone, tasting courgette and poppy seeds, a hint of Parmesan. The salty tang of seaweed. 'This is delicious. Did you make it?'

'My mother,' she whispers. 'Don't tell.' She puts her fingers to her lips and backs away, disappearing into the throng. He cranes his neck for Skuld, who might be helping, but she is nowhere in sight – perhaps she's in the lab, working late.

A burst of laughter pulls his attention towards the doors of the balcony, where Jenny and Ted are talking in a little group. Jenny looks tanned, better than the last time he saw her, nearly two years ago. Time and success have restored her, at least partly, at least outwardly. Ed holds hands with his pretty fiancée. A man with a thick mop of red hair lounges at Ed's other side between him and his father, his eyes focused on Ted. He looks familiar – Beth's foxy journalist from the paper, surely, Jake somebody. Albie moves towards them, wanting to catch Ted, but the journalist, Jake, is now resting a hand on Ted's shoulder and murmuring in his ear. Ted's mouth opens wide in a noisy, unfamiliar laugh. The younger man leans to embrace him, Ted reciprocates, a bear hug. Albie stares; Ted only hugs family. He is still staring when Ted glances in his direction. Jake's gaze follows his as if intrigued. Albie smiles but Ted's eyes narrow, his eyebrows draw together, his face seems to contract. He has seen that look before, when Ted is about to perform a difficult operation and is weighing the risks. It lasts a second, maybe two. Despite the pressing crowd and the deafening noise, they could be facing each other in a darkened room; all he can see are those glinting eyes. Albie's heart begins to beat fast, as if his body senses a threat that his mind hasn't grasped. Ted turns away and raises his glass. 'A toast to the engaged couple.'

Glasses are lifted, congratulations shouted. Albie joins in the toast but the champagne tastes bitter, a little flat; he should have drunk it sooner. Ted is different tonight, as if with his family and this journalist fellow, their own friendship counts for less. He feels snubbed, like a child at a party left out of a game. He must find Beth, they should leave. It was a mistake to have come, they were both too tired. He will talk to Ted in the morning.

'. . . head up the laboratory for a year, with immediate effect.' Ted is looking straight at him again. He missed the start of this speech and the words hang in the air on their own in a moment of silence. Albie feels his neck and shoulders relax. Ted is making good on his promise after all; he'd been waiting for the right moment and hence the searching glance. Albie steps forward, assembling an acceptance speech. As he waits for the clapping to die down, Ted switches his gaze back to Ed, who ducks his head, smiling. Albie halts, confused, like a man at a crossroads where the signs have been changed, unsure of his direction.

'We feel very lucky he's accepted. This role will be challenging, but he has youth on his side. He will be helping to guide projects in the lab and will be taking forward some exciting commercial interest as well.' Ted smiles at his son and his voice deepens with affection. 'It comes at an auspicious time for Ed as we celebrate his engagement to our lovely future daughter-in-law, Sophie Valance.' More clapping. Sophie hides her face in Ed's shoulder. An orthopaedic surgeon standing next to Ed cheers loudly but Ted holds up his hand for quiet. 'Perhaps I should add that Ed was the unanimous choice of the selection board for appointments. He will be in charge; I'll remain on hand but in the background.'

Ted's words scythe through Albie like a weapon used in combat, rough-edged to do maximum harm. He is motionless to contain the hurt. He probably looks the same but his hand is shaking to the wild rhythm of his heart and the room has dimmed. He is conscious of movement nearby, a circle forming around Ed and Sophie. Ted has turned his back, as if, having struck a fatal blow, he can afford to ignore his rival, felled and no longer a threat. Is that what he's become without realising – Ted's rival? Perhaps he's always been a target, robbed at every turn and now dispossessed. Albie finishes his drink, slopping some. He must leave, go home and staunch the wound. He begins to shoulder through the throng, looking for Beth. He glimpses a slim girl through a parting in the crowd, her platinum head turned away in conversation with Owen: Skuld. His little spy. Did she know? Why didn't she warn him? He manoeuvres himself closer and taps her shoulder; the head turns, a lined fifty-year-old face stares into his, plucked eyebrows raised high. He stammers an apology and backs away, nodding in response to Owen's friendly smile. His face is sweating; he has to get out.

Beth is in a corner near the window, talking to a tall Indian girl, whose arm is around Jake. Albie looks at him with dislike.

'There you are.' Beth turns towards him as he approaches; she sounds relieved. 'I couldn't find you anywhere so I went outside to look. I missed the speech.' She takes his hand, drawing him into the little group. 'This is Jake and Gita. It was Jake I was talking about when I spotted that newspaper article, remember? I've been congratulating him on his piece.' Jake gives a little bow. 'Jake's Ed's best friend; it's his sister Sophie that Ed's marrying.' She smiles at Gita. 'Gita and I have been discussing gardens.'

Gita's pink sari is bright against her skin; her black hair sticks up in little points over a finely shaped skull but there are dark lines under her eyes. 'Beth's been suggesting what trees to plant for our son to look at from his pram.' She smiles but her voice trembles. 'He has hydrocephalus, so—'

'I hear you're a neurosurgeon, like Ted,' Jake cuts in, looking at Albie.

Albie stares at him blankly. The words jar. He isn't like Ted; he's not a thief or a liar, he doesn't break promises or cheat on his wife. Jake's pointed nose lifts at the tip, as if scenting the air for a problem. Close up his eyes are coloured differently, one brown, one green. It's hard to know which one to look at. Albie takes Beth's elbow, 'Excuse us, we have to leave straightaway.'

Beth glances at him; her eyes flick between his eyes and mouth, reading him. She slides her hand into his. As he draws her away, she turns back to Gita. 'Don't forget, a cherry tree, for the blossom.'

They are at the door when Ted's voice calls from the crowd. 'Leaving already?' He approaches, holding a champagne bottle in one hand, a glass in the other, his black tie askew. Albie stares at the angle of Ted's jaw where the tanned skin is stretched smoothly over the mandible, the place where in movies, fist meets flesh with a crunch of bone. But they are not in a movie; they are neurosurgical colleagues standing in the middle of a party. He wants to hurt Ted but he doesn't know how.

'. . . know how busy you are, Albie; you implied as much when I mentioned the post. It left an impression.' Ted's voice is a little slurred, his words run together. 'Ed's got more time to run a lab than you have.'

'You gave that job to me, Ted; it's mine.' Albie's face is burning. 'I'm managing the two-dose trial, remember?' He has never spoken to Ted like this before but the man is half drunk; he can say what he wants. Ted won't remember a word in the morning.

'Nothing was signed to that effect.' Ted sounds regretful. 'And as you've heard, turns out the lab wasn't mine to give.'

He's lying. Ted heads up that selection board; he could have achieved whatever outcome he wanted. Ted takes a step towards them. Beth instantly presses into Albie's side, he puts his arm around her; she is trembling as if with fever.

'Don't worry.' Ted smiles cheerfully. 'Though Ed takes over the running of the trial from now on, you'll still get your payout from the Viromex deal, plus royalties; that's if it all goes to plan. You modified the virus, after all.' Then he shrugs. 'There'll be no deal if it fails, of course. Ed would design a new trial in that case, and any payout and royalties that follow would be his.' His voice deepens. 'I'll take responsibility for this trial as it's already started, that's only fair while he's so new to it all. Ed's aware that the buck stops with me.' Then he laughs. 'Don't look like that, Albie. I thought you'd be relieved. The trial is more complicated now there are two stages to manage.' He glances at Beth, something sharp flickers across his face: anger? Regret? It's gone before Albie can analyse it. 'Lovely woman. She understands.' Ted lurches towards her and Albie tenses, bunching his hand. Ted's intoxicated, it wouldn't take much.

'Let's go, Albie.' Beth turns a white face up to his and he remembers the investigation she underwent that morning; he should get her home. He guides her through the door, but when he glances back, Ted is still staring after them. The smile has vanished and his face is quite empty.

Beth is sleeping; her lavender scent lingers in the room and on her skin.

His hands rest as if in prayer between her hips. They made love, a brief, intense coupling, and then, as though released, he'd talked into the night, tracing out the pattern of Ted's betrayals. They seem so obvious now; the smaller ones that were the forerunners of this larger one. The theft of his patent nearly two years ago, then his PhD. Now Ted has stolen his job. Albie has accommodated everything until this point, made allowances, tried to understand, to take the long view. Now there is no view; Ted has blotted it out.

Sleep doesn't come. He eases his arm from under Beth's body, gets up and slides the window open as widely as it will go. The night is cold, there's a harvest moon. He smells diesel fumes, decaying leaves, rubbish. A fox barks from somewhere close by. He hadn't realised how quickly the year was passing, summer has disappeared. Journeys between home and work take place in the dark, the seasons have become invisible. The old wood of the lintel is damp, the paint flakes beneath his hand. Everything is in jeopardy.

The lab job has gone; without a body of research to his name, the chances of a consultant post anywhere will be diminished. All his plans to make a difference could come to nothing. If the rats in the virus trial survive he'll at least own that research. His application for the next job will be strengthened, he'll have a future; if any die, the work will be dismissed and his position weakened. Ed will devise other treatments, he'll take the credit and the money. Without that money and without the salary from the lab to fund the mortgage, the house itself will be at risk. There will be nothing left for fertility treatment should they need it after all. Loss after loss.

The moon is obscured by cloud; as he gazes out at the dark trees his mind touches every shadowy possibility. He can hear Beth's words again, as clearly as if she were beside him, whispering them into his ear.

What if the chances of a reaction could be eliminated?

That could only happen if the rats were to receive the virus once, rather than twice; his thoughts begin to slide towards a plan as if down a sloping path that Beth has already smoothed for him.

There might be things that can be altered.

The protocol is set and the virus ordered, but no one would know if the rats were injected with an inert liquid, saline for instance, instead of virus in the first round of injections.

The fox barks again, the noise lengthening into a scream. Another shriek cuts across the first; it sounds like a fight. The noises are getting nearer. When the virus is given to the rats on the second injection, it would be as if for the first time. There would be no reaction, the treatment would be judged successful, Viromex would release the payout as promised and the trial would go forward. If any rats were to die during Viromex's own trials, the treatment would be terminated at that point, no child would ever be at risk. By then, at least he'd have the payout. If Viromex were to blame the Institute for a misleading trial, the blame would attach to Ted, who shoulders the responsibility and might even have to leave. The consultant job would fall vacant, and he'll be waiting, next in line.

A fox jumps on to the wall and runs lightly along it, a small shape hanging wriggling from its jaws. A bird? A rat? The spoils of a fight. The fox jumps through the air as though flying, lands smoothly and disappears behind the tree next to the shed. If he follows this plan he'll be stepping into wild territory where the shadows are thick, away from the straight path he has followed until now. He lifts his head, catching a faint iron tang. The victim has been laid open. He knows the scent of blood in all its guises, fresh in the operating theatre, putrid on a bandage, dried in the morgue. The wind blows the clouds from the moon and stirs the boughs of the pine tree next door; they lift and thrash like limbs. The garden becomes brighter in the moonlight.

Karim was smiling in the review clinic today, transformed. There will be others like him if the treatment can progress, generations of children to save. He owes it to them to take the research forward. He steps back and shuts the window then slides into bed. The warmth from Beth's sleeping body envelops him.

The noise of the coffee machine wakes him early. Beth is in the kitchen at five a.m., her work uniform beneath her coat. A jug of squeezed juice on the table is turbid with fragments that stir as if alive.

'I was thinking back to our discussion before the party.' She hands him a cup of coffee. 'I wondered if you'd thought any more about it.' She scoops up the stiffening tea bags that have been left to bleed in brown pools and tips the orange peel away.

He nods, wrapping his hands around the cup, the heat stings his palms. 'You were right, there are things that could be altered.' He drops his voice. 'Substituting saline for the virus in the first round of inoculations could be one of them . . .' He stops, uncertain. The words sound wrong in the bright kitchen – they belong back in the night, in the silence and dark – but Beth's eyes narrow instantly, she nods.

'Those kinds of changes would have to be done soon, before Bruce starts the trial. It will be too late after that.' She extracts toast from the toaster, butters the slice and passes it to him. Her mouth shines with lipstick, her hair is pinned neatly with a clasp. She looks fresh after her night's sleep, moving rapidly as though impelled by her thoughts. Harris sits by her feet, staring fixedly at her. She takes his biscuits from the cupboard, weighs a handful then pours them clattering into the bowl. The dog crunches them down in seconds. 'After my theatre list I'll start planning what we need to do.' She turns to him. 'We'll need to know if there are any CCTV cameras in the lab, perhaps call in to check if you have time.' As she walks about the kitchen, clearing the table and replacing milk in the fridge, the ring on her finger catches the light and a green splinter dances on the wall. He gazes at it as he bites into the toast, his thoughts veering wildly.

She kisses him goodbye, then the door closes behind her. His list starts later than hers. He dresses slowly, pulling his clothes from a heap on the bedroom floor, the black silk dress crumpled amongst them. The plans that seemed so clear last night are muddled now, the way ahead tangled with doubts. He replaces the towels on the bathroom rail, glancing in the mirror. His lips are stained red with her lipstick. The taste is unfamiliar. He scrubs his mouth clean with the flannel, looks round the untidy bedroom and, closing the door on the mess, hurries from the house.

13

London. Autumn 2017

Scalpel. Wound retractor. Forceps. Diathermy. She knows the order by heart. The surgeon next to her is trussed into crackling cotton like a warrior into armour. He doesn't look up but holds out a gloved hand into which she places instruments, slapping them against his palm one by one. They act with precision as if shadow-dancing while images from yesterday rise up to bob against her mind: the swollen tubes on the screen, Albie's joyful face and later his stricken one; Ted lurching towards her.

The surgeon glances up. She hands him the bone saw, handle first, and an ear-splitting whine fills the theatre. She swabs blood and rinses debris; the images submerge again. When the leg is removed, it is passed to her, the weight heavier than she'd expected, much warmer; she hands it on to an assistant, then turns back again, passing the diathermy instruments, needles and thread. Stitching draws the wound edges together as neatly as a zippered purse. When the operation is finished and the patient has been attended to in the recovery room, she follows his bed to the ward and delivers the notes and instructions before descending again to wash white bone dust from her face. Leaving the hospital, she looks about her for a moment as if she has stumbled ashore in a strange place and is wondering exactly where she is. She walks part-way back, needing sun and air after a morning of artificial fluorescence and the rusty scents of blood and bone. Once home she changes into her oldest tracksuit and ties her hair high. Her eyes look different in the bathroom mirror. They shine more brightly, her jaw seems sharply defined, as if the muscles have grown from clenching her teeth in her sleep. She turns away from that pale, determined face.

The kitchen first. Order seems necessary for the task ahead, like her trolley of instruments before the surgeon goes to work. She clears shelves, scouring the sticky rings and throwing away broken strands of pasta and grains of rice. As she scrubs and sluices, the stain of her encounter with David yesterday seems to fade a little. She sweeps dog hair, blackened fragments of meat and translucent slivers of cheese from the corners of the floor. Harris watches from the door, whining softly as she works; after a while he settles to sleep, nose on his paws.

There are bones behind the compost bin in the garden where she dumps the waste, blackish faeces, a musky smell. Foxes. She leaves their mess untouched, not wanting to scare them away. What if there are cubs about? She walks back to the house, glancing around at the garden as she goes. There are more trees now, a large vegetable patch in the corner behind a hedge, but she hasn't thought of flowers for the spring. By then Albie's trial could be done, the children will be improving; Albie will be feted everywhere, Ted's betrayals fading. They'll need to gaze out on celebratory yellows and oranges, colours that cheer and heal. Leaving the kitchen floor to dry, she shuts Harris in the house and walks round the curve of the road to Rosslyn Hill. Her feet crunch on the curled leaves that drift on the pavements as she hurries to the village, out of breath by the time she turns into Flask Walk. At the flower shop, she squats to fill a bag with hard cream and brown daffodil bulbs from an open sack on the floor, scooping them up in handfuls.

'Beth?'

It takes a couple of seconds to place the smiling face bending towards her: the party last night, the tired girl who wanted to plant trees for her baby. Gita.

'This is so amazing. I've just ordered that cherry tree.' Gita leans forward and kisses her, then straightens, revealing a baby strapped against her chest in a stripy papoose. 'Meet Billy.'

Beth would have seen something was wrong even if Gita hadn't mentioned Billy's hydrocephalus. His large head lolls against the side of the sling; his features crowd together under the swollen dome of his forehead.

'I might have known you'd be here,' Gita continues happily. 'What are you buying?' She peers into Beth's bag.

'Oh, just a few daffodil bulbs for next spring.'

'Gosh, how organised. I wouldn't have a clue.'

Beth smiles, calculating how soon she can say goodbye; she wants to plant the daffodils, then sit at the table in her clean kitchen, a list in front of her. Albie will need equipment to take to the lab, an excuse for his presence, an idea of the time it might take.

She walks rapidly to the till. 'I should pay for these.'

Gita follows, leaning her elbow on the counter to watch as Beth picks up seed packets of carrots, beetroot and lettuce, and as an afterthought, parsley. Gita fingers the little paper envelope. 'My mum always says that parsley only grows in a house where the woman rules.'

Beth nods, hardly hearing; she pays and turns to go.

'Come round for coffee,' Gita proposes suddenly. 'I'll take you. The car's round the corner.' She touches Beth's arm. 'My mum sent some special biscuits.' Her other hand is cupped over Billy's head; a pleading note has entered her voice.

Gita's flat is on the ground floor in a modern block on the main road in Crouch End. She waves her hand airily to the patch of grass in front – 'For the cherry tree,' she laughs. Inside, they navigate their way through a room full of toys to the kitchen. The surfaces are littered: glasses with crimson dregs sit alongside bowls containing dried cornflakes beached above puddles of milk. A kitten drowses on a cushion near the sink.

'The mess!' Gita exclaims, as if proud of the disorder. 'We need a bigger place but we can't afford it; Jake doesn't have a regular salary. He's freelance and very picky; he only works on things he thinks are important.'

'Like that story in the paper?'

'Exactly. He worked on that case for years. His tenacity is great, but more space would be nice.' She leans forward to rest the papoose on the counter. Releasing Billy, she holds him high in the air, turning him a little to show him off, like a new kitten or puppy. As Billy smiles, a stream of mucus falls from his mouth to Gita's cheek. She laughs again, and shifts him to a hip to wipe her face, humming as she walks round her untidy kitchen. The child seems part of her body, as essential and taken for granted as a limb. Beth looks away quickly. A cork board on the wall is covered with photos of every size: a younger Jake and Ed on a painted canal boat, Jake with a guitar and Sophie playing an accordion, another revealing a large family group in a restaurant, Ted and Jenny among them.

'That was the night Ed proposed to Sophie,' Gita says, glancing over. 'His family were thrilled, specially Ted. Sophie marrying Ed completed the family in his eyes; he'd more or less adopted Jake already.

'Jake? Why?'

'Jake met Ed in rehab. You may not know that Ed

was an addict as a teenager. Jake was too but he was older; he took him under his wing. They went through it together. Ted credits Jake with rescuing Ed, since then he can't do enough for him. He paid for Jake's journalism course.' She glances down at Billy. 'Daddy's a lucky boy, isn't he?' She grins. 'You should see Jake and Ted together, like big kids. It's sweet.'

Jake should take care. Ted's generous if he wants something, but once he's taken what he needs everything changes. It happened to his wife and then to her; now it's Albie's turn. Last night his eyes were black with pain.

'You okay?' Gita puts a hand on her arm.

'Sure.' She points quickly to another photo: a beautiful white-haired woman in a dark blue sari next to an older version of Gita in pink carrying a bundle in her arms. 'Who's this?'

'Me as a baby, my mum and grandmother. They adore Billy.' She puts her lips to the boy's forehead. 'They'll all be here at Christmas.'

Christmas. Families gathering, children celebrated; the bright colours in the photo blur. The shriek of the kettle makes her jump.

'Oh sorry, it'll have to be tea; we've run out of coffee. Could you take Billy?'

He weighs more than she'd thought – not a kitten or puppy, more like a small sack of damp sand. His mouth is a perfect circle of surprise, the large head smells of warm toast. His heat penetrates to her skin and she is hit by a wave of longing so intense she sways on her feet. Gita doesn't notice. She is humming again, dropping tea bags into mugs and opening a tin of diamond-shaped biscuits, speckled with sugar. 'Mum is forever sending food parcels, as if we're starving. Does yours still do that?'

Beth shakes her head, holding Billy more tightly. The last food from her mother was twenty years ago. Baked beans in front of the television, followed by a kiss on the cheek, wet with alcohol, the door closing, stilettos tapping down the stairs. A car door slamming, the engine revving; her parents had been, the police told her later, precisely five minutes from their deaths.

'I can't resist.' Gita crunches into a biscuit. 'Breast-feeding makes me ravenous.'

Billy begins to grizzle. Gita holds out her arms and Beth hands him over. The place where he had rested feels cold, a little damp, empty; she smooths her crumpled shirt.

Gita pushes up her jersey and her red lacy bra, Billy pummels her breast and then there is peace. Beth watches his small toes curl. The veins in the stretched skin of his forehead seem to bulge rhythmically, as if filling with liquid at each mouthful. Beth watches the way the small lips close round the nipple, the cheeks hollowing with each suck, and her own nipples begin to ache with memory.

After a few minutes, Billy jerks his head back and

he begins to cry. Gita lifts him to her shoulder, patting his back. 'He has a problem with digesting his feed; there are lots of problems, to be honest.' She stands to rock him, looking weary. 'I shouldn't complain. Ted helps with all the medical stuff. He's a saint, don't you think?'

'I wouldn't know.' Beth glances to the photo of Ted surrounded by his family. 'You'll have to ask Albie.'

Gita looks surprised. 'So I guess you medics must be too busy to socialise much amongst yourselves.' She gestures towards the dirty glasses. 'Jake parties with his mates all the time.'

There would be music, jazz maybe, talking, dancing, the smell of exotic food. It would be warm and crowded. The rooms in their flat are deserted, a little cool. No one comes; she hasn't wanted friends. Albie is enough. Albie is everything, but slim as a scalpel slipping between her mind and these certainties is the sense of missing something, of being mistaken, of being too late. Too late for laughter and parties, too late for a family. The stilettos tap to silence and the door in her mind slams shut. 'I should go . . . the dog.'

As she fumbles by her feet for the bag of bulbs, the front door crashes open.

'In the kitchen,' Gita calls.

Jake comes in, a compact shape moving swiftly across the room. He pauses to glance at Beth as he takes Billy from Gita. Billy begins to cry again. Cradling his son,

Jake comes close to Beth. 'Hi there, it's good to see you again.' His odd-coloured eyes probe hers as if to find out why she's in his house. He is bouncing on his feet to soothe the baby but the movements seem faintly aggressive, like the dance of a boxer.

'You too.' Beth turns away, unsettled. Why did she come, after all? Gita had been insistent but she could have refused; perhaps she'd simply been following the baby.

'I'm off now, Gita, thanks for the tea.'

'Let me drive you.' Gita gets up and, pushing her breast back into the bra, starts hunting for shoes.

'It's okay, I'll catch a bus.'

Jake walks to the door and holds it open for her. Billy has stopped crying. He regards her unblinkingly; his eyelashes are clumped together in small, wet points.

'Bye, Billy.' She touches his foot quickly.

'It was good to meet your husband the other night.' Jake jogs from side to side, his body blocking her from leaving. 'You know, Ted put the drainage system in Billy's head. He lets us phone him if there are problems and sometimes he meets us on the ward at Great Ormond Street Hospital.' He sighs. 'But he's mostly in the States now, so we were wondering, as Albie's doing his locum . . .'

'I'll ask him.'

Jake steps away from the door, nodding his thanks. So that was why Gita was so friendly and why she'd invited her round. It wasn't about making friends at all. Beth understands, though. She would have done anything to have helped her daughter to survive, anything. She walks swiftly past Jake without saying goodbye.

Her aunt would have said to plant the daffodils neatly, two bulb-widths apart, but she wants a random blaze of colour and throws handfuls of bulbs on the lawn. She digs out cones of grass-topped earth where they fall, drops in a bulb and replaces the turf, pressing it flat. A robin flutters to the fence in the dusk, attracted by the smell of earth, watching for worms. She sits quite still but he flicks away into the trees next door. Wet from the grass seeps through her trousers; it's too dark for more planting now. She is tapping compost into a plug tray on the draining board in the kitchen when Albie returns. He watches as she scatters the ridged brown parsley seeds over the soil, and then he sits down, whisky in hand.

'Hungry?'

He shakes his head.

'How was your day?'

He shrugs. There are dark lines under his eyes, his days are relentless. 'How was yours?'

'An orthopaedic list, then I cleaned, planted daffodils, that sort of day. I met Gita at the flower shop.'

He looks through the window then away again, as if disappointed not to see yellow flowers blooming in the dark autumn garden. 'Gita?' he echoes absently.

'From last night, Jake's partner.'

He doesn't respond; he must have forgotten. She won't pass on their request to help with Billy just yet, he seems tired. She covers the little seeds with brown granules of vermiculite and pours water over them.

'Did you notice if there were CCTV cameras in the lab?'

'There were none the last time I looked; I didn't have time to go today.' He closes his eyes.

She pulls cling film from the roll, stretching it tightly over the tray; he's still undecided. 'I was thinking you might need some equipment, syringes, needles, a sharps box.' She drops these ideas lightly, seeds scattered on to compost. 'Gloves, maybe, things like that.'

Albie says nothing but pushes himself out of the chair, pours himself another drink and hands one to her.

'Just what I needed, thank you.' She smiles up at him and carries the tray to the window sill then washes her hands.

He sits down again and drains his glass. 'Criminals wear gloves,' he says at last.

'They're the criminals, Albie.' She walks over, kneels by his chair and speaks softly. 'Ted is a thief. He has stolen everything he possibly could from you, but this trial is yours by right; yours and the children's. You need to make sure the outcome is positive or your work will stall before it's had a chance to reach them. You have to, Albie, for the sake of those children. You know there's a safety net in place.'

He seems to be listening, but as she leans to kiss him, his eyes are full of struggle. 'I'm here to help whenever you need me,' she whispers. 'I'll do anything you want.'

He looks at her as if seeing her for the first time that evening, then stands and lifts her against him. She slips her hand between the belt of his trousers and the warm skin behind. His response is immediate, a match to kindling. He pushes up her skirt, unbelts his trousers and treads them down. She steps out of her pants and he lifts her, carries her a few steps to the wall, holds her as she curls her legs around him, the weight of his chest pressing against hers. Then he is inside her, she stifles a cry, his face is buried in her neck, he is absorbed, panting, quick as an animal. He comes in shuddering gasps. She clings to him, stroking his hair. Tears of pain are wet on her cheeks but she doesn't care. It seems to her that she's signed her name to a pact.

In bed that night they make love again. He is tender this time and very careful; he strokes her hair, murmuring to her, watching her face as he waits for her to climax first. Afterwards, lying side by side, they hear the fox, a high-pitched, unearthly sound. She pushes herself up.

'Foxes,' he tells her.

'But this sounds noisier than normal.'

'A vixen on the prowl. Lie flat, sweetheart, don't move.' He puts a pillow under her knees; he is thinking this will make the sperm's journey easier.

'How do you know it's a vixen?'

'The females always scream.' His voice slurs, he is sliding into sleep. 'If it worries you I'll get rid of it. Foxes are shot as vermin in Jura.'

'Don't do anything, Albie. What if she has cubs?' Albie doesn't answer. His face is turned into the pillow. He is asleep.

14

London. Autumn 2017

The glass doors of the private hospital slide back soundlessly. Albie enters, leaving behind the damp world of wet leaves and grey skies as he walks through the luxuriously furnished spaces of the reception area to the untidy changing room, transforming from man in the street to doctor as he goes. As he puts on the blue cotton theatre clothes and slides his feet into a pair of bloodstained plastic clogs, the metamorphosis completes. With the clothes he becomes the surgeon, life simplifies.

He scrubs up with Betadine, the tarry scent recalling the pines in summer behind the house in Jura, though at this time of year the trees will be tossing in autumn storms. As the season deepens, life on the island strips back to weather and food; the struggle for survival becomes elemental. The deer come off the hill and group in the conifers. He'd give a lot to be there now.

He glances at Sabat, his theatre nurse, scrubbing up alongside. His wife had a baby last week, he looks half asleep. A young nurse steps forward with his gloves, her fair hair plaited and pinned like a milkmaid. She opens the paper envelope containing his gloves so that once scrubbed, he doesn't need to touch the paper which would desterilise him. He slips his hands into the gloves, working the fingers to fit, and then the automatic doors swing open into the theatre and he steps into the innermost circle, the bright heart of the building, of his work, of who he is. He stands a little apart. Owen is talking to the patient while slowly depressing a white-filled syringe connected to the cannula in the old man's arm; the replies mumble to silence and his eyelids flicker shut. He is swiftly intubated.

Albie checks the scans. The degenerate discs are obvious; one block of bone rests directly on another below, which has thickened to take the weight, trapping the emerging nerve. In front of him is no longer a man's neck, stretched out for a knife, but an operating field, to be cleansed and made ready. He swabs the neck with a sponge on a stick dipped into prep fluid and lays out the green wraps as simply as if organising the repair of a broken machine. Sabat hands him the scalpel and in less than a second he has incised the skin of the neck. In this opened flap lie the carotid artery, the recurrent laryngeal nerve and the brachial plexus. Injury to any one of these would be catastrophic; moving the structures aside with his fingers, he dissects to the spine. The remnants of the disc are removed piecemeal like so many fragments of crabmeat; then he drills the bony spurs away from the surrounding bone, freeing the trapped nerve now glistening in the widened canal. He inserts an artificial joint between the vertebrae, forcefully pressing it in place. Checking the clock, he is surprised to see almost two hours have passed.

He closes up the wound then strips off the tight gloves, his hands damp with sweat. He writes up his operation in the patient's notes, then walks into the coffee room, circling his head and shrugging to ease the stiff muscles. His shoulders burn. His own discomfort is irrelevant: in a short while the patient will turn his neck cautiously from side to side, open and close his hand, realising his movements are free of pain.

Sabat has made coffee for him and fills a glass of water for himself. They sit next to each other, both sighing with relief. He takes in his friend's contented smile.

'How's life with the baby, Sabat?' he asks, ignoring a lightning stab of jealousy.

'Fine, thanks. My parents are with us; my father says prayers of thankfulness every day. It is the first grandchild.'

'Prayers,' Albie repeats. The word seems as incongruous as 'evil' did at the lecture; it has been years since he prayed. He wouldn't remember the words.

'He is a priest, so is my brother,' Sabat continues. 'That's what I was supposed to become, but I chose this work instead. My other brother is a social worker.'

Good people, then; good imbibed from childhood,

as simple and transparent as the water in his glass, though the water in Jura tastes different in different rivers, salty like the sea or coloured brown with peat. His father stopped them drinking from mountain streams in case an animal might be decaying higher up, out of sight. Albie looks through the window into the bleak garden outside the coffee room, the bare flower beds covered with rotting leaves. His ambitions aren't simple any more. Ted's betrayals have muddied them, or perhaps they've revealed how he felt all along. Doing good isn't enough, unless it contains the possibility of doing well. Recognition and reward: the salt in the water, the silt at the bottom.

A nurse puts her head round the door. 'They've sent for the next patient, Mr McAlister.'

As Albie re-scrubs, the same nurse opens another packet of gloves. The elements that underpin his life seem as tightly twisted as her plaited hair, the drive to do good so interwoven with the need to do well that even if he could disentangle the strands, both would be distorted. Nothing seems straightforward any more.

The next operation is lumbar spine decompression, harder work; the bones are bigger. After an exhausting tussle, the nerve roots are freed and, as in the case before, he sees the shining white length of the nerve running freely in its canal. While he is sewing up the skin, the message comes through that the next case is cancelled. The patient has been accidentally fed. Back in the changing room, he is undressing when the door opens then slams shut. Loud voices and raucous laughter spill into the silent room. Those who have entered begin to change their clothes, chatting unseen behind a row of tall lockers. One of the voices belongs to the orthopaedic surgeon who cheered for Ed at the party. Ambushed, Albie sheds the last of his clothes and steps swiftly into the shower, turning on the water. He doesn't want to meet Ted's friends.

'. . . Six o' clock?'

'You'll beat me hollow. Ted's away, I'm out of practice.'

'Is he any good?'

'Won the cup last year.'

A pause. The sound of a belt or buckle being undone.

'. . . certainly on great form at that engagement do.' The voice is effortful, as if the man is bending to unlace shoes, '. . . surprised me.'

Albie instantly turns the water to a trickle and draws the shower curtain back, straining to hear more. The reply is muffled, the speaker must be pulling a theatre top over his head and speaking through fabric.

'. . . very young . . . well of course . . .'

This is about Ed and the lab. Albie's body becomes rigid.

'. . . keeping it in the family . . . naturally . . .'

He'd been family or so he'd thought; his jaw clenches.

He hears laughter, the sound of a locker being opened then closed, more words, buried in more laughter. They are laughing at him, he is sure of it, the dupe who did the work, and was cast aside like a dog left to howl in the dark outside a locked door. Albie puts his fist against the wet tiles, the walls close around him. Water trickles on to his head and down his neck; he begins to shiver. Minutes pass before he hears the stamping on of clogs then footsteps walking through the room. Plastic doors slap shut, cutting off further sounds.

He turns the dripping water off with difficulty, fumbling the heavy tap. He waits a moment or two to be sure that no one returns, then, pushing the curtain fully aside, he steps out of the shower into the warmth of the changing room, and in that moment, steps into his decision. He binds the towel tightly round his waist, takes another and rubs his cold body, tingling with resolve. The choice is made. He dresses quickly and, visiting the recovery room with his briefcase, calmly helps himself to gloves, needles and syringes, a bag of saline. He does this methodically, making no attempt to hide what he's doing. He puts the items into his case while the anaesthetist and nurses are busy with the patient; they don't even look up. He phones Bruce outside the recovery room, suggesting lunch, but Bruce's sentences are muddled and punctuated by long exhalations, he sounds distracted or high. Drunk, maybe. His project is impossible, he says, the results don't add up to anything sensible. He is on the point of giving up.

Albie seizes his chance. He offers to help, today if it suits, he has time. Maths is his strong point. Bruce accepts, he sounds on the brink of tears.

Albie retrieves his car from the hospital car park and heads south, driving fast; if the trial has been started already – as Beth warned – he could be too late. As he weaves rapidly through the traffic, he turns the radio on, tuned to Classic FM. The clear notes of a flute fill the car; the clean sound marries with the image of the glistening nerve running unimpeded in its canal to its destination.

15

London. Autumn 2017

The stage looks empty; don't be fooled.

Scuffles and squeaks, the odd squeal as the night animals rouse. This is their time, but something is different and they sense it; someone is working, if you can call it that. He is invisible, no one sees him for who he is. Almost no one. As we said, the stage looks empty.

We won't punish him; we won't need to. He'll do that on his own.

The needle penetrates the tough rubber bung; he withdraws the fluid then pauses, syringe in hand. This, after all, is theft. This could be murder if the odds are against him, child murder, a massacre of the innocents. The kind of thing Sabat's family would entreat their god to prevent at all costs. Then Albie leans over the basin and ejects the contents carefully down the plughole. His fears are groundless, the product of stress. There will be no need for prayers because there's no chance of problems, as Beth reminded him, a safety net's in place. He is speeding the process, that's all. Viromex will repeat the trial; any dangers he is bypassing now will come to light then. He continues to work his way through the row of vials, peeling back a corner of the foil tab over each rubber bung and then draining them one by one.

Bruce's left leg had been jigging up and down when Albie entered his room three hours ago. He glanced up irritably. His skin was pale, a couple of pustular lesions glowed beside his nose, his hair was greasy. The foppish appearance had slipped.

'Finally,' Bruce muttered.

No welcome, no thanks for making the effort. Albie's tension dissipated. Bruce was distracted; his guard would be down.

'I've got a few hours,' Albie told him. 'We could make a start on sorting out these results of yours. What's the problem?'

'I'm in such fucking trouble.' Bruce turned back to the screen but he'd been logged out. He swore, rapidly tapping in his password with nicotine-stained fingers, his long nails clicking on the keys. *DEAD RATS.* Albie looked away, wincing. Typical Bruce.

'They don't make sense.' Bruce stared at the rows of numbers, scrolling up and down. 'My father funded this PhD. I'm the last fucking hope of a fucked-up family, but I won't get it.' His voice was thin with panic. 'Nothing adds up.'

'Have you or Ed started the rerun Ted wanted yet?'

Bruce stared blankly back at him.

'Injecting virus into the abdomen of those rats – you must remember, Bruce, the ones who get a second dose later?'

'Christ. What does he expect? Fucking miracles?' Bruce exploded. 'Of course we haven't. Home Office approval only came through two weeks ago. Ed's in Berne looking at stem cells. He's left everything to me. I'm screwed, Albie.'

'Anything is possible if you take it step by step.' He felt weak with relief; there was still time. He smiled at Bruce. 'As I remember, you've grown up five tumour cell lines in petri dishes, all subtypes of glioblastoma from different biopsy samples?'

Bruce's eyes were bloodshot. 'I can hardly remember anything. I haven't slept for two nights.'

'And you are testing the efficacy of differing concentrations of temozolomide and irinotecan, right?'

'Don't mock. It may sound simple, but the numbers are muddled. The bloody graphs don't work.'

'Meaning?'

'You'd think that the stronger the concentration of drug, the quicker the tumour cells are killed, but it doesn't work like that. There are random anomalies which skew the results.' Bruce leant over the desk, gesticulating at the screen; the smell of stale sweat was intense. His leg began to bounce again.

This would be easy, easier than he'd dared to imagine. Bruce was unravelling before his eyes.

'Go home. Eat something, have a bath and go to sleep. This won't take me long.' Albie paused. 'By the way, I don't think it would help your PhD if it got out that someone else had written up your results. I promise I won't tell anyone I was here tonight if you don't.'

'My lips are sealed.' Bruce eased off his chair, performing a stumbling victory dance and saving himself by holding Albie's shoulder. 'I owe you.'

'It's the other way round.' Albie looked Bruce in the eye. 'I'm grateful you're running that trial. Frankly I'm relieved to be out of it. Time is short. I've taken over Ted's private patients too, so—'

'You always were a greedy bastard,' Bruce butted in with a short laugh.

He had wanted to punch Bruce then. He puts the syringe down, letting the surge of fury subside. He was never greedy; it was never just about the money. The private work is incidental. What he is doing now concerns the future of treatment for brain tumours in children. In a few months he, Albie, will be the author of miracles. His presence will be requested as the key speaker at international conferences, the acknowledged leader in the field. No one will take his success away after that; it will be Ted in the audience then, listening in the dark.

Before he left, Bruce had reached for an untidy stack of green notebooks pushed against the wall at the back of the desk. 'The data is all in here, if you want to double-check anything.'

Albie opened the first page; numbers stretched down the paper in messy columns, figures crossed out several times, notes scrawled alongside, with pencilled arrows pointing to different sums. He turned a few more pages, trying to mask his surprise.

'It's on the screen as well.' Bruce was watching his face. 'If you're going to be anal about it.'

Albie accompanied him down the corridor, glancing at the ceiling. Still no CCTV cameras. At the door Bruce turned. 'You're a mate.' He stepped forward and launched himself at Albie. The musky smell of cannabis was overwhelming, followed by a fainter wash of alcohol and nicotine.

Albie made a cup of coffee in the staffroom, heaping in the granules. It would take a while to correct Bruce's project, then the work of the night could start. No one else was about now. He felt as excited as a student with a deadline, as determined. Back then, he'd spent whole nights in the Glasgow research centre, hiding behind the door from Hilary, the laboratory manager, while she prowled her labs, checking for lingerers. Once she'd gone, he worked through his rat stress experiments, free from the censorious gaze of those narrow hazel eyes. It was unpleasant work, the rats had frozen with fear under the strong light then scrabbled to get away, tearing each other's coats. There were casualties, but despite his guilt he persisted. The bigger picture was the one that counted, he told himself, the longer view. In time he would make a difference; he held to that.

A row of keys hung on hooks under the cupboard of mugs. The one for the animal fridge had a red tab – that's where the vaccines would be, with the tumour solutions and chemotherapy agents, all carefully labelled.

Light footsteps came down the corridor towards the coffee room. He stepped swiftly away from the keys as Skuld came in; she glanced at him incuriously as she reached for a glass on the shelf above the sink.

'Oh, hi there, Skuld.' His heart had plummeted. This was worrying, he'd reckoned on an empty lab. 'You're working late tonight.'

She filled her glass from the tap but didn't reply. He studied the slim back view.

'I'm correcting Bruce's PhD; it's a bit of a secret.' A quick laugh. 'I wouldn't want anyone to think he'd been cheating.'

Her head tipped back as she swallowed; a listener, he reassured himself, not a gossip.

'It's good to see you,' he continued. 'I've been wanting to ask if you knew about the lab being handed to Ted's son? You go to those meetings; I'm mostly in the hospital these days, but if there was anything to tell me, you could always leave a message with the departmental secretary and I'd come to find you.'

She turned, her fair eyebrows slightly raised as if puzzled. She shook her head silently.

'Well, it doesn't matter now.' It does matter, it still hurts. It will always hurt. 'I just wondered, that's all. Things are busy, it's probably for the best.'

A smile flickered over her face; encouraged, he smiled back.

'I thought I saw you running on the Heath with your sisters a while ago now, a glimpse but—'

'Take care.' The words were breathed quietly, like a wind on a summer night, light enough to be imaginary, cool enough to make you shiver.

'Sorry, what—'

'See you.' She walked past him and the door swung shut behind her; a faint scent of summer grass lingered in the air.

He stood still, staring at the door. She couldn't possibly have guessed what was afoot. *Take care* is simply another way to say goodbye, like *see you*. His coffee had gone cold and he topped it up from the kettle. She didn't mean he should be careful any more than she meant she would see him.

Back at the desk, Albie checked the numbers on the screen against those in the notebook and saw a mismatch on the very first page, another on the fifth. He shook his head in disbelief. Bruce had simply failed to translate the correct numbers from page to screen; basic errors, though enough to spoil the expected trend. He must have been high on drugs and alcohol for weeks, too confused to think clearly; the errors were those of a tired child. Bruce might be brilliant, but he'd forgotten fundamental accuracy, and a single mistake would be enough to wreck the results. In three hours Albie had checked every number and corrected several more copying mistakes. He began to feed the corrected information into the computer, generating graph after graph. They all demonstrated the predicted relationship between concentration of drug and destruction of cancer cells; by midnight the last one had been completed. It was time to start the real work of the night.

He glanced in the animal room; Skuld had gone home. Wearing the gloves he'd stowed earlier, he retrieved the keys and unlocked the fridge. The labelled boxes were on the middle shelf: *Primer varicella solution: Batch 82297X for intra-abdominal inoculations* was clearly written on the cardboard in blue felt tip. In matters like this, Bridget took no chances. The other boxes were labelled with orange felt tip: *Varicella solution for intracerebral inoculation.* It was that easy. He removed the blue-labelled box and took it to Bruce's room. If the night porter came by on his rounds, he should have time to push it under the counter.

He's halfway there. He removes the bag of saline from his case, withdraws a syringeful then refills each vial to the previous level marked on the side. He takes care to use the puncture point he made before and presses the silver foil top down afterwards, smoothing it flat. He bends close to inspect the vials; they look exactly as they did before he began. No one could possibly guess at the change. Bruce will drain them again in a day or so, unwittingly delivering a quarter of a millilitre of saline into the abdomen of each rat. Intracerebral dosing will follow, Viromex's tests and later, the children's trial. His part is over.

He replaces the vials in the box, then the box in the fridge, locks the fridge door, puts the key back on its hook, then stows the syringes and needles in his case along with the gloves and empty bag of saline. He checks the sink is swilled out and tidies the pile of notebooks.

'Done,' he mutters, exhausted. 'All done.'

Ted's coat is still hanging behind the door in the locker room, untouched for the last two years, the underground car park pass still in the pocket. He removes the card, takes the stairs to the ground floor and continues to the lower ground then basement. His presence on the CCTV cameras in reception earlier won't matter, but exiting now could attract attention. The dark car park is empty. There is a ramp leading to the exit, which might have CCTV cameras in place. He begins to walk around the perimeter. He is being overcautious – Ted's training again. No investigation will ever be necessary; he knows that. Nevertheless, he doggedly continues his search until he finds a door in the corner with the slotted metal box. He swipes the card rapidly: nothing. He wipes the plastic against his sleeve and tries again and this time the door opens with a dull click. He steps into a dark cul-de-sac which leads to an alley; another turn brings him out to Great Ormond Street.

The sky is lightening over the Heath as he drives up Haverstock Hill, but in Hampstead Hill Gardens, all the curtains are still drawn. He gazes up at the house, his grandparents' house; safe now. The mortgage will be paid by the end of the year. Their children, their children's children, will grow up here. He walks down the steps by the side of the house to the garden door and lets himself into the kitchen quietly. Lit candles on the dresser gutter in their holders. Beth has fallen asleep in a chair, legs tucked under her body, but her eyes snap open as if she can feel his gaze on her skin. She smiles sleepily and stretches to retrieve a champagne bottle in a bucket of melting ice on the table by her side.

'Something a little unexpected happened . . .' He takes the champagne glasses from the dresser and gives them to her.

'Unexpected?' Her smile falters.

'I hadn't realised Skuld would be in the lab so late at night.' He shakes his head. 'She didn't see anything, but if there are problems further on, it might come out that I made an unscheduled visit just before the trials were due to start.'

Beth sets the glasses down and picks up the champagne bottle. 'What problems could there be, Albie?

Viromex's trials will uncover any risks. There won't be any problems. Relax.' She removes the cork with a deft twist as if she's been practising in readiness for just this moment. She proffers his glass, lifting her own high.

'Congratulations, sweetheart, it all starts now.'

Act Two

16

London. Spring 2018

The day everything changes is their second wedding anniversary; it starts with silence and light. The ladders, dust sheets and buckets have finally gone. The absence of radios and cement mixers confers peace, like a blessing. The house is the same and different, like the shift in a friend from youth to middle age. The bones are the same, the eyes and the hands, but everything else has changed. There are no separate rooms in the basement now, their old bedroom has vanished. Instead a large kitchen opens into a sitting room that looks over the garden through sheets of glass and folding doors. The walls are rough brick, the table shining steel. The dresser has gone. Copper saucepans gleam from a low hanging rack; there is a boiling tap and a fridge the size of a small room that clatters ice into drinks at the touch of a button. Upstairs the newly painted walls shimmer like the inside of a shell. The view reaches to the trees on the Heath, blue-green in the distance over the rooftops. Sometimes Beth takes Harris for walks up Parliament Hill, where Albie goes for his run, but twice now joggers with dogs, thin women rushing past, have almost pushed her off the path. Children are everywhere, in prams, with kites, dragging on their parents' hands or running down the slopes. She prefers the village and takes Harris along little side streets, dawdling to look at the gardens.

There are more plants in their garden; the daffodils are over, but roses and clematis cover the high trellis. Pleached limes grow against the wall. She has started a gardening journal, recording everything she's planted; she writes it up while Albie designs trials in his notebook. The leather binding is a little cracked these days, some of the pages are loose. It's almost full but he won't hear of a replacement. She has taken it from the shelf and placed it next to her gardening journal on the side table in the hall; easier for him to pick up on the way to work, secretly she likes the way they look side by side, her flowery notebook, his leather one, touching each other.

The lab's two-dose rat trial had gone to plan. Bruce gave Viromex the data six months ago and they ran their own trials, which went smoothly, according to Ed. Albie had been speechless with relief. When the payout arrived, Beth bought champagne. The countdown to the children's trial has begun. She left her job; the money isn't needed now and she'd far rather be in the garden. Occasionally she catches his glance up and down her body when he thinks she isn't looking, in the bath, or as she reaches for her clothes in the morning. He doesn't say anything, and she doesn't either. The encounter with David Smith has receded into the past, undiscussed and buried deep.

Today is perfect for gardening. Brightness beats from a white sky. Gulls circle high up; their sharp descending calls filter through the air. She glances at her journal; the jobs for the week are neatly listed: fertilise beds, plant beans and herbs, earth up the first earlies. She trundles the wheelbarrow full of fish, bone and blood fertiliser to the flower beds and forks it in, Harris scrabbling alongside. Later she plants beans in neat holes, covers them with soil and attaches cotton to twigs pushed into the ground against the birds. She earths up the potatoes and fills an old terracotta pot by the back door with compost, pushing a cutting of rosemary into the soil. She is interrupted once for a delivery, a woman bringing the special cake she ordered. She asks her to leave it in its box in the kitchen and carries on, working to the rhythm of the garden, one hour slipping into another.

Later the front door bangs. She replaces her trowel and spade in the shed, catching the musky smell again, foxes about. Albie is sitting on the sofa, watching the news. She pulls off her boots and pours him a glass of whisky from the last of the hoarded Jura bottles. *Prophecy* is written in thin black letters on the gold label. Looked at through the glass, the room becomes refracted in amber and Albie gilded, a little out of focus. 'Make it last, sweetheart,' she tells him. 'We're down to the last bottle.' He glances up, his eyes travel over her tangled hair, bare feet and muddy clothes. Nowadays she prefers to be without make-up, without heels and tights; more connected to the garden, though sometimes she wonders if he minds.

'We'll be there in a month. I can spin it out till then.' He raises the glass to her.

Jura in four weeks. Engrossed in her planting, she'd forgotten; she bends to receive his kiss. 'You taste of the garden,' he says absently, taking a leaf from her hair. His eyes drift back to the screen. A medical case has gone to court, a woman accused of murdering her child when it was a cot death all along. Beth moves away but Albie is absorbed; he doesn't ask her about her day and she's glad – the satisfaction in digging and planting, the way the hours stream by unmeasured, none of it would fit easily into words. In the kitchen, she slides the cake out of the box on to a plate; two swans are entwined in pink icing next to 'Happy Anniversary' written in gold lettering on the smooth white surface. She collects plates and a knife.

He looks up from the television. 'You should watch this, sweetheart, it's fascinating. I could swear I saw that journalist friend of Ed's outside the Old Bailey with a banner . . .' He glances at the cake, then claps his hand to his forehead. 'Oh God, I forgot.'

'It doesn't matter.' She cuts him a slice and hands him the plate. She doesn't want to hear about the death of a child, even if Jake is among those campaigning for justice. Whatever took place, there was a small, lifeless body, a funeral and sorrow that will last a lifetime.

'You look upset.' He kisses her. 'I'm so sorry, sweetheart; it totally slipped my mind. And you made a special cake.'

'I didn't. It was a catering company, one of those cards that come through the door. A woman delivered it today.'

'I don't suppose it was a woman with red hair, mid-twenties?' he asks, looking amused.

She shakes her head. 'Sixties, jollyish. Why?'

'Skuld's sister caters and delivers, a long shot.' He takes a bite of the cake and gazes out at the garden. His eyes shine with content. 'Right now it feels as though I'm planing.'

'Planing?' She tests the unfamiliar word; it means nothing to her.

'A sailing term. It used to happen to Jamie and me in Father's Wayfarer off Jura. The dinghy would catch the bow wave and we'd be accelerated forward through the water, as though we were flying. It feels like that now. My clinical work's going well. The rat trials were successful, the house is a triumph. It's all coming together.' He finishes his slice of cake and holds out his hand. 'I haven't been in the garden for weeks. I want to see everything you've been planting.'

They step outside. Harris runs past them to the hut, barking and sniffing around the base.

'Rats or foxes, I expect. I'll get poison.' Albie sounds resigned.

She leads him away to the vegetable patch. 'Look, new potatoes, your favourite.' But as she points to the heaped row of earth, just visible in the dusk, a message pings through on his phone.

'Ted. He wants me to phone – odd timing. It's probably about his private patients; I'll need the computer.'

He runs across the grass and half stumbles into the house; she watches as he hurries to his desk and the computer screen lights up. The torch is on the second shelf in the shed. Albie has his back to the garden, the phone to his ear. The corners of the shed are suspended on square stones; as Beth lies down, she hears chirping noises like the sounds of baby birds. She angles the beam through the gap between the ground and the wooden base. The torch beam picks out small heads, the sharp tent of an ear; six red points of light are reflected from three pairs of eyes. Fox cubs. She replaces the torch, shuts the door and leans back against it. Albie needn't know about this little family; foxes are shot as vermin in Jura.

The lights have come on across the garden from buried sockets in the grass. It was Albie's idea to floodlight the lawn. She doesn't like it; the light will confuse the birds and now the foxes. Nevertheless she feels content; she has a garden that shelters foxes, a husband who is happy and successful. So this is planing: when the elements of your life fuse and you feel as though you are flying. As she walks towards the house, she sees Albie has left the desk and is staring into the garden. The earlier happiness has gone. His face is full of horror.

17

London. Late Spring 2018

He sees her walk towards the house, flickering in and out of the strips of light across the dark lawn, arms swinging. He wants to freeze this moment, so that she is always walking towards him, always happy, always approaching an evening of talk, wine, food and love. She lifts her head towards the window, and then she starts to run; another second and she is inside.

'It took them two weeks to die, maybe less.' He is conscious of her eyes moving over his face as she takes his hands. 'The children,' he tells her in a hoarse whisper. 'The children.'

He struggles to encompass what he has brought about. There would have been behaviour changes at first: food refusal, tiredness, crying, nothing specific. The GP's advice might have been Calpol and plenty to drink, but the fever would have steadily mounted.

'Ted said the headaches were so bad they screamed like animals.'

There would have been vomiting, followed by fits. By then the child would have been in hospital, parents by the bedside, watching helplessly as the treatment escalated. Antivirals, steroid infusions, a bed on intensive care. The child would have become floppy, then paralysed, before slipping into a deep coma. Death would have followed swiftly.

'There were nine children altogether; two have died. There are three more in intensive care.'

Beth frowns, shaking her head, as if unable to absorb the news. It is dark in his head, dark outside. He can't see his way from one moment to the next. Beth pours him more whisky and he drains the glass.

'Encephalitis.' He puts his head in his hands. 'How could this possibly be? Viromex's tests were fine, completely fine. I was so sure—'

'It could have been the cancer itself,' Beth interrupts, 'rather than an immune response, especially if the tumour was rapidly expanding.'

'It wasn't cancer.' He walks to his desk to look at his computer screen. 'Ted sent me the path report: "Dense lymphocytic infiltration of the brain, typical of acute inflammation mediated by an intense immune response. Appearances consistent with acute encephalitis." Ted's flying back. He'll go to the lab, then he's coming here, tomorrow or the next day.'

Sitting still is too difficult; he paces to the wall and puts his hand against the glass. This room was constructed for light; they didn't think about the dark, about how it would feel to be surrounded by blackness pressing in.

'New treatments are always risky, Albie—'

'Risky? It was a death sentence.'

'Their death sentence had been passed already. What you did brought treatment closer.' She reaches to take his hand but he buries his fists deep in his pockets and continues to pace. Her logic is muddled. He didn't bring treatment closer, he pushed it further away. The phone begins to shrill. When he picks it up, a male voice crackles aggressively in his ear.

'Mike Stevens from the *Mail on Sunday.* I wonder if you have any comment on the recent deaths of children following a new treatment in the US? It's our understanding that a Mr McAlister was part of the original research team responsible for its development here in London. We are reliably informed that the work took place at the Institute of Neurology, Queen Square.'

He covers the receiver and mouths, 'The press.'

Beth steps forward and takes the phone from him. She rests her other hand on his shoulder.

'Can you repeat your question, please? . . . Ah, you have been misinformed. The initial concept was my husband's but he left well before any experiments were carried out . . . Yes, over a year ago now, to pursue his clinical career.' She slides her hand from his shoulder and links her fingers with his; he can hear the persistent quacking down the phone.

'Correct.' She smiles. 'No involvement whatsoever . . . Ah. That would be Professor Malcolm . . . Naturally, as director of the laboratory, Professor Malcolm has oversight of all the projects . . . Total responsibility; the Professor has always insisted on that.'

This will be death to Ted's career. He looks up at her. She is transformed, her cheeks burn with colour, her eyes glitter. She is drawing on the skills she learnt as a child, making sure they both survive, but to anyone else she would appear to be exulting.

'Not at all. You're welcome.' She replaces the receiver. 'Courage, sweetheart.' Her voice is warm in his ear. 'It will be Ted's name in the papers, and maybe Ed's, but not yours.'

He puts his hand over his eyes; he wants to weep.

Two days later on Sunday morning, Albie is in the kitchen on his own. Beth has gone to the garden centre, aiming to be back before him, but he ran as though pursued by demons and reached home first. Physical effort blots his thoughts. Since he heard the news, only operating has given him that sort of respite. He does little else; he hasn't made a single entry in his notebook or done any sketches; designing a trial would be beyond him. He is swallowing orange juice when the bell sounds, three impatient notes. When Albie opens the door, Ted pushes through without a greeting; his face is flushed. He glances behind him into the street, the Sunday papers under his arm.

'Fucking journalists,' he mutters.

On the pavement two girls trail a fat poodle, but beyond them, a man is sitting in the driver's seat of a green Mini parked on double yellow lines. He lifts his phone in both hands, pointing in their direction. Albie closes the door quickly. Ted walks past him and down the stairs into the sitting room. His gaze sweeps the room and the garden outside, as if, despite the engulfing crisis, he is assessing the worth of what's in front of him. Albie waits, his heart thudding in his mouth. Has Ted found out the truth somehow? Has he come to blame or even attack him? Ted turns to face him; framed by so much glass, he seems shorter than he used to be, older too, though his stare is defiant. A fighter past his best and knocked against the ropes, who thinks he can somehow still win.

'We have a crisis on our hands, Albie,' he says expressionlessly. 'I hope you don't mind me turning up; I couldn't think of anyone else I'd prefer to be with.'

Ted doesn't suspect him; in fact Ted has turned to him for comfort, rather than to Ed or even Jake. Albie feels a passing moment of gratification laced with guilt. 'I'm glad you're here, Ted.' Midway between a lie and the truth. He stares at Ted, unfamiliar pity stirring.

'Any coffee going?' Ted turns back to the garden. 'You've done well.' His tone is accusing as he indicates the velvety lawn and ordered planting. He's approaching the tragedy slowly like the Hindu mourners Sabat once described to him, ritually pacing round their dead in circles. For a few terrible seconds, Albie sees child corpses piled on the shining floorboards in the centre of the room, small hands curled, heads thrown back and blue lips open, as if death came while they were still gasping for air.

He walks into the kitchen area. 'Beth did it all.' He tips coffee beans into the machine. 'She organises everything in the garden, the house too.'

Ted removes his jacket and loosens his tie with a vicious tug as he takes in the leather chairs, the rough woven rug, the sleek wood burner and the brick walls covered with large black and white photos of a Jura storm. Ted hasn't been here since Beth moved in; it would be unrecognisable to him now.

'Beth,' Ted echoes wonderingly. 'Who would have thought?'

'You sound surprised.' Albie looks up from the dark ribbon of coffee streaming into the cups from the spout of the machine.

'I never realised she could do things like this.' Ted glances back into the garden, his face turned from Albie; there is a complex edge to his voice, regret or shame, and something sharper, like anger.

'And I never realised you knew her that well.' As Albie hands Ted his coffee, Ted's eyelids lower; he sips the thin layer of golden froth from the surface.

'She was my theatre nurse, once.'

'She never told me. That's strange; unlike her to forget something like that.' The silence between them stretches; the faint alarm bell he heard before has started up again.

'I don't suppose I really knew her, though.' Ted's grimace is sudden, as if registering a spasm of pain. 'You can't know other people, you can't even know yourself.'

This is nothing to do with Beth after all; this is about the daughter who never came back, the wife who retreated. 'Sit here, Ted.'

Ted lowers himself into the chair; he moves cautiously and seems older. Albie takes the sofa opposite.

'This situation must be rescued,' Ted tells him.

Albie stares at him as he tries to imagine what rescue would be possible for the families of the dead children. Ted puts his coffee down and squeezes his hands together till the bones crack. His face is bleak. 'Nothing will bring the children back, but we have to understand what has happened. Child deaths were what I most feared when you found that original report; it was precisely why we repeated your work. And yet, unimaginably, two have died. I am at a loss.'

'I can't understand what happened at Viromex,' Albie says. 'I thought—'

'They are analysing every vial they've ever sent us. Including a batch of spares.'

The fear is instant; Albie can hardly speak. 'Has Bruce kept the vials he used?'

'I'm told those have been incinerated. Clinical waste.'

Albie stands and moves back towards the kitchen in case the relief shows on his face. 'More coffee?'

'Thanks.'

'I really meant Viromex's own trials,' Albie calls out above the noise of grinding. 'The ones they did to confirm our findings. Ed told me they were fine, that's what I can't understand.'

'My God, didn't anyone tell you?' Ted gets up and begins to pace backwards and forwards, running his hand through his hair. 'I thought you knew. It turns out that there were no reruns of our trial.'

'But Ed said—'

'He was misinformed.' Ted is shouting now. 'Some bloody junior researcher at Viromex who couldn't give a fuck got his facts completely wrong.'

Albie slops burning coffee on his hand and holds it under cold water. There had been no safety net then, nothing to save the children from what he did. It means he killed them as surely as if he had stood them together side by side and shot them, one after the other. He turns off the tap and wipes his hands slowly, his mind spinning with guilt.

'Viromex relied completely on our data.' Ted's voice is quieter again, much flatter. 'Our lab has such an excellent reputation they decided not to bother with their own trials, despite promising to do so. They got permission from the Federal Drugs Administration to proceed straight to the children's trial on the back of the rat data we handed them; they made their case on the grounds of urgent clinical need.'

Albie is silent. Just six months ago he had been in Bruce's room meticulously removing the viral solution from each little bottle and swilling the fluid away, unaware as he did so that he was signing two death warrants, possibly more. He puts the coffee on the table near Ted and sits with bowed head, listening to the countdown to disaster.

'By the time we'd finished, Viromex were all ready to go. Ethics committee approval took less time than they thought. Then the permission from the FDA was hurried through; not bothering to run the trial on their own lab animals saved more time. I guess they couldn't wait to get their money.' Ted pauses, his eyebrows knit together in a solid bar. His voice quietens, 'Once the trial finally got underway, things happened quickly. The children became ill just days after the brain infusion.' He takes a gulp of the coffee then spits it out. 'Jesus, it's boiling.'

Albie fetches a towel from the kitchen. Ted stands to wipe his shirt and then sits again, making a visible effort to compose himself. He puts both hands on his knees and leans forward.

'Viromex have approached a contract research organisation to do a retrial on a fresh batch of rats with brain tumours. It will take three weeks minimum: the first immunisation, two weeks to develop immunity, then the intracerebral inoculation.' He lifts his face to the ceiling and closes his eyes as if in prayer. 'If their rats survive, I'm in the clear. If they die, our results will look faked, in which case, game over. I'm fucked.'

'Even though you weren't in the country?'

'Doesn't matter. My lab, my responsibility.'

'And Ed?'

'He'll be okay, thank God. I was always going to be responsible for this trial, remember – he was new to the lab, and away in Germany for most of the time anyway.'

'What about Bruce?'

'I spoke to Bridget about Bruce on the phone yesterday, we couldn't meet in the lab, no one's allowed in for a month. The Board have commissioned an investigation; the police are involved.' His face tightens, he pushes himself to standing and begins to pace. 'Bridget told me Bruce had been stressed. She was worried he'd make errors in the trial, so she supervised every inoculation and recorded it all. He performed faultlessly, I'm told. He's no more to blame than you – and you, of course, were gone before the trial finally kicked off.' He glances at Albie ruefully. 'Thank God for that at least.'

Guilt rises like vomit but Albie swallows it down. He stares at Ted, telling himself that if Ted hadn't given the lab to his son, none of this would have happened, that he has brought this on himself. The door opens and Harris sits up, tail beating the floor, as Beth comes into the room clasping a pot which holds a small tree. Her face is screened from the room by pink blossom. She navigates past the sofa and bends to kiss Albie.

‘Look what I found.’ She sounds happier, more determined. ‘I’m going to plant it near the shed, so we can see it. I thought we needed cheering up—’

He interrupts quickly, ‘Ted’s here.’

The pallor is instant, for a moment it seems she might faint. In the midst of despair his thoughts spin to hopes of a pregnancy; if she’s started a child, she shouldn’t be carrying a heavy load. He takes the tree from her, while Ted gets up and comes forward, leaning as if to kiss her at exactly the same time that she steps away.

‘I can manage.’ She pulls open the folding glass door, takes the tree back from Albie and walks out into the garden. Ted straightens, his face expressionless.

‘Gardening seems to be all she can think about right now,’ Albie tells him.

‘I respect passion.’ Ted’s eyes follow Beth. ‘It must be good to immerse yourself in a garden. I envy her, I envy you both.’ He picks up his jacket. ‘I’ve bribed my lawyer with Sunday lunch, we’re going through my options.’

Albie opens the front door; the green Mini is still parked opposite, the driver staring across at them.

‘Hell,’ Ted mutters, stepping back. ‘They never give up. I can’t escape. They’ve even staked out the cottage in Dorset.’

‘It might be easier for you back in the States.’

Ted shakes his head. 'Once the results of the contract research team are out, I'll have to meet representatives of the Medical Protection Society and the consultant board at the hospital who think I've cheated and lied. I'll need to return to the lab when it's open and hunt around, though I doubt I'll be allowed much freedom; they've already asked for my resignation. Most of all though, I long to escape the bloody press.' His eyes rove the room as if searching for a hidden door.

'Come to Jura with us. We're going in three weeks,' Albie hears himself saying. Ted's company on Jura is the last thing they need, but the idea catches hold. They'll be leaving for Scotland before the lab reopens – if he's with them, Ted won't be able to search for evidence, should any exist. Beth will see the logic, though she's never liked him. He puts a hand on Ted's shoulder, feeling the sharp outline of bone through the jacket. Ted has lost weight. Pity flares, a thin, hot flame. 'I'll text you the details. You'll be safe from the press up there.'

'You know, that might just save my life.' Ted pats the pockets of his jacket and draws out keys and mobile. Albie opens the door again; the green car has gone. There is a discreet clunk and a flash of lights from the red Mercedes parked further down the road. 'Thanks, Albie, I'll be in touch.' He walks to his car and opens the door, then ducks into the thickly upholstered seat, phone to his ear.

The *Mail on Sunday* is lying where Ted tossed it on the sofa. Albie turns the pages, scanning each column. He finds what he is looking for on the fifth page. The title is lurid.

EXPERIMENTAL BRAIN CANCER TREATMENT KILLS TWO CHILDREN

He reads on, feeling nauseous. *Professor Edward Malcolm of London's National Hospital oversaw research . . . rats given tumours . . . miracle cure . . . sold for undisclosed sum to US pharmacy giant Viromex . . . one year later in a Boston hospital, children began to die.*

There is a grainy picture of Ted smiling as he shakes the hand of a man Albie recognises, a tanned man with a crew cut. *Exciting new treatment on its way for children struck with deadly brain cancer* runs the caption dated two years previously. *'We are delighted to partner Prof Malcolm to take his thrilling treatment forward' says Viromex chief.* Below that another picture: an emaciated child in a hospital bed. *Grieving parents want answers.*

Albie puts the paper down; a headache has started. In the garden, Beth is digging a deep hole and is oblivious of his approach. The little tree has been freed of its pot and placed on its side; white roots curl round and round in the compact drum of earth.

'Should you be doing that, sweetheart? For a moment back there I thought you might faint.'

'Fine.' She is breathless from digging. 'Forgot breakfast, that's all.'

'Not pregnant then?' He attempts a laugh.

She shakes her head and, taking a knife from her pocket, starts to slash at the drum of earth. His headache is intensified by the blade stabbing into the soil.

'Surely you are slicing through the roots?'

'That's the point. You need to sever them; the cut ends will be stimulated to grow outwards and anchor the tree to the ground.'

She lifts the tree with both hands and then lowers it into the hole. Albie holds it steady as she tips the soil around the trunk, stamping it firmly down. She replaces the spade in the shed and walks towards the house. 'Is Ted still here?'

'Gone to see his lawyer. Beth, listen. Viromex didn't repeat Bruce's tests after all. They took the results for granted.'

She faces him; there is a pause while her glance flickers over his face. Her expression hardens. 'So it's their fault. Not yours. Not ours. You trusted Viromex would do their tests—'

'I've asked Ted to Jura,' he interrupts. He wants to stop her talking, blaming Viromex won't bring the children back.

She stares at him in silence, her eyes unreadable.

'I know you've never liked him,' he says slowly. 'But we need him out of harm's way. The lab's closed for now, but I know Ted. He'll turn it upside down as soon as he's allowed in.' He doesn't talk about guilt or pity; she seems tense, she might not understand.

'Of course, Albie, though it could be awkward. I don't know him as well as you do.'

'He told me you were his theatre nurse once.' He frowns, feeling wrong-footed. 'You must be reasonably acquainted.'

'Oh, that. I was just one of his team for a while.' She turns away and steps into the house; he follows. 'You know what it's like in theatres.' She picks up the empty coffee cups and takes them to the kitchen. 'No one gets to know anyone very well.'

He thinks of Ted in theatre telling stories, joking, keeping the team going; of the hours Ted spent teaching him, patiently watching and guiding. In theatre he'd felt he knew Ted better than at any other time. Through the window he looks at the little tree, standing in its circle of mud. He closes his eyes, trying to shut out the image of the flashing knife, slashing and cutting the strands of root tissue.

There is a phone call at midnight exactly three weeks later. Beth passes him the phone. Ted's voice is slurred. He tells Albie that the results from the contract research organisation are out. Eighty per cent of the rats inoculated with attenuated varicella died when they received the cerebral infusion of the same virus later. Pathology reports showed a massive inflammatory infiltrate of the brain. In the opinion of the

General Medical Council, the trial from Ted's lab was grossly misleading. The children should never have received the treatment. The Trust has suspended his employment; he may be facing criminal proceedings.

Albie is silent. He had wanted revenge but this is extreme. He imagined his success trumping Ted's; he never envisaged prison.

'Jura in a couple of days, Ted.'

'I have a meeting at the Trust headquarters on Thursday. I'll follow you up at the weekend.'

Albie is unable to sleep after the call. He gets up and roams the house, turning his laptop on then off again. He can't face emails, but then he remembers his notebook, neglected since the news. Not work – something different. A drawing might soothe him, he could sketch Dunbar, settled into its curve of land as if it had grown with the landscape. He knows the shapes by heart. He walks to the hall but his notebook is not on the table; he stares at the empty surface, treading down disquiet. Beth's journal has gone too; she must have moved both to polish the wood. He's too tired to search now. He picks up a book of poems he doesn't read, and makes a cup of tea he doesn't drink. As he is drifting into sleep an hour later he hears a scream from outside. Foxes again.

Very early the next morning, he wakes in the dark, his heart thumping. At four a.m. he gets up to search for his book. He looks in his desk and the kitchen and on every surface in the house. The notebook contains all his thoughts and clinical plans, his future trials. It's a record of his working life, past and future, part of who he is. Panic washes through him at the thought of its loss. He pulls the books from the bookcase, emptying each shelf, and tips out all the drawers. He turns out the kitchen cupboards; the clattering pans wake Beth.

'Why is everything all over the floor?' she enquires sleepily on her way to make tea.

'My notebook's missing.' The admission feels dangerous; he can hardly get the words out. 'Have you seen it?'

'Not for a while, sorry.'

'Your gardening journal's not there either—'

'I think I left it in the shed the other day. I did notice that yours had gone, but I assumed you'd taken it to work,'

'When was that?

'I can't remember.'

'Wish you'd said.'

They sit in silence over breakfast that neither eat; she is gazing into the garden when her face clears. 'If it helps I do remember the last time I saw your book, Albie. It was our anniversary, the day that turned out to be so terrible. I checked my journal before I went into the garden to do some planting. I'm sure yours was next to it then.'

Three weeks ago; grief and regret have emptied his mind since then. He simply cannot remember where he put it down. He has an operating list later but continues to rummage at haste through the loft, the airing cupboard, in wardrobes and under rugs. In a box in the tool cupboard he comes across the rat poison his father gave him years ago for an infestation. Out of date, but he hurries into the garden to slide a tube under the shed before he leaves. He asks Beth to search when he's gone, to keep searching; he'll look on the wards and in theatre. A notebook can't simply vanish into thin air.

18

Jura. Late Spring 2018

Glasgow is hotter than London, darker. The air feels heavy. The man hired to garage Albie's Range Rover removes his glasses to wipe his sweaty face; he winks at her in a friendly way. An ordinary-looking chap, square-framed in blue overalls, a decent man. If he knew exactly why the children in the newspaper headlines had died, the smiling face would darken; he would spurn their money, spit on the ground and drive away.

Albie settles himself behind the wheel and begins to drive in silence. He hardly said a word on the flight. Rain begins to spatter against the windscreen near Loch Lomond, the Trossachs loom towards them in the greenish light. Inveraray passes on the left, then the long, grey gleam of Loch Fyne. By the time they arrive in Kennacraig, the black and white ferry is docked and waiting, its funnel scarlet against the grey sky. Albie installs them in a corner of the dining room, buys sandwiches, opens his laptop and starts to work. Her eyelids droop in the stuffy heat. Sleep closes in; she is in a hospital ward, one she vaguely knows.

Parents are crying by a bed; as she approaches to comfort them, she sees writhing movements on the pillow where a nest of rats squirm together as if in pain. She wakes with a gasp of horror. Albie is focused on the screen and doesn't look up. She walks unsteadily to the window; dark grey waves swell beyond the dirty glass. She has hardly dared think of the children. After the initial shock Albie hasn't talked about what happened; he has barely talked at all. The disaster is still too raw for him, the damage too great. He is not used, as she is, to burying tragedy. A young man in a green vest with a mauve shock of hair walks by, a baby held close to his chest; the child is wrapped in white, tufts of dark hair just visible. The past heaves under her feet. She holds tight to the window sill and after a minute walks slowly back to her seat, summoning resolve. The mothers of the trial children had them for longer than she'd had her baby, they saw them grow before they died, they have more memories to treasure than she does. She sits down nearer to Albie. There will be a way to encompass this, she will find them a way. Albie doesn't look up; she doesn't touch him though she wants to. They will have time before Ted arrives; she has brought him a volume of poetry and a new notebook to use until his own turns up. There's a soft rug for the garden in her holdall and silky underwear in her case. When he has slept his fill, he will read in the garden, they'll make love. Somehow they will draw together again.

The boat docks in Port Askaig in Islay, a cluster of white houses that huddle close around the harbour and then thin out down the road; the white line is broken by the red of a telephone kiosk and the peeling beige of a dilapidated pub. Albie fills the car from a small petrol station by the dock; his phone rings as they join the second queue for the Feolin ferry to Jura. He is still listening as he eases the Range Rover on to the ferry. An unshaven workman in stained oilskins waves them in to park close up behind a blue van. Albie finishes the call, but when they get out to stand by the rail, the man scowls at him.

'Is he angry because you were on your mobile?'

Albie shakes his head. 'It's an old Scottish belief that men with red hair on board a ship bring bad luck.' He would have grinned at this absurdity once, but he is focused on the sea ahead of the boat where white birds drop like bombs into the waves. His face is tense. 'That was Ed on the phone, by the way. He's coming up with his father, along with Theo.'

'The boys are coming? I didn't know you'd invited them as well.'

'They invited themselves. Does it matter?'

She shakes her head, pushing down apprehension. Ted will keep quiet about the affair, he has so far. Ed saw them together once but was sworn to silence by his father. He might have forgotten by now. Theo never knew, or so Ted promised at the time.

'. . . can't let him out of their sight,' Albie is

continuing. 'He's become so depressed they feel he should be watched all the time.' He glances at her. 'You know how I feel about him, Beth, but I can't forget I'm responsible.'

The sun has emerged, a hard, high ball of light between the clouds. Her eyes hurt with the low dazzle off the water. Jura draws closer. They are at that precise distance when the smooth grey beach becomes individual pebbles, the green of the hill turns into grass and trees and heather. The risks are very clear. Guilt is tying Albie to Ted; it could create a bond tighter than affection, more lasting. She might get pushed away, pushed out.

'It's your house, Albie. We can clean the attic rooms for the boys. Is Sophie coming?'

'Our house.' His expression softens. 'Sophie's staying behind to organise the wedding, but Ed is bringing Jake along. Ted's fond of him. I should have known you wouldn't mind.'

She does mind though, she minds about Jake especially. His eyes had been very watchful, but some battles are only worth fighting if you know you can win.

They climb back into the car as the boat pulls into Feolin, a simple dock with a low brick building and a shelter, a couple of waiting lorries. They drive off the ferry, bumping across metal plates, and follow the other cars, which speed down the road and vanish as if swallowed up into the island. At Craighouse, Albie disappears into the shop, leaving her in the car. She lowers the window. The smell of whisky is as strong as ever, but the village is quiet; no one is about. The silence feels oppressive. When Albie emerges from the shop he is talking to a bearded man in tweed who waves cheerily as he walks away.

'The new doctor.' Albie puts shopping bags in the back of the car. 'Seems nice.'

They drive out of Craighouse, passing Lowlandman's Bay, then the bungalows at Lagg. Albie has lapsed into silence again. No one else comes from the opposite direction, June is early for visitors. The house smells stale when they arrive; despite the heat outside, the rooms feel cold, a little damp. Albie forgot to let Iona know they were coming; there are mouse droppings by the kettle and cobwebs on the window frames. Later Albie walks round the garden on his own in the dark.

The next morning, Beth leans from the window. The day is already warm. The garden has grown wild in their absence, the grass turned to hay. Her silver birch trees are taller, cow parsley foams at the base of their white trunks. The sea is as blue as she remembers, but swimming with Albie after breakfast, she feels frightened again. The pull of the waves seems stronger than before, the water colder. Afterwards they lie in a hollow in the springy grass on the cliffs above the beach, their bodies absorbing the warmth.

'I thought it would feel better here, but it's worse,' Albie mutters. 'I associate this place with happiness but that's all gone. The sea and the wind are forces for good; it makes what happened even worse.' His voice fades to a whisper. 'I can hardly remember why I did it now.'

The mountains gleam darkly in the distance; the shrivelled trees at the back of the beach look beaten by the wind. The waves crash against rock, retreat and crash again; the forces here feel hostile rather than good. She moves closer to his warmth, propping herself on an elbow to look at him.

'You took a risk, Albie. You couldn't know Viromex would fail to repeat the trials. It didn't work but it might have done.' He glances at her and she continues. 'You learn, you move forward, you will succeed and other children will benefit in their hundreds.'

She is leaving out the rules he broke and the part she played. All the same, he nods and closes his eyes, seeming to accept what she says.

The sun is hotter the next day, far hotter than is usual for June on the island. The air seems swollen with moisture. Clouds form at the horizon but dissipate by midday. They eat all their meals with their backs against the warm stone of the house, tracking the light on the sea as it turns from platinum to cobalt then gold. In the garden yellow irises, harebells and geraniums are growing wild among the grass, secret things of beauty, hidden for now. In bed they lie apart, though when he sleeps she rests her hand against his back.

On the fourth day, Albie puts on a shirt, pushes his feet into sandals and vanishes without a word, returning later with bulging plastic bags. He dumps them all on the floor and disappears. Outside an engine splutters into life, then he walks past the window pushing a dented mower. Two chickens, cheese, bacon, butter and great sides of venison steaks have to be fitted into the fridge. The wine and whisky go in the pantry along with bags of potatoes and peas. The smell of diesel comes through the open kitchen window, sharpened by the scent of cut grass. Stacking jars of coffee in the cupboard she remembers the wild flowers and runs outside, but the grass is spiky under her bare feet, everything has been mown down.

The next day he is up early again, tossing rugs through the upper windows on to the grass. They strip beds and wash sheets. Beth pins them on the line in the garden where they hang unmoving in the heat. Albie cleans the salt-spattered windows while she sweeps the floors, clears dead flies from the pantry shelves and scrapes at the limescale crusting the taps.

'I'm not sure why we're doing this. We don't have to impress Ted.' They are sitting outside with their sandwiches. The air is stifling; she holds her glass of water against her neck. 'The point of this place is the simplicity, he likes simple things.'

'How would you know what Ted likes?' Albie stares at the silver birches with narrowed eyes. 'I thought you didn't know him very well.'

How stupid to let the past slip in between them again. 'Surely everyone's the same as us, trying to escape from their complicated lives.' She gets to her feet. 'Look, those sheets should be dry enough to iron now, it's like an oven out here.'

The pile of laundered linen grows and she stacks them by the stove. The sheets smell very fresh. She touches her tongue to one; it tastes faintly of salt. She must be careful, very careful. She won't mention Ted again; she'll avoid him as much as she can when he arrives.

They hear the car at six. They stand at the door; the warm air presses against her face and dries her throat, she can hardly breathe. Ted's red Mercedes comes to a smooth halt outside the gate. Ed gets out; for the first time she sees Jenny's symmetrical beauty in his dark blue eyes and straight brows. He turns to support an old man who emerges slowly. His face is gaunt, the eyes sunken, his hair mostly white. With a little shock she recognises Ted. He has aged years in just a few weeks; his face cracks into a smile as he sees Albie, who moves forward to greet them and lead them towards the door. Despite his appearance, it is all she can do not to shrink back as he passes in front of her, the enemy, being ushered in. Meanwhile Theo has climbed out of the back seat and waves at her as he clambers on the bonnet and stands to look at the view. His cheeks are thickly freckled, his fair hair blows back. He is wearing shorts and grinning widely. Ted must have looked like this once, years before she knew him. Jake pushes open the other door and gets out, stretching and looking about curiously; he doesn't comment on the view.

'Hi there.' He approaches, his eyes searching hers, as if looking for something with which to amuse himself.

'Welcome,' she remembers to say, hoping her smile seems genuine.

'Beth, this is wonderful, wonderful,' Theo shouts. 'Look at that sea! Come on, Jake, we have to take a dip right now.'

'You go ahead,' Jake calls back then turns to Beth. 'I'll stay with Ted.'

'Oh, I think it's okay, Jake.' The longer she can keep him at bay, the better. An outsider, he might detect some nuance of the affair that has passed the family by, and if he does, he could tell Albie. She feels frightened. 'Ed's with his father. Go with Theo, you might enjoy a swim.'

'Ted's like a father to me, I'm part of the family too.' He turns abruptly and disappears into the house; her heart sinks as she follows. Ed is drinking water at the kitchen table. He glances up when she comes in then swiftly down; colour flares in his cheeks. He's forgotten nothing then.

Albie leans against the fridge. Ted is nowhere in sight. 'He seems so much worse than when we saw him just a few weeks ago.' Albie's forehead is furrowed.

Ed looks up again, his face miserable. 'He went downhill fast when he was forced to resign from the lab. The GMC enquiry is in a month; he's convinced he'll be struck off for conducting a fraudulent trial. For a man like Dad, it couldn't be worse. He's been living on alcohol and Diazepam.' There are tears at the back of Ed's voice. 'He's mentioned suicide more than once.'

Albie is listening attentively; his lips tighten. He seems to feel sorry for Ed; if he harbours resentment towards him for taking over his job, he has put it aside for now.

Jake sits next to Ed, looping an arm round his friend's shoulders. 'Granted Ted's tired but I thought he seemed better today; it was the way he was sitting in the car on the way here – more upright, looking out.'

Ed shrugs but doesn't reply.

Just then, footsteps come slowly down the stairs and Ted enters the room. 'My contribution.' He puts a couple of bottles of whisky on the table; his voice is slurred. 'Anyone care to join me?' He glances straight at Beth; aware of Jake's watching eyes, she leaves the room abruptly to find a towel for Theo.

The mood is subdued at supper. The conversation lags, everyone seems too tired to talk. Ted slumps in his chair. Ed is watching his father, but when she gets up to refill the water jug his gaze flicks to her, an assessing glance as if wondering whether the woman his father once loved will be a help or danger; a moment only but Jake catches it. Those brown and green eyes look from her to Ed and then Ted. He has picked up something already. Albie, talking to Theo, seems oblivious. She fills the jug, finds ice in the freezer and adds sprigs of mint from the box by the sink as she composes her face. She replaces the water on the table then makes her excuses; she is tired and will leave them all to chat. As she walks to the door she is conscious of Jake's gaze following her across the kitchen.

19

Jura. Summer 2018

The crash jolts Beth from sleep. The landing window, left open in the heat, has slammed shut in a night breeze. Fastening it, she hears the murmur of voices from the kitchen. She tiptoes down the stairs barefoot, wrapping her dressing gown tightly around her. The kitchen door is ajar, she creeps close to listen.

'. . . America maybe?'

'Funding's been withdrawn.'

'I know you resigned from the lab, but what about the consultant job?'

'When they found me in the hospital last week, I was practically escorted off the premises.'

'I'm sorry, Ted.'

'Don't be. I found something in the lab the other night; the porter's a friend, he let me in.'

The terror is instant. CCTV evidence after all or a missed syringe, rolled into a corner of the room? Did Albie leave a glove behind?

'Anything helpful?' There is fear beneath Albie's lightly curious tone; she moves to the doorway, he will need her help.

‘Not sure yet.’ Ted’s voice is reticent. ‘It could be evidence of some kind.’

Beth slips into the room. ‘Don’t mind me, you two. I couldn’t sleep, I’ll make us a drink.’

‘Bless you.’ Ted watches her walk across the kitchen.

‘If you can tell me what you found,’ Albie leans forward, ‘we might be able to help.’

Ted stares into the fire. Albie must have lit one specially to comfort him; the nights can be chilly here, even in summer. A log falls with a soft crash. Beth slides the kettle on to the range and pours a glass of whisky.

‘It might be nothing,’ Ted mutters.

Beth bends over him, she smiles into his eyes and hands him the whisky.

‘Bless you,’ he repeats softly, staring at her, motionless, as if mesmerised. Then he drains the glass and shifts his position to pull a roll of tissue from his trouser pocket. He unrolls it carefully and tips the contents into his hand. Two small glass tubes clink together on the wide palm; each has a foil-topped rubber bung and a white label. She looks down into his hand masking dismay, conscious that behind her Albie is motionless.

‘I was told the vials Bruce used had all been destroyed, but later he remembered he hadn’t needed quite all of them. I searched everywhere: my office, the animal rooms and then I started looking in the fridge, in all the boxes on every shelf.’ He is smiling as he talks, spinning it out; a storyteller who knows his tale ends satisfactorily. She waits, sweat pricking in her armpits, her heart pounding. 'There were hundreds of vials. I found these after three hours; I knew the batch number I was looking for, you see. They'd been put in a box with a set of chemotherapeutic agents by mistake.'

'What's on those labels?' Albie asks.

'Live attenuated varicella vaccine. Batch no 82297X,' Ted replies without looking. He knows the numbers by heart; his voice has lifted. Jake was right, Ted is happier, he has allowed himself to hope. She suppresses a shiver.

'I daren't let them out of my sight so I brought them with me in a bag with some ice,' he continues cheerfully. 'This evening I looked at them properly for the first time. Interestingly, a corner of the foil has come away.' He points to the top of the vial. 'It looks as though it has been peeled back and then stuck down again. I'm convinced there's a puncture mark in the top of the rubber bung.'

Beth bends to look at the vials. 'I can't see anything. Perhaps those kind of tops loosen a little in the damp of a fridge.'

'Or perhaps they've been got at,' Ted replies. 'My porter friend searched the CCTV by the entrance of the Institute, but there were no unusual comings or goings around the time this could have happened. It's a mystery so far.'

'What do you plan to do?' Albie asks.

'Test them.'

Beth touches Albie very lightly on the back.

'Let me get them analysed for you.' Albie holds out his hand. 'It might be difficult for you, given the situation.'

Ted closes his fingers round the vials. 'I worry they could get lost in the system, things go astray so easily. Ed can take them straight to Chem. Path. when we get home.' He lowers his voice. 'Maybe I'm being paranoid, but I can't get rid of the thought that someone was out to sabotage my work.'

'What do the boys think about that?' Beth asks.

'I told Ed before supper. He thinks I'm bonkers.'

'It does sound a little unlikely.' Albie smiles.

Ted doesn't reply but carefully wraps the vials in tissue again.

'Give them to me, I'll put them in the fridge for you,' Beth offers. 'They probably need to be kept cold.'

'They might get chucked away by mistake. I'm going to find somewhere extremely safe. They could give me back my future.' Ted looks round the kitchen. 'I could use something better to wrap them in, though.'

Beth reaches into the bottom of the cupboard under the sink and pulls a couple of blue plastic freezer bags off a roll and some sheets of kitchen towel and hands them over.

'Did you show these to anyone in the lab?' she asks lightly. 'For their advice, I mean.'

'I phoned Bruce but no one else, I'm not sure who I can trust,' Ted replies. 'He wasn't much help. I thought I'd get the contents analysed and leave any questioning to the police.'

'I hope it works out. I'll say goodnight, it's very late.' It should be easy enough to find a couple of blue plastic bags tomorrow, hidden among Ted's things. She is halfway up the stairs when she catches Ted's question.

'. . . so beautiful. When are you two starting a family?'

She is held as though nailed to the wall.

'That's the thing . . .' Albie's voice is low-pitched; she presses her ear tightly to the wall. 'It's not happening, I'm not sure why . . .' She can see the regretful twist to Albie's mouth as clearly as if she was facing him.

'Plenty of time,' Ted replies, she detects complacency. Perhaps he is secretly congratulating himself, the alpha male who impregnated the female, preventing others from doing so. There isn't time, though. He is wrong, her time ran out years ago. Anger sluices through her, cold like the sea, her hands tingle with rage. It was Ted's fault; he has yet to pay fully for what he's done. She flattens her fingers against the wall. The old paint feels faintly damp and silky smooth, like skin, like a child's skin.

The next morning, Ted sleeps in but everyone else is up early. Theo stretches in the kitchen; his large body and extended arms seem to take up all the space in the little room. He glances at the Paps through the window, where the mountains are gleaming in the early sun.

'I'd love to climb those; anyone up for an expedition?' Theo seems happy to have escaped the London life of a professional photographer; perhaps the trip feels like a family outing to him.

'Great idea. I'll tell Jake.' Ed runs upstairs, a slice of toast crammed in his mouth.

'I'll come along too,' Albie tells Theo. 'It's harder than you think to find the way up. We'll need sunscreen and water, anoraks in case of a storm – they can arrive out of the blue on this island. Coming, Jake?'

Jake has entered the room; he is checking his phone. His mouth is pulled down, he looks like a sulky boy.

'Everything okay?' Beth asks.

'Billy's fretful, nothing new.' He shrugs. 'Not much I can do from here. Think I'll join the climbers, I like a challenge.'

Gita might be worried or lonely. Beth finds some old water bottles in the pantry and washes out the traces of grit and two curled spiders. Jake seems focused on his own discoveries, perhaps he doesn't understand how fragile a child's life can be. If her baby had lived long enough to be fretful, she would never have left her, not for a second.

Albie opens the map to show Theo where they are going; he is smiling, the first time he has smiled for weeks. She registers a quick beat of happiness; they'll be together, they can hold hands like before. As she reaches for her anorak, Albie whispers in her ear: 'Ted is sleeping; someone needs to stay behind to keep an eye on him.'

She unlaces the boots and hangs her anorak back on the peg. Ted is in the way as she'd feared; the guilt she thought Albie might feel is already elbowing her out. She follows them to the gate to see them off. Theo's hand waves from a window as the car disappears. The morning is already oppressive. Thunder clouds are mounting in the sky, mosquitoes dance in the air. It would be a relief if a storm breaks. She walks down to her birch trees and leans against a trunk, looking at the sky between the leaves while her thoughts race. Ted is clever; he has guessed that the vials have been tampered with, though not yet who is responsible. Once it's established they hold saline rather than vaccine, the blame will shift. There will be an internal investigation at first. Bruce might reveal that Albie volunteered to help with his PhD one night and was on his own in the lab for hours, at a time that preceded the first inoculations. They could cross-examine Skuld. It wouldn't be long after that; Albie would lose everything and so would she. They have no option; they have to find the vials.

Back in the house, Ted is sleeping in the sitting room. He must have come down in her absence and has fallen asleep again in the chair. A cup has overturned by his feet, a shining puddle of tea lies on the hearth. He is snoring loudly. She takes a cloth, kneels down by his side to wipe up the tea and at the same time slips her hand carefully into the gaping side pocket of his trousers. Her fingers touch tissue but he stirs and she withdraws her hand. His eyes open and immediately close, he lapses back into sleep. The snoring starts up once more.

She climbs the stairs and enters his room, searches his case, the drawers, beneath the pillow and under the bed. She finds nothing and descends to the kitchen again. Ted is still snoring. She clears the table and begins to pod peas into a colander on the draining board in front of the window. She runs a fingernail down the green join, splitting the tight-skinned pods and releasing the pale green peas one after the other into the colander. The task is calming. A plan will shape itself soon, it always does. Something will slip into her mind if she quietens her thoughts. She can see the Paps from here; Albie will be climbing towards the summit, looking down at the tiny box of their house, thinking about her perhaps, as she is of him. She smiles. When a hand slides around her waist, the shock empties her mind. She twists away and the colander tips; green peas fall and bounce on the floor, scattering to the corners of the room. There is a guttural protest, it must have been hers, and she finds herself facing Ted as she holds to the wall, struggling for breath.

'Jesus. What was that about?' His tone is innocent but his cheeks are scarlet. He pulls out a chair by the table and sits down. 'I thought you might . . . you know . . .'

'Might what . . . ?' She manufactures an incredulous smile. She won't give him the gift of her outrage though her heart is thudding in her mouth.

'Be glad of a hug.' He grins, the bright colour already fading from his face, he is recovering quickly. 'I know you, Beth, I sensed tension last night. I thought to myself maybe things between Beth and Albie aren't working out; if that's the case, well, someone has to cheer her up.'

He's lying. She heard his conversation with Albie last night; because they have no children, Ted would have concluded she and Albie don't sleep together, he's trying his luck. She stares at him, her body slowly filling up with hate. He is still smiling. His teeth seem longer than they used to be, the lips looser. She glances at his hand resting on the table. The fingers are thin skinned and brown splotched, even the nails are dirty. Years ago as Ted's theatre nurse she'd been transfixed by longing as she watched those hands, moving with delicate precision, knowing they would be on her body later. Now she shudders with distaste. He'll continue to pursue her; once he gets something in his mind he never lets it go. It will be the same with the vials; he'll discover the truth, he'll destroy Albie and then destroy her.

She walks out into the garden, leaving Ted at the table. The hot air is a wall against her face, the distant hills swim in the stifling heat. If there are deer, they will be in the wood where it's cool, safe for now. The killing season hasn't started yet; the stalkers arrive in late August. And then it comes to her. The idea falls into her mind as sweetly as the peas fell from the pod into the colander. She wipes her sweaty face with her forearm. She will say nothing to Ted, not one word of anger or recrimination, she will ignore him completely. Albie might find it hard to do what it takes, though he wants his career to progress more than he wants anything, almost. She smooths her skirt over her abdomen, which is as hard and flat as a stone under her hands, the abdomen of a woman who has never carried a baby to term, and she knows exactly what she will say to her husband. It won't be complicated; the truth never is. Lies are far trickier. She bends to pick a handful of wild thyme growing in the stony crevices of the wall, sets her face to look calm and walks back up the garden and into the kitchen as the first drops of rain begin to fall.

20

Jura. Summer 2018

Albie halts just inside the doorway, his arms full of logs. The hair rises on the back of his neck, like a dog scenting danger. Something is happening in front of him that he can sense but not see, as though invisible threads are tightening across the room. The air is dense with the scent of thyme, cooking meat and drying cloth. Anoraks drip on stone, muddy boots lie in a jumble. Beth is chopping herbs. Ed and Theo are playing cards either side of the fire. Jake is leaning against the bookcase, absorbed in a book. Ted is drinking wine, glancing across the room to Beth, looking away, glancing back; her face is turned from his, a pale shield tilted as if against arrows.

Albie dumps the logs on the hearth, the crash halts conversation. Beth looks up, the threads snap. 'Supper's ready.' Her voice is brittle.

She's tired. It would have been a long day alone in the house with Ted. Albie pushes logs into the fire then leans back from the heat. He won't leave them alone together again.

Ted sits at the kitchen table, sighing and stretching

his legs. 'I wish I'd come with you.' He stares restlessly around the room. 'I need fresh air. Anyone want to join me in a walk after supper?'

'Where would you go now, Dad? It's dark.' Ed stares at his father across the table.

'It's not dark. It doesn't get dark here.' Ted gestures towards the window where thunder clouds are massing in the sky above the cliffs.

'Save your energy, Ted. I'll take you to the Corryvreckan whirlpool tomorrow,' Albie interjects. Ted is far too drunk to go anywhere tonight.

'I need to stretch my legs,' Ted insists. 'Lend me a coat, for Christ's sake, and don't fuss.'

'I'll lend you a coat tomorrow.' Albie braces himself for a fight but Ted shrugs, muttering under his breath. Beth puts a handful of cutlery on the table but Ted catches his foot in the cloth and sends the knives and forks clattering to the floor. She picks them up and dumps them back, her face expressionless. When Ted leans from his chair and opens the oven to look at the bread warming inside, she closes it with her foot. Jake's eyes follow every move. Ed's face is shuttered as he passes the cutlery around. There is a dance going on in front of Albie, something has happened he doesn't understand. Beth carries the casserole to the table and Jake sits down next to her.

'It was like we were on the moon at the top of the mountain today,' Jake remarks conversationally. 'That view was stunning. Miles and miles of nothing.'

'I disagree.' Ed leans forward, fist on the table. 'The hills were full of light and shadow, there were buzzards circling. Wild flowers everywhere. Detail; you just had to look.'

Ted used to be the same, argumentative, combative even. Albie glances at Ted who is staring at Beth; he would have joined in a conversation like this once but now he seems preoccupied.

'You like detail, I go for the bigger picture.' Jake smiles round the table, his glance lingering on Beth before moving on. He swirls the drink in his glass. 'Woods and trees come to mind,' he murmurs before downing his wine in one gulp, grinning to himself. Albie stares. Jake must be drunk; after a day in the fresh air the wine has gone straight to his head.

'What do you mean? What picture am I missing?' Ed glares at Jake.

'The one in front of you, always the easiest to overlook,' Jake tells him.

'What the hell are you talking about now?' Theo punches Jake's arm lightly.

Jake shakes his head, smiling, then turns to Albie. 'It was a great day, thanks, Albie.'

'Glad you enjoyed it,' Albie nods briefly.

'Yeah, thanks, Albie.' Theo's freckled face beams across the table. 'Wish you'd been there, Dad.'

'Me too.' Ted shakes his head. 'It turned out to be a disappointing day here, all in all.'

Beth stands abruptly, retrieves the bread from the

oven and thumps it down on the table. Ted reaches out to spoon stew at the very moment she moves the pot towards Theo, and the spoon tips a trail of dark gravy on the white cloth. Beth swears under her breath. Conscious that Jake's eyes have narrowed, Albie leans forward; like the plot of an obscure play, a secret is unravelling in front of his eyes. For a while everyone eats silently; the chips, a mound of rustling shards, are passed around.

'This is delicious,' Theo remarks. 'Thanks, Beth, it must have taken ages to put together.'

Beth doesn't reply. Albie takes in her silence, the resentment on her face. He's watched her prepare casseroles often; slicing through meat and chopping onions usually seems to soothe her but now he detects simmering anger. Does she mind that he asked her to stay behind today?

'Beth.' He leans towards her, speaking quietly. 'I hope you—'

'So how was the day for you two home birds?' Jake cuts across him as his gaze travels between Ted's flushed face and Beth's pale one. Neither answers and the question hovers. Albie finds himself waiting for the answer, Ed sits forward and even Theo looks interested.

'I cooked,' Beth answers shortly.

'And I managed to upset everything,' Ted adds with a guilty laugh, glancing at Beth who has averted her face.

'Why is Ted feeling so guilty?' Jake stares at Beth,

his tone challenging. Ed looks at his father, worry in his eyes. Albie glances from Ted to Beth then Jake, unease growing.

'Oh, I don't think Ted feels guilty,' Beth replies, her eyes are very dark. 'I was podding peas; Ted gave me a shock and I dropped the colander. The peas went on the floor. That's all.'

'I'm intrigued.' Jake turns towards Ted. 'Did you sneak up behind her and shout boo?'

Ted is still staring at Beth but her head is turned away. Jake's smile deepens. Without being sure why, Albie needs to wipe that smile off Jake's face.

'Hey, Jake, how about you and I clear the table?'

Jake's gaze snaps to him. 'Right, sir.' He puts his fingers to his forehead in a mock salute and gets up to clear away. Albie and Theo stand too. Ed moves to sit next to his father and puts an arm around him. Ted smiles at Ed; Ted and his son, together. Albie feels the quick, hot squeeze of envy.

When all the plates and pots are piled on the side, Beth puts a pie on the table. 'Apple,' she says brusquely. 'I didn't make it, Albie bought it from the shop.'

Ted gets up and walks unsteadily to the fridge, then pulls out a magnum of champagne.

'Knew there'd be something to celebrate,' he says, removing the cork with an expert twist. Albie frowns; the deft movement is familiar. Ted pours the champagne clumsily into glasses, missing some. He sits down again.

'To apple pie, not homemade.' His voice is slurred.

Jake raises his glass to Beth, smiling. 'And to love, wherever you may find it.'

She stares at him, the strain evident on her face. Albie has had enough. Jake is unsettling everyone.

'Back off, Jake,' he says evenly. 'I don't know what the problem is, but we're all tired—'

'The perfect moment for a love song,' Jake interrupts. 'One that's sad and romantic at the same time; who knows something that could fit the bill?'

Unexpectedly Ted stands, clears his throat and starts to sing.

> 'Are you going to Scarborough Fair?
> Parsley, sage, rosemary and thyme . . .'

Theo joins in, then Jake, although Ted's powerful baritone easily dominates. Albie's anger ebbs as he stares at Ted wonderingly; he had no idea Ted could sing like this. He sips his champagne as he listens.

> 'Remember me to one who lives there,
> She was once a true love of mine . . .'

Beth gets up, tips her champagne away and, picking up the plates on the side, clatters them into the sink. Ted's voice gets louder as his eyes follow Beth while she walks backwards and forwards collecting glasses. Albie has never seen him look so sad – angry, depressed, bored and defeated maybe, but the expression on his face now speaks of heartbreak. Albie's head begins to throb. The climb and the alcohol add to the guilt and the grief for the children that floats on everything, like an oil spill at sea, contaminating all it touches.

When the song comes to an end, Albie stands up. 'Sorry, folks, the day has caught up with me. We need to make an early start tomorrow to catch the incoming tide if we're to see the whirlpool at its best.'

He senses rather than sees the white disc of Beth's face turn to follow him from the kitchen. When she enters their bedroom ten minutes later he is still sitting on the edge of the bed, summoning the energy to undress. He looks up wearily.

'I don't like Ted either. I don't trust him an inch, but surely he's been wounded enough. Can't we pretend to forgive him, at least while he's a guest under our roof?'

'Wounded animals are dangerous,' she flashes back. 'They close in for the kill. When he works out what has happened, he'll come after us with everything he's got.'

'We'll search his room tomorrow; the vials can't just disappear. Once we organise a thorough hunt they'll turn up.'

'What if they don't?' she hisses. 'I've searched his room already. Ted's clever, if he's hidden them it will be in a place where we wouldn't think of looking. We won't find them. Once he gets them analysed, Bruce or Skuld might talk; the trail will lead to you. You'll lose everything and so will I, starting with our freedom.'

'Someone will hear you.' He puts a hand on her arm. 'The vials have to be somewhere—'

'You're not listening.' She wrenches away. 'You're facing public disgrace and prison and you're still talking about hide and seek.'

He buries his head in his hands. Beth stops talking and in the silence he hears the wind get up outside, the trees begin to move with a harsh rustling noise. When he looks up he meets her gaze, but now it's as if she is looking inwards; her eyes seem full of secrets. Disquiet prickles his neck. He watches her take the matches from the mantelpiece and light the white sandalwood candles on the window sill. Her movements are slow and deliberate as if preparing for a role she has rehearsed many times. She sits down in the chair, pulling a blanket about her shoulders, and then she starts to talk.

Her voice is soft, but as she speaks the room begins to turn around her, the dense nucleus at its centre, the point where darkness gathers. He is unable to move and unable to look away. The wind rattles the windows and gusts through the gap by the hinge, extinguishing the candle. She lights it again.

'Seven years altogether . . .' she finishes quietly. The wick catches and the glow spreads, gilding her face.

His heart is thudding violently. He feels rigid with shock as though mugged in the street. Her lips come together to blow out the match, like a kiss. She must have kissed Ted thousands of times, seven years' worth of kisses. Seven years of fucking. Their bodies together in bed, mouths together, Ted inside her. The pain in his chest is intense, his throat constricts. Was she with Ted when they met? When they first slept together? His thoughts plunge further into darkness. Is there anything between them still?

'It had been over for at least a year before I met you,' she says, keeping pace with his thoughts. 'He left me when I was pregnant.'

The word he has waited years to hear: Beth pregnant, but with Ted's child. Thin arrows of rain hit against the windows; he looks up, confused at the sound. The howling wind echoes down the chimney but the noise seems to be coming from deep inside him too. Her voice continues relentlessly.

'. . . had left me before, when they lost their daughter, but he was back after a few weeks.' Her lips twist as if she is tasting something bitter. 'I followed him to London when he bought the flat; I lived with him until I fell pregnant.'

That word again, the word that means everything.

'It all changed when I told him. He said his family needed him, but the truth was he couldn't countenance another child. He left to go back to Jenny. The money for a termination arrived later online.'

She shifts in the chair and her voice gets quieter. Her eyes are lowered, her face very still. Beth, the Madonna. 'I lived in a hostel till I found a flat, I waited on tables in the evenings to pay rent. It was tough, on my feet night and day. I bled a little sometimes but it always stopped. I thought it didn't matter but labour came at twenty-two weeks. A girl. She died after half an hour.'

He kneels at her feet as though asking forgiveness for a sin that wasn't his. After a while she gets out of the chair and stands by the window; he follows. In the murky green-grey light, crows, dislodged from their nest, are tossed round the trees, black cinders from a fire. It could be November, not June. Wings of anger beat in his head, dark birds trapped inside his skull.

'I discharged myself against advice, and after that, I became very ill.' He takes her hand; she feels cold. 'It was a pelvic infection. I got antibiotics in the end but by then the damage was done.'

'Damage?'

'Tubal scarring. I can't have another child, because of Ted.'

When he was a boy a shelf he'd tried to fix came loose; a whole set of his mother's best bone china came smashing to the floor. That same long, splintering crash is filling his head now. Sharp-edged fragments fly loose in the dark of his mind. Beth continues to talk but he can't hear properly, he moves closer.

'. . . know what you'll say, Albie; and you'd be right, there are things we could try, but I don't want a baby at any price.' Her voice has thickened, she is holding back tears. 'I can't stand the thought of IVF; people end up trying again and again and again. It can destroy them. What if I managed to get pregnant and then lost the baby for the second time? I wouldn't survive that.' She looks down. 'It was her birthday in January, she'd be four by now.'

'Why didn't Ted help you? He could have got you antibiotics immediately.' His lips are stiff, speech is difficult.

'Ted kept away; if he thought about it at all, he must have assumed I'd had a termination.'

The crows beyond the window flap and wheel in the wind, a trail of pain plumes inside his skull.

'Why didn't you tell me? Why not let me know this years ago?'

'I didn't know about the scarring until the scan.' A flat little sentence, flat enough to be the truth. 'I'd told you too many lies by then.'

'You could have told me about Ted at the start.'

'I waited until I could trust you, but by then we were in love.' Her eyes swim. 'There was too much to lose. I was scared you'd leave me if you knew or else that you would confront Ted and ruin your career. Every day I knew I should tell you, but every day was later than the day before; it went on and on, always being just too late.'

'Yet you are telling me now . . .'

'Because you think he's harmless.' She pulls her hand away. 'You expect me to act as though I forgive him when I know he deserves everything that's happened.'

'It's all right, Beth—'

'It's not.' He can hear the wind howling at the window, feel her breath on his skin. 'When you were safely out of the way today, your wounded colleague made a pass at me. He put his hands . . .' She doesn't finish.

He is drenched in rage, breathless as though a bucket of ice has been thrown at his face.

'How dare he?' His eyes are as wild as a tiger who is crouching to attack. 'How is he not afraid of what would happen if I found out?'

'Ted doesn't waste time being afraid. He relies on your ignorance. He knows I'd want to protect you.'

'Protect me from what?'

'The rage you would feel.' She slides a cold hand into his. 'The revenge you might want.'

Revenge. The tubes he implants are as narrow as a hair, as delicately constructed. Chemicals pass down them into the brain, altering every cell they touch; her words have slipped deep into his mind, transforming everything he thought he knew about Ted.

'You will have to stop me,' he says into her hair. 'Because if you don't, I honestly think I'm going to kill him.'

Outside the wind has dropped and the sky is clear. The words fall into silence,

'I'm not going to stop you, Albie.' She pulls back to look at him, her eyes shining in the moonlight. 'I'm going to help you.'

There is silence while the world shifts; everything changes in the space of seconds.

'Who knows about you and Ted?' he asks.

'Ed saw us together just once, a long time ago. Ted swore him to secrecy. I don't think he will have told anyone, not even Theo. Jake seems to have picked up something, but I doubt he knows for sure.'

He is silent. They have reached an agreement and for a while at least there is nothing more to say. She seems exhausted now. She undresses and falls asleep quickly, though she turns restlessly as if engulfed in a nightmare, the tangled sheet winding around her legs. Her naked body in the candlelight is as smooth and slim as a blade. She is as heart-stoppingly lovely as she was the night they met, arriving into his life as if from nowhere. Ted must have been watching that evening, watching ever since. Tomorrow. It doesn't matter that he doesn't know exactly when or how, he will have his revenge tomorrow.

They wake the next morning into sunshine. The triangle of sea between the sloping cliffs is already a deep turquoise blue. The storm has passed in the night; it will be a glorious day.

21

Jura. Summer 2018

Jake stands on the highest point of the cliffs, framed by sky. He bows to the circle of watching faces in front of him and begins his recitation. He speaks with foreboding.

'. . . many stories are woven around the swirling water of the Corryvreckan.'

He has brought the *Legends of the Western Isles* from the house and has insisted on reading one aloud before the picnic; a good story, he promised, about love and lies and magic.

The sun gleams off the rounded boulders that are scattered about the grass as if dropped by giants. Beth leans against a rock, Harris at her feet, Theo and Albie on either side. Beyond Theo, Ted sits on a boulder, leaning forward, a pair of binoculars swing from his neck. His face is turned towards her. Ed sits on the ground close to his father. Albie looks drawn, his eyes are bloodshot as if he barely slept. Beth slips her arm around him.

'There was a Norwegian prince called Breakan,' Jake continues, glancing round to check he has everyone's attention. 'He was in love with a girl from a noble family. To gain her father's consent for her hand in marriage, Breakan agreed to a test of courage; he had to anchor his boat for three nights in the Corryvreckan whirlpool.' He gestures beyond the cliffs where a wide circle of choppy water is visible against a calmer background; the crested waves swirl and heave as if they were alive.

'Breakan sailed back to his homeland where three wise men advised him to have anchor cables made: a plait of hemp, one of wool and one that had been spun from the hair of maidens.'

Beth's hair is blowing across Albie's face in dark, whip-like strands; there had been a girl with plaits at school, larger than the rest of them, more outspoken. The daughter of visiting Americans who were trying the state system for a year. She gathered a gang around her, whispering that Beth wore funny shoes, that her father was a drunk. Her fat blond plaits hung down over the back of her chair, in front of Beth's desk; in an art lesson Beth leant forward with scissors and cut across them with a crunch she can still sometimes hear. Albie leans to tuck her hair tenderly into her collar; the pale oblong of Ted's face turns towards the sea.

'Breakan returned to Corryvreckan and anchored his boat.' Jake strides up and down on the grass as he reads, his voice building to a crescendo, 'On the first night, the hemp rope snapped. During the second, the wool cable broke. On the third a storm swept across the sea and the last rope, whose strength lay in the purity of the maidens, was torn apart.'

His voice drops as the story draws to an end. 'Too late, Breakan realised the maidens were not as virtuous as he had been led to believe; both he and his boat were engulfed in the whirlpool and drowned.'

Jake bows deeply, everyone claps. Ted stands to cheer him, Ed stands too, smiling as he gazes at Ted. He looks relieved; his father seems to have improved. Beth walks to the edge of the cliffs; the fall is precipitous. Far below the waves champ at the rocks like teeth. The prince in the story wouldn't have had a chance, no one would.

Theo and Ed have spread a rug and a white lace tablecloth on top of that, then laid it with sandwiches that Theo made. There are tins of beer, a pile of apples and a fruit cake that Sophie sent up with Ed, carefully wrapped in foil. Afterwards as they stand and stretch and walk to the cliff edge, Beth begins to pack away; she wants to go back, there are plans to make. She wraps the remains of the cake in the foil; it was perfectly cooked, dark with fruit and alcohol. Sophie will make a wonderful mother for Ed's children. She will bake for them. She will never send them to school hungry or in the wrong clothes. She won't take to the road with a drunken husband, leaving her child alone in the dark.

Ed squats beside her, offering beer. He is less surly

than yesterday; now that his father seems happier it's as though he has called a truce. 'Look.' He picks up a stem with pearl-like white fruit, another with thicker leaves and tiny catkins. 'Hey, Jake.' He opens his palm. 'This is what I meant by detail; isn't it pretty?'

'And there's the bigger picture.' Jake waves his hand to the cliffs and the sea. 'Incredible.'

'That water would take you under in moments.' Albie speaks for the first time that day. 'The rocks would cut you to pieces.' He takes a can of beer and walks away from the group.

Ed gets up to join his father while Jake comes to kneel beside Beth as she crams apples into the side pocket of the rucksack.

'I hope you weren't bored by that story.' The green and brown eyes gleam; she turns away, stacking plates together. 'Same old thing: love, betrayal, the lies some women tell.' He grins. 'Funny how these ancient myths come up fresh.'

'Jake, come here. I want to take a photo of you posing with your book, whirlpool in the background.' Theo gestures to a rocky vantage point on the edge of the cliff. Jake grins, pushes himself up and saunters towards Theo. Jake was rooting for information, he knows nothing for certain. She begins to push plates into the rucksack, elbowing Harris from the remains of the sandwiches. A hand covers hers, Ted's. She snatches hers away.

'This reminds me of our picnics in Cornwall.' He

kneels stiffly beside her. 'Do you remember the day it poured and we had to—'

'Chatting up my wife?' Albie is behind them, his voice trembles.

Ted pushes himself to standing, catches his breath and smiles. 'Just helping her,' he says cheerfully, winking at Beth.

'Dad, bring your binoculars over here,' Ed calls from the cliff edge. 'I swear I saw a sea eagle just now.' Ted walks to join him, grinning to himself; despite everything that's happened, his old sexual confidence seems intact. Albie's cheeks are burning, he looks murderous. She puts her arms around him, drawing him close. 'Be nice,' she whispers. 'You have to be nice for a little longer.'

The muscles of his shoulders are tight under her hands, he is breathing rapidly. 'Wait,' she says into his ear. 'Wait till this evening.'

On the way back the sun disappears behind the clouds, the weather is changing rapidly again. In the distance a dark curtain of rain is drawn across the sky. Albie leads the way. Ted is tired, his stride wavers behind Albie's easy lope, but then Albie knows the terrain; he has stalked all over the island. Ed and Jake follow. Theo is just behind them, whistling and taking shots of the approaching storm. Beth is at the back with Harris. They reach home a few minutes before the downpour. Ted drinks the last of the beer and sleeps in the chair but Albie is claimed by Ed and

Theo for a game of cards; the moment for planning slips away. Jake reads on his own. He seems tired and doesn't approach her again. By supper Ted has woken and is restless, pacing as he drinks; in the long silences she hears the wind get up again and begin to whistle down the chimney. After the meal, Ted starts rummaging amongst the pegs by the door. 'Where's your coat gone, Albie?'

'Not that again, Dad.' Theo sounds weary. 'The storm's come back. It's not safe. You might get lost.' He leans to kiss his father goodnight, his freckled face vivid against Ted's lined visage, the one a fresh copy of the other.

'I need to sleep,' she hears Ed murmur to Albie. 'Can you keep an eye on Dad till he goes to bed? He seems better, but you never know.'

When the boys have disappeared, Beth slips out of the room. Albie follows her, leaving Ted on his own, searching for coats. They stand close together in the bedroom, there's hardly any time.

'He's determined to go out,' she whispers. 'This is our chance . . .' She doesn't repeat his words or hers from the night before; they will have been in his head all day. He looks out of the window; sweat gleams in minute drops along his hairline, but he doesn't move.

'He has the vials, Albie; he holds our future in his hands. You have to go after him.'

She can tell by his breathing that he is listening to her, but still he doesn't move.

She steps closer. 'He'll take everything. You'll lose your career, all your work, your houses. We've already lost our children.'

He turns at that and his eyes stare into hers; they seem to look through her, as if searching for the children they will never have, their children's children, and beyond them, the line of offspring that are lost for ever. He touches her hand; his signature on the pact. Surprising, after so long, how easily an idea slips from thought to action, how silently an end can be encompassed.

'Here's your coat.' She unhooks it from the back of the bedroom door. 'I'll take it to him.' She comes back in a few minutes, another jacket in her hands. 'This is for you. He's about to leave. I showed him the path on the map, the one that leads to the high cliffs on the next headland.' She kisses him, he still hasn't said a word.

'A life for a life, Albie. A life for many lives.'

Downstairs the back door bangs shut.

'Hurry.'

The quiet pad of his footsteps descends the stairs. From the window she sees him leave the house; a few moments later his figure disappears as if swallowed up by the rain.

22

Jura. Summer 2018

He has to run in bursts to keep Ted in his sights, but he stops now and then to crouch in the bracken and catch his breath, the tough undergrowth scratching at the skin of his fingers. The figure up ahead appears then disappears through blowing veils of rain.

An owl shrieks twice from the trees to his left, but Ted doesn't falter. By the time the slope flattens on to deer-nibbled grass, he has gained ground and is close enough to see Ted's scalp through the strands of white hair, the green of the borrowed jacket. Ted's face is turned towards the sea where a dull silvery yellow stains the horizon. The wind is fierce. The acrid scents of dung and salt catch his throat; an image of the autopsy room slices across the cliff and is gone. The waves are crashing on to rock forty feet below; quiet earlier today but now churning and roaring.

His boot strikes the lichen on a half-buried lump of granite and Ted turns at the noise. In the murky light Albie could be staring at his older self, a beaten, late middle-aged self.

'It's you.' Ted sounds relieved. 'I had the sense of

someone behind me all the way but thought I was imagining things. The storm plays tricks. I'd have waited if I'd known.'

Albie's heart is beating in his mouth. The blood in his head sounds like the sea. He wipes his eyes clear of rain with his wrist. At the edge of his vision a dark bird, large as a child, lifts from a spur of rock and rises silently on a downward beat of wings. Both men turn to track it as it disappears; the snowy tail feathers leave a white echo in the misty air. Sea eagle, scavenger of the dead.

'So close . . .' Ted says. 'I was watching for one today.'

'I followed you from the house.' Safe to admit that. Ted trusts him, though even that thought makes him angry: the eternal lieutenant, too biddable to be dangerous.

'It was good of you.' Ted smiles, a lopsided version of his former grin. 'How like you to worry, but there's no need.'

'I wasn't worried,' Albie replies but Ted isn't listening; perhaps he has never really listened.

'I wouldn't do anything stupid, though I admit I've come close at times. Early mornings are the worst,' Ted continues, pulling Albie's jacket more closely around him. He glances to the edge of the cliff where the grass ends in a line as if cut by a knife. 'Those vials have made a difference, and then of course I'd never leave my boys . . .'

My boys. After all, it comes down to children: what Ted has and what he stole. The churning in Albie's head gets louder; blood will be flowing fast through the arteries of his brain, the dark stream expanding all the twisting vessels. Rage rises to his throat. They are inches from the edge.

He reaches out to grip Ted's upper arms. Ted smiles and covers Albie's right hand with his left, acknowledging the gesture; his friend is comforting him. Even as he is lifted off his feet, he gives a surprised laugh. Does he imagine that he is being pulled in for a hug?

Albie swings him close, their faces almost touch, and in the violence of that motion Ted lets out a grunting noise of protest. His mouth has fallen open, the beefy red of his tongue works to make a sound. His pupils have dilated. Albie spreads his legs; the decision becomes absolute. Mustering force, he pushes Ted backwards over the edge.

There is a noise, a sharp flap or shout as though the molecules of wet air through which Ted is falling are vibrating with sound. Albie hunches forward, watching, arms still wide as though about to tackle a monster; through the misty grey air he sees the head meet rock, then the torso roll and bump between dark ledges so fast the body is a blur. He doesn't see it disappear beneath the broken surface of the water; he must have absorbed the sight but that moment is too rapidly over, too terrible to register. A tern startled from its perch wheels, screaming against the black rock. Albie stays where he is, panting heavily and scanning the empty waves as they move back and forth far below.

Act Three

23

Jura. Summer 2018

'I look just the same.'

Beth watches him watch himself in the small gilt-framed mirror on the chest of drawers. His summer-looking skin and blue stare reflect innocence while she swims ghost-like in the dark behind him, her eyes in shadow. His face creases with distress as he turns away and lowers himself to the bed. She wrenches off his boots.

'When I grabbed hold of him, he thought I was hugging him. Christ.'

'It's done, Albie.' She helps him out of his anorak, then sits by him and lifts his wet hand to her mouth. Her heart is light; her body feels as if it could float away. She kisses his palm again and again. 'It's over.' She puts her arms around him. 'We are safe now. Nothing can touch us, we are free to do whatever we—'

'Free?' He twists away, staring at her as if he hardly knows her. 'I'm not free, I'm trapped in that moment. I can't get it out of my head. Ted didn't believe it was happening even when he began to fall—'

'Don't think about it. Block it out. It's a relief . . .'

She glances away from his furious stare. 'It's a relief you are safe, sweetheart. That's all. I was so scared when you went after him; now you are safely back, I hardly know what I'm saying.' She gets up and touches him on the shoulder. 'Get some sleep. I'll bring you a cup of tea then I'll leave you in peace.'

The map is still on the kitchen table. When she traced the path for Ted, his face was bent near hers, his eyes were focused. Those eyes will be vacant now, the skin of the cheeks scraped to muscle. Her mouth tightens as she folds the map. She makes a cup of tea and fills a hot water bottle. In the bedroom, Albie has pulled the duvet around him, his blank gaze follows her as she puts the cup on the bedside table and slips the warm bottle next to him. She retrieves his mud-caked clothes and boots, turns off the light and closes the door quietly. She puts the clothes in buckets in the pantry, hiding them under a towel, but there could be other evidence: traces on the cliffs, a dropped glove or a boot dislodged by the struggle. Harris positions himself at the door as she laces her boots. Outside, the metallic gleam of puddles outlines the path to the cliff; she follows it to the end, passing between high outcrops of rock where the sound of the sea and the birds comes at her in a screaming roar. The grass and heather on the clifftop look empty; she searches but nothing has been left behind, not even footprints. She daren't look over the edge but turns and jogs home as the sky lightens.

The house looks asleep, the curtains still tightly

drawn, but in the garden the shadows fall differently. Something has changed. She takes in ragged stumps and branches scattered across the grass and then she understands: the storm has snapped her silver birches in the night. Albie's wedding gift, smashed to pieces. Tears press behind her eyes as she hurries into the house, Harris at her heels. In the kitchen she puts her clothes with Albie's, wipes her anorak and rinses the cloth she used to wipe it with. All traces of the morning's effort gone, she climbs the stairs one by one. She won't tell Albie about the trees just yet.

He wakes at her touch. 'Is he back?'

'Who, Albie?' But she knows who he means and she feels frightened.

'Ted.'

She shakes her head slowly.

'Oh God.' He turns his head away.

'You'll need to get up soon.'

Downstairs Harris begins to bark.

'Jesus. Someone's coming, They've found him.' Albie's face loosens with fear.

'You must pull yourself together. I'll go down.' She puts on a jersey and dry trousers then turns at the door, making an effort to speak gently as to a child. 'Wash your hands and face, sweetheart. It will make you feel better.'

Harris runs up to her in the kitchen barking, unusually disturbed. She opens the door but there is no one waiting outside. He settles in front of the stove, whining softly. She lays the table for breakfast but her hands shake, spilling cereal. In the sitting room the drawn-back curtains reveal the wet fields, the shadow-shrouded trees, the puddled path, the normal island landscape at dawn. No one could guess a man was tracked up that path in the dark. She glances swiftly up the hill, as if half expecting to see Ted's tall figure stumble into view. She turns to shake out cushions, replace books on the shelves, straighten the rug. If she tidies and clears and cleans maybe the night will fade, maybe she won't have to think. Picking up a mug she turns to go into the kitchen then jolts violently, the mug tumbles from her grasp to shatter on the hearth. Jake is sitting silently in the chair by the fireplace watching her every move.

'Jake.' Her mouth is so dry it's difficult to speak. 'You gave me a shock.'

'Apparently.' He smiles; one leg is crossed over the other, foot swinging. He seems to be enjoying her discomfort. She picks up the pieces of china and walks into the kitchen, her heart thumping. That was why Harris was barking, Jake must have frightened him too.

'Coffee?' she calls.

Jake follows her.

'Have you been down here all night?' She tips away the broken mug and turns on the kettle. What might he have seen or heard?

'Just long enough to hear your voices in the bedroom just now.' He smiles his mocking smile again.

Their luck had hung by the slenderest of threads, then; if he had come down earlier he might have met Albie returning or seen her go out. She makes a jug of coffee and hands him a cup, hoping he doesn't notice that the surface of the liquid trembles.

'Thanks.' He leans his back against the stove, still watching her. She turns away to open the window. Gulls are circling in the sky beyond the cliffs, their cries come into the room. She watches them float as if suspended in the air. Ted must have heard them as he fell. If time slowed for him as people say it does, he might have wondered why Albie had done this, before it came to him in the last half second of his life that it was her – of course, it was Beth. Did he have time to scream out her name?

'Where's Ted?'

'Sleeping in. He's tired out.'

'I'll take this to Ed, then.' He fills a cup from the jug and disappears.

She follows as far as their bedroom. Albie is sitting on the bed, half dressed. His shoulders are bowed, his face very pale.

'Jake's up already,' she whispers as she sits next to him. She takes his hand; the skin is clammy. 'You'll have to come down in a minute.'

He shakes his head.

'It's easier than you think, sweetheart. Just be yourself.'

He stares at her, bewildered, as if he has lost all

sense of who that might be: friend, colleague, doctor, host, schemer, murderer? She reaches to touch his face but he recoils and she pushes herself to standing. 'We have to get through this, Albie. There's no turning back.'

He puts his head in his hands and doesn't reply.

Jake is in the kitchen again making fresh coffee. 'Ted will be hungover after last night. This is extra strong, specially for him.'

'I think Ted needs rest more than he needs coffee,' she says lightly.

'Ed says we should get him up for a walk.' Jake disappears up the stairs again but returns in moments. 'He's not there.'

'He must be.' Upstairs she opens the curtains in Ted's room, bangs the bathroom door shut. By the time she re-enters the kitchen, Albie is sitting silently at the table. He looks haggard.

'Jake's right; Ted must have taken himself off somewhere.' She drops a kiss on Albie's head and sits next to him, smiling cheerfully.

Ed enters, glancing round the room, followed by Theo, sleep-tousled and yawning.

'Dad up yet?' Ed asks.

'He wasn't in his room,' Jake tells him. 'And his bed's not been slept in.'

Ed's dark brows draw together, Theo looks puzzled. Beth pours three fresh mugs of coffee and sets them on the table.

'I expect he made his bed before he left, then. He'll be down on the beach, looking at the sea,' she tells them.

'Dad hasn't made a bed in his life.' Ed's eyes meet hers, a sharp-edged glance that takes her aback. Of all people, that look implies, his ex-mistress should have known that. 'I've been doing it for him since we arrived,' he continues. 'Where the hell has he got to?' He walks around the kitchen, into the sitting room and back again, studying his watch. Jake is frowning as he feeds bread into the toaster.

'Dad's always going off on a whim,' Theo remarks peaceably, sipping his coffee. 'He'd disappear for hours at a time when we were younger, remember? Mum tried to pretend she wasn't worried; no one knew where he'd gone but he always came back.' He smiles at Beth.

Those were the times when he came to see me. She senses Jake's quick glance but keeps her face steady. Theo's expression is artless; he has no idea that she and his father were once lovers. Ed protecting his brother from the truth; theirs is a family that is good at keeping secrets.

'If he's taken himself off like the old days, he has to be feeling better,' Theo finishes.

'Or worse.' Ed sits down, tapping a number into his mobile.

'Anyone seen those poor trees?' Jake asks, nodding towards the window as he butters slices of toast and props them up on the table. 'Broken in two by the storm. I shouldn't say this but it would make a great photograph. You ought to shoot them in black and white, Theo.'

Theo looks out of the window and whistles with surprise.

'Send me the images,' Jake continues. 'I'm doing a piece on climate change and summer storms are part of the story. Damage is everywhere, no one seems to notice.'

'Fuck. His phone is unavailable.' The worry in Ed's voice is palpable.

Theo offers his brother a piece of toast. 'It'll be fine, Ed. It's Dad after all. Try not to worry.'

'His bed's not been slept in; he's not answering his mobile. He was drunk last night, and he's been very depressed. How can I not worry?' Ed replies angrily, ignoring the toast.

She mustn't add to anything that's being said or thought, mustn't suggest that suicide is a possibility or breathe a word about accidents. She stands by Albie's side, waiting to see how things fall.

'Did he say anything to you about going out last night?' Jake puts a hand on Ed's shoulder.

'I left him in the kitchen with Albie and Beth.'

'He told us he was turning in soon, he wanted to study the map,' she says, following where Ed's thoughts are already leading him. 'We went to bed; we presumed he would follow.'

Jake stares at her closely as if testing her words for the truth, but Ed has sprung to his feet. 'Shit. Did anyone hear him leave?'

'It was stormy,' Albie says. 'The wind was howling. You couldn't hear yourself think.'

'I'm going to look for him now.' Ed pulls out his walking boots and laces them up. 'At the very least he may have fallen and twisted his ankle.'

'Or found a sheltered spot to sleep it off,' Theo says hopefully. 'I'm coming too. Jake?'

Jake nods silently, winding a long scarf around his neck.

'I'll join you; I know every inch of this island,' Albie says. He turns to Beth. 'You'd better wait here. Phone immediately if he returns.'

She nods without replying. It's happening again, she could have been quite wrong after all. There might never be an escape from Ted; his hold on Albie might be stronger now he's gone.

'Anyone seen my jacket?' Albie fumbles among the layers of coats by the back door.

'Maybe Ted took it,' Beth replies. 'He wanted to borrow it the night before last, remember.' It's as if they have rehearsed their lines. It might be important later, proof perhaps that Albie didn't leave the house – he wouldn't have gone out without a coat in the storm.

They walk off in a straggling group, heads lowered. No one talks. The day is warming up. She checks through Ted's room once more, but in vain. In Theo and Ed's room the beds are neatly made, the clothes hung tidily in the wardrobe, but she finds nothing. In Jake's room, the clothes are strewn on the floor and on the unmade bed. It takes longer to search but the result is the same. No vials. Outside Ted's Mercedes is unlocked. There are car documents in the glove compartment, CDs and phone chargers; her searching fingers touch something soft, buried deep. She draws out a fine red scarf, hers from long, long ago. She puts it to her face, the faintest smell of lavender still lingers in the silk. When she wore it he had called her his scarlet woman. She crushes it in her hand and opens the door of the stove to thrust it into the flames. Another hour passes in a fruitless search through cupboards and shelves; she is turning old wellington boots upside down when her mobile rings.

'We haven't found him.' Albie's voice is terse. 'I've contacted Iona, she's phoned the Search and Rescue Team on Islay. They're sending a helicopter; the police may call at the house. We're carrying on looking.' He cuts the call before she can reply.

She retreats to the garden and sits against the wall of the house. The vials have gone; they must have still been in his pocket when he fell and would be in slivers now. Harris puts his head on her legs and her eyes begin to close, but a roaring noise fills the garden, pulling her back from sleep. She cowers while above her the huge, glinting beetle shape of a helicopter passes low over the house. She glimpses the pilot in dark glasses. A violent trembling starts; she downs two glasses of whisky, then runs a bath and sits in water as hot as she can bear. Gradually the trembling stops. Dressed and downstairs again, she forces herself to think of food; they'll be hungry when they return. Not meat, a quiche of some kind maybe. She is rubbing butter into flour when a man in uniform knocks and steps through the door.

'Sergeant Carmichael.' He removes his cap and bows formally. She stares, shocked to silence, her floury hands deep in the bowl, taking in bulk, badges, a wide nose growing hairs at its split tip.

She rinses her hands, the wet flour clumping on her fingertips. 'Have you any news?'

'We've been called to assist in the search for a Professor Edward Malcolm,' he replies stolidly. 'We were given this address. You are a relative?'

An ex-mistress doesn't qualify, even if you knew your victim as well as any wife. She shakes her head as she dries her hands. 'Friend. He is a colleague of my husband, staying with us.'

'You may need to sit down.'

She doesn't move. 'Tell me.'

His wooden expression solidifies. 'I regret to inform you that I was notified on my way over here that a body has been found on the shore towards the north of the island.'

She has to sit down after all.

'We have reason to believe it's the missing individual,

though the body had been in the sea for a while. It will need to be formally identified.'

'Oh God . . .' she whispers. Less time than she thought; the discovery should have been weeks hence, on another island or at the bottom of the sea. The policeman is watching her closely, as if braced for hysteria.

'What exactly happened? I mean . . .' She stops, uncertain of the difference between the kind of questions a friend might ask and the sort a murderer would need to know.

'That is information I am not party to. There will be a post-mortem.' The small eyes behind thick glasses are not unkind. 'I understand his sons are staying with you.'

'They are out looking for him now, with my husband.' She doesn't add that his wife Jenny is hundreds of miles away in a Dorset village. The woman she used to envy and pity would have had enough of police when her daughter disappeared, and enough of her husband's former lover. The boys should break the news, not the police – certainly not her.

The sergeant finds the kettle; he seems used to this, to bringing bad news to women in their kitchens, to making tea for them. He stands as he waits for it to boil, legs apart, firm as if planted, while her fingers shake as she scrolls down for Albie's number. Her voice is hoarse. 'They've found a body; they think it's Ted.'

'Ah.' A sharp downward exhalation, as though he has finished a race but one he's just lost; had he been hoping that Ted would survive against all odds?

Sergeant Carmichael has made the tea, orange and over sweet. She tips hers down the sink while he walks around overhead in Ted's room, his footsteps creaking loudly.

Ed is first through the door, eyes screwed up and panting as though mastering great physical pain. Jake must have fallen; his glasses are spattered and his hair stiff with mud, there are tear marks on his cheeks. Theo is crying, leaning against Albie who looks at Beth, his face stripped of all expression. She moves towards him but he holds up his hand to ward her off; perhaps he's afraid if she touches him he will break down, or worse, confess. Sergeant Carmichael informs them that the body of a white-haired older male in a green jacket has been found on the shore further north. Approximately six foot four inches in height. Brown trousers, watch with black strap. No shoes. He doesn't mention the contents of the pockets.

'Did anyone try to resuscitate him?' Ed asks. Jake stands near, gripping his arm.

'It was clear he had been dead for a while, sir,' the sergeant tells him. 'He had been injured. The sea was rough, you understand, very cold.'

'They should have tried anyway,' Ed persists. 'In the hospital we always—'

'The injuries were severe.' Sergeant Carmichael

pauses as if deciding whether to continue and then he does. 'Part of the skull and the underlying brain were missing.'

Ed's face pales. Theo turns and vomits into the sink. Jake wipes his mouth with a cloth and leads him back to the table, like a father; it's easy to forget that Jake has a son. She watches him pull a pack of tobacco from his pocket and make a roll-up with trembling fingers.

'We need to tell Mum,' Theo says through his tears.

'I've told her already,' Ed says. 'I rang her on the way back to the house.'

Had Jenny been in her little studio or walking in the Dorset hills? Perhaps on the shingle by the sea, probably on her own. Beth pictures that lovely face crumpling, the tears beginning to fall.

'Do you have any idea how he came to be in the water?' Jake asks, his eyes narrowing as he blows out cigarette smoke.

The policeman glances at him. 'There is no way of telling at this stage, sir. We do know there was a bad storm last night. We also know that cliffs can be treacherous in the dark. Anything else would be speculation.'

'Christ,' mutters Jake.

Sergeant Carmichael clears his throat ponderously. 'We will need identification.'

Theo looks up quickly. 'So it might not be Dad?'

'Identification is a necessary formality. The body has been taken to Bowmore police station on Islay.'

'I'll come.' Theo gets to his feet, his face running with tears and mucus.

'Me too.' Ed stands, Jake with him.

'I should advise you that the station closes at six p.m. I am sorry for this unfortunate turn of events on your holiday.' They stare at him incredulously. Beth wonders if he has any idea how his words sound, though of course there are no words that would comfort Ed and Theo, or even Jake.

'I'm sorry,' he repeats, sounding more human. He walks out with a measured tread and shuts the door quietly. They hear a car start up and move away.

'I'll drive you,' Albie says. 'I know the way.'

'No.' Jake's voice is decisive. 'I'll take them.'

No one says anything else. There is nothing to say, everything is being felt. The family seems to have drawn together, as if closing ranks against outsiders. Albie leaves the room and Beth retreats to the kitchen, quietly assembling a tray of glasses and a bottle of whisky. They begin to mutter together; she pads about barefoot, focusing on every word.

'God . . .' Theo is still crying. There are comforting noises from Jake and footsteps as someone paces, probably Ed. He is making inarticulate sounds as if he is swearing or sobbing.

'What the fuck are we supposed to do?' Theo asks after a while. 'I don't want to stay here now . . .'

'Dorset,' Jake murmurs. 'Jenny will need you.'

'Yes.' Ed's voice. 'Of course. We must go to Mum.'

'If we are going to Islay, it makes sense for us to pack up here and leave for good when we go,' Jake continues.

'Why did that man say "anything else would be speculation"?' Theo's voice quavers. 'Dad must have fallen, mustn't he?'

There is a long pause. 'I think he was telling us some people might think he did this on purpose.' Ed sounds cautious, protecting his brother again.

'He was more cheerful recently, though.' Theo has begun to weep again. 'Better since we arrived than he's been since those children died.'

'That's because he'd convinced himself he had the evidence to prove his innocence. I wish—'

A glass slips from her fingers and crashes on the tray. The boys look up through the archway into the kitchen, Jake gets to his feet. Beth proffers the tray quickly.

'Have something to drink. It might help.'

Ed looks away, his face is dark with grief but not suspicion. Not yet. Jake shakes his head silently. Theo takes a glass but doesn't drink.

'We need to get our stuff together,' Jake tells the brothers. All three walk past her and climb the stairs in silence.

She makes cheese sandwiches for their journey and a thermos of coffee, but in the pantry the remains of Sophie's fruit cake are now a pile of dark crumbs. Closer, she sees mice have been at work. They must have been swarming all over the cake: dark droppings like miniature bullets are scattered on the plate and the table. She searches the shelves for apples or a packet of biscuits instead, jolting when the back door slams. In the kitchen Albie is standing with the sandwiches in his hand, the thermos still on the table with the bowl of half-mixed flour and butter. They listen to the sound of the car roar up the hill, then he goes to the bin and throws the sandwiches away, a violent movement.

'That's a waste, Albie.'

'A waste?' His laugh is new, hollow-sounding, more of a sob than a laugh. 'That's rich. It was a sandwich, Beth, that's all. A fucking sandwich.' He walks into the garden and the door slams again.

24

Jura. Summer 2018

Albie leans against the bonnet of his car checking ferry times on his mobile, his case by his feet. Beth brings out two cups of strong coffee on a tray, caffeine to keep him awake for the drive. He has been sleeping poorly, waking often. They walk into the garden, pausing to sip from the steaming cups. The wet grass shines with a thousand tiny rainbows but dark splinters of shade are scattered beneath the trees. She is scared. Albie's silence feels dangerous; since the boys left two days ago he has hardly talked at all. They circumvent the branches still scattered on the lawn, their leaves withering. This morning her face looked parched in the mirror, the lines by her mouth more deeply etched, as though something had broken inside her and she had begun to wither too.

'How long before you come back?'

He shrugs.

'I'll be fine. You mustn't worry about me. I won't have a car, of course, but there's plenty of food . . .' She's rambling and she never rambles; she doesn't want him to leave.

The sea shimmers beyond the cliffs, the colour reflecting the sky, that endless blue of infinity. The space around a murder is larger than you think: the time before can stretch for years; the time after might do the same. She walks with Albie up and down the garden, he turns and turns like an animal in a cage that's too small. She wipes her eyes quickly with the back of her hand; he hasn't noticed her tears. She is tired, that's all. She's hasn't slept either; these are the tears of exhaustion.

'Are you sure I have to stay, Albie? I'd far rather come home with you.'

'The police will come back. Someone needs to be here. Ed will return for his father's things at some point.'

The marks under his eyes are dark green, his face is white. He starts muttering but he doesn't look at her, he seems be talking to himself.

'I'm almost but not completely certain that when he hit his head on the rocks he would have been killed outright.'

Almost but not completely certain; there are gaps between those words where you could stumble and be lost. She puts her hand into his palm and curls her fingers to hold on.

'The policeman said part of his skull was missing; if it happened then, he wouldn't have felt the impact of the sea. He wouldn't have experienced drowning.'

'Yes,' she says. 'It must have happened then.'

'I tell myself we all die of brain damage, the brain dying as the blood stops. We don't feel that, or do we?' He doesn't wait for an answer; his eyes are wild. 'Maybe we do; the language centres might die before consciousness does, so no one can tell us what happens or if it hurts.'

They walk back and forth on the lawn. The grass is getting longer now, the little flowers have gone, though thyme still clings to the walls. She can hear the old song as clearly as if Ted were singing it to her in the garden.

> Tell her to find me an acre of land
> Parsley, sage, rosemary and thyme
> Between the salt water and the sea strand
> Then she'll be a true love of mine.

How many true loves are you allowed? One? Two? Is your true love the first one, someone you loved when you were young, or the man who would do anything for you, no matter what you ask? What happens if they both leave?

'. . . but perhaps he didn't hit his head.' Albie's voice is strained. 'The light was bad; it might have just looked like that, from the top of the cliff.'

He has pulled his hand away and is walking so fast she has to run to keep up.

'So if he was alive when he entered the water, would that shock have been enough to make him unconscious?'

He is muttering; she can hardly make out the words. 'Or perhaps he survived that too; Ted's a survivor. He would have had time to hate me then.'

'I don't suppose he was conscious—'

'Though even Ted wouldn't survive the swell against the rocks; his skull would have opened like an egg.'

'You have to stop this, Albie. What's done is done.'

He stares at her as if she were a stranger he can hardly recognise.

'You've been through a traumatic time—'

'Ah. I thought that was Ted.' A harsh laugh.

'When my parents died, at first I saw continuous images of crushed bodies strewn across a road.' She glances at the branches around them. 'But after a while it became like a film that I watched sometimes, about people I didn't know.'

'So that's how you coped, by distancing yourself?'

'It's how everyone copes.'

'No, it's not.' He sounds angry. 'If you block out the terrible things that happen, how will you ever come to terms with them?'

She stands under a tree, trembling. They've never had an argument like this before; they've never even had an argument.

'At some point you have to let them go.'

'We are completely different, then.'

'Ted would have said the same.'

'What?' He turns on her in fury. 'Do you dare offer me advice from your experience together?'

'You told me that,' she falters. 'You said he advised you to put everything out of your mind when you had to operate, focus ahead.'

'You're right,' he replies after a pause. 'I'm forgetting what he taught me already.'

You're not forgetting, she tells him silently; it hasn't occurred to you yet to use Ted's advice to cope with his murder, the murder you are already regretting. She feels fresh tears sting and turns her face away.

He looks at his watch. 'I must go.' He walks to the car and she follows. 'I'll come back when I can. There'll be stuff to bring home in the car, curtains, seat covers, all the linen. Things go mouldy here over winter. He glances around as if saying goodbye to the house and garden, but he doesn't look at her. 'After that I doubt we'll return till next summer.'

Will they ever want to come back? She watches him settle in the car; he turns to look at her through the glass but he doesn't smile.

'Safe journey, my love,' she says, but the car has already started to move and he is looking ahead to the road.

25

London. Summer 2018

'It was easy, Albie. Dead easy.' Is that supposed to be a joke? He can't tell if she's laughing or crying. Both, maybe, hysterical perhaps.

'Wait a minute. I'll go somewhere quieter.'

With the phone to his ear, he walks from the ward to the Department of Neurosurgery. The tab bearing the inscription *Professor E. Malcolm* is still fixed to the third door on the left. Loss jolts, the unexpected shock from an electric fence. He shoulders his way in, dumps his briefcase and sits at the desk. The locum has been extended; he is officially 'holding the fort', that's what he was told by the selection committee. They have to advertise the consultant job, shortlist applicants, hold interviews. Rules were rules but he was privately assured the job would be his from now on.

He has barely been into this room since his return two weeks ago, has not yet sat in the chair. Ted's chair. Ted didn't sit much either, now Albie understands why. He is on his feet constantly running the wards and the lab in Ed's absence. Ted had insisted he'd given the lab to his son because he knew Albie was too busy – could that have been, after all, the truth? Doubt opens, the gulf beyond a cliff; he steps back.

A family photo stands on the desk in front of him. Framed in silver, it shows Jenny, with darker hair, Ted laughing with his arm around her. The two young boys pulling faces, and a teenage girl with fair hair in her eyes. Ten years ago at least, a happy family, though Beth was seeing Ted then, sleeping with him. She had lied to the wife and children in the photo, she had lied to him. How many more lies have there been? He turns the photo upside down on the desk.

'Albie? Are you still there?' Her tone is sharp.

'You sound different.' When he left, she had looked different too. Her composure had vanished, along with the smooth Madonna face and the way she lowered her eyes as if guarding secrets – which she had been, of course, for years. 'Are you eating enough?'

'I'm all right.' Her voice softens. 'I miss you. Ed hasn't turned up yet. Have you seen him?'

'He hasn't been in touch. No one knows where he is or even if he's coming back.' He turns up the sleeves of the white coat; he'd forgotten his and Ted's swamps him. 'Bridget asked me to head up the lab for now so I'm doing that too.'

'Everything you wanted.' Her tone is flat, as if she has reached the end of a journey but the destination isn't as she'd hoped.

'Everything we wanted,' he corrects, but he

understands how she feels, he feels the same. The day Ted asked him to do the locum, he'd been transported to the cliffs of Jura, gazing up at the stars, his career about to launch. He moves on the hard seat, trying to get comfortable. The last time he was on those cliffs, he had been staring downwards instead to the churning water far below.

'I was telling you about the police,' Beth continues. 'It was easier than I'd thought. They simply listened and took notes. They searched the house, I'm not sure why – nothing turned up. They said they might need to return to check details.'

'And the vials?'

'No sign. I've looked everywhere twice now; I've been in the loft and the shed where you keep the mower.'

'The cliff path? The cliff top?'

'I went up again yesterday. If I missed anything the first time, it's not there now. All gone.' Again the strange, sharp laughter.

He looks about the room. The files on the shelves are stacked high, Ted's framed certificates cover the walls. The years of study, the operations, the hours of research have vanished now. Ted's dreams, his friendship, the man himself – all gone.

'Are you still there, Albie?'

'I've got to go. I need to check equipment for some trials I designed, start over . . .'

His beloved notebook is still missing despite

searching since his return. He will have to start from scratch, design everything again.

'More trials.' A quiet sigh comes down the phone. 'Well, we got away with it, Albie.' She sounds exhausted rather than triumphant.

'Try to sleep,' he tells her. He's exhausted too, a bone-deep tiredness; his sleep is still broken by nightmares.

'How much longer? It's strange here on my own.'

'Wait till Ed's visit, I'll come up after that.'

As he walks towards the lift, it's as though he is walking away from her or she is moving away from him, becoming a small figure getting smaller all the time, in a room in a house on an island in another country, far away.

He leaves the hospital for the Institute next door; the new trials must start soon if the lab's reputation is to be restored. The stands and automated syringes he ordered months back have been stored in Ted's room, still in boxes. Unlike his hospital office, though, Ted's room in the lab is now locked. Down the corridor he glimpses Bruce's face turn towards him then away, a door is opened and Bruce disappears from sight.

Albie walks down the corridor and enters without knocking. Bruce is sitting behind his computer; he looks up, the wary expression is replaced by a swift smile. 'Good to see you, Albie.'

Albie nods. Bruce is lying. He is not glad to see him; he had scurried into his room like a rat. This is the first he's seen of his friend since his return – Bruce, slacking again. It's time he was moved on.

'Where have you been for the last two weeks, Bruce?'

'Managerial course, Birmingham. I was there when I heard the news actually; poor Ted. Bloody awful.' His eyes fill with tears. 'I gather no one has a clue what happened.'

'That's right.' Uninvited, Albie sits opposite.

'Bridget thinks it was suicide; as lab manager she feels partly to blame. She's upset she wasn't more sympathetic about the trial results. I told her Ted would never have taken his own life.'

'No?'

'He thought the trial had been sabotaged. It gave him hope. He'd planned to talk about it with you.' Bruce stares at him; beneath the sorrowful overlay, Albie detects a harder gleam. His friend is sounding him out.

'Sabotage wasn't mentioned,' Albie replies. 'Though I gather he'd searched in the lab for clues. Has anything been found since then?'

'There have been a couple of official searches but nothing's turned up. Meantime, I see myself as the standard bearer, taking things forward,' Bruce continues, looking down modestly.

Is this a joke? Bruce lifts his head but his gaze is unsmiling. 'You know how fond of me Ted was, from the very beginning.'

Albie stares. What other fictions does Bruce tell himself?

'You look startled,' Bruce murmurs. 'He trusted me with your virus technology three years ago.'

The unforgettable moment that was followed by all the other moments. A day of sun and hope; the autumn trees, Ted's hand on his shoulder. Skuld, whose words all came true.

'It all started for me back then,' Bruce says complacently. 'You passed on some gossip from Skuld. You won't remember—'

'I'm surprised you do.'

'Because it made a difference. A seed had been planted though I did my best to ignore it at the time.' He shakes his head, looking rueful. 'I almost failed my PhD; then I remembered that scrap of gossip: someone had believed in me. I worked like a dog from then on.' He laughs briefly. 'Skuld has always refused to give me more details about what she overheard.'

'Have you seen her recently?'

'She left a couple of weeks ago to work at the Royal Free, but those words seem prescient now.'

'You'll have to remind me what they were.' He watches Bruce clear his throat, a fussy, self-important sound.

'A mark, Albie. She told you I would make my mark.'

'Does that involve a takeover?' An attempt at a joke, but his voice trembles with anger.

'Hardly necessary. Ed seems to have vanished and I've cleaned up my act. Killed the booze and the fags.' He leans forward and whispers, 'No more porn.' He sits back again, wriggling to make himself comfortable in the seat. 'I got top marks in the leadership module on the course last week.'

A pulse is beating in Albie's head. 'Surely you know Bridget asked me to hold the fort?'

'Temporary measure, I'm told. I've asked for a meeting with the board members tomorrow.' Bruce sounds different, determined. His hair is neater. Close up, his skin is clear, he smells of aftershave. He glances at his watch. 'I need to do a cell count on the SP 9271 culture lines. Hang around, we'll do lunch.'

'How long will you be?'

'An hour.'

'I'll wait; meanwhile I need to get into Ted's room.' Albie rises. 'Have you a key?'

A complicated expression passes across Bruce's face, annoyance and satisfaction both. 'No one can go in; police orders. There was a fire in there just over two weeks ago. The furniture was wrecked. It was all over the news, animal rights were implicated. I'm surprised it didn't reach you.'

'The internet is patchy on Jura; we didn't buy papers . . . what happened to my boxes of equipment?'

'Carbonised, I'm afraid.'

He feels sick. 'How the bloody hell did this happen?'

'Remember the fire in my room that everyone blamed on me? The police now think it was the same bunch, though this time the fire alarm had been disabled. It gets worse, I'm afraid.' A smile flickers, quickly suppressed. 'That breed of immune deficient rats you'd earmarked for your next trial have disappeared. All eighteen of them.'

'They stole my rats?'

'It's almost as if they knew about your trial.'

'No one knew, Bruce. The designs were in the notebook which I kept with me, always.'

The notebook which has nevertheless vanished completely; he's looked everywhere: at home, Bridget has searched in the lab on his behalf, he's gone through the wards and even theatres. Someone might have found it in the changing room while he was operating and used it to target his work; a jealous colleague, perhaps. A protester could have followed him to the tube and stolen it from the seat next to him. It might be in a taxi. It could be anywhere, but it has his name inside; he'll see it again if he waits long enough.

'. . . similar case of fires breaking out in an Oxford lab about three years ago.' Bruce is continuing. 'The police think that was animal rights protesters too, they're linking the two episodes. They advised the installation of CCTV cameras and took fingerprints. Mine, Bridget's, Skuld's. Everyone was cleared, of course.' He gets up.

Albie stands with him, thinking fast. This bad luck

could be turned to his advantage. The lab is vulnerable. Bridget has never understood the importance of security and animal rights protesters have taken advantage. Ed has disappeared; this could be an opportunity to present himself as the stable, experienced candidate for the long term. Bruce doesn't deserve to waltz into the job that was originally promised to him. There has to be something he can do. Bruce has prepared his fortifications well, but every castle has a weak place if you search long enough: a drawbridge left down, a door that's unmanned. They leave the room together. Bruce doesn't bother to lock up; he is only walking round the corner to the lab. Albie enters the lift, closes the door, descends to the ground floor then re-ascends, and walks swiftly back to Bruce's room where he shuts the door then locks it.

He begins to leaf among the papers on the desk, looking for information, a strategy to hijack, contacts he can anonymously email with unhelpful information about his friend. His eyes roam the room seeking lists or numbers; catching instead a picture of a naked girl on the cork board, he moves closer. Bruce's professed interest in young girls is something he could use. The girl straddles a scarlet motorbike on a calendar; she's young, probably younger than she looks, and a plan begins to shape itself from the racing thoughts in his head. When his mobile sounds a second later he answers without glancing at the caller's name on the screen. Muffled sobs come down the phone.

'Can it wait, Beth? I'll phone you back in an hour.'

'It's Gita, Albie. Billy's ill.'

'Billy's ill?' He is back in his other world, where illness rules and doctors are helpful to their patients. 'How can I help?'

'He's off his food; he's been sick a couple of times. The nurse at the practice thinks it's just the usual sort of virus going round, but I know Billy. Jake's away. Ted usually . . . Oh God, Ted. It's so sad. How terrible for you all.'

'Yes.' It had been the most terrible moment of his life. 'Tell me about Billy,' he continues quickly. 'Is he hot? Sleepy?'

She pours out a list of symptoms, though none seem particularly worrying. He invites her to bring Billy to Ward Three at Great Ormond Street Hospital and then contacts the staff asking for a side room. One of Prof Malcolm's special patients, a member of his family, almost; the little boy with hydrocephalus. Yes, that's right, Billy. He'll see him himself. He's unlikely to need admission.

This will be some minor problem. Gita is on her own, everything will seem worse. He turns off his phone and, opening his briefcase, retrieves the gloves he stowed long ago. It doesn't take long to find Bruce's personal laptop behind the door. He unzips the case and slips it on to the desk. New, top of the range.

Bruce has given himself a present in advance of the salary rise he imagines will be his. All Albie needs is the password; offering up a silent prayer that Bruce has the same one for personal and hospital use he taps in DEADRATS. He is in, immediately. Then he pauses, conscious he is navigating a path that's leading him into a dark forest. He could step off the track now, put the laptop back in the case, meet Bruce as planned, work out some compromise. He sits, sweating with indecision, but here in Bruce's office, Bruce's face comes easily to mind: falsely modest, fresh as if he slept well, untroubled by plaguing nightmares. Bruce hasn't suffered for this, as he has. He hasn't committed terrible crimes. Albie reaches swiftly for the memory stick that is jammed into a mug with felt-tip pens and a cigarette lighter. Slotting it into the side of the laptop, he begins to search on Google, typing in terms which make him shudder. 'Child images . . . Young sex . . . Pre-pubescent naked child abuse images.' He trawls each website for images and scans them, feeling sick, though by some standards these images would be mild. He would probably have to pay for the worst ones or join the dark web; these will be sufficient for his purpose. He saves whole web pages to the memory stick, downloading fifty. He removes the stick, zips up the laptop and replaces it behind the door. He sits in front of Bruce's hospital desktop, slides in the stick and taps in the same password. It takes moments to copy the images on to the home drive. Finally, he brings up Google and taps in 'Child porn'.

Immediately a red message fills the screen: ACCESS DENIED.

He shuts the computer down and slips the stick back into the mug. He pulls a handful of tissues from a box on the desk and wipes his face. Every week, at least once, the hospital computer checks for highly sensitive words, searching all transactions. A month ago, a pathologist was sacked for looking at pornography. This is child abuse, incalculably worse. The abortive Google search on the hospital computer will alert them and all Bruce's files will be meticulously explored. Those obscene images will be quickly discovered.

Albie puts the gloves back in his case and leaves the room as he found it. He descends to the underground car park as before, then walks back to his office in the hospital. He checks his watch. An hour has gone by, an hour to wreck a career. After five minutes he phones Bruce to explain he has been held up on the wards. Next week should be easier. Thursday?

'Fine.' Bruce sounds cheerful. 'I should have lots of news for you by then.'

Albie sits back in his chair. His shirt is sticking to his skin. By next Thursday his friend could be in custody. He feels increasingly nauseous. The path he was travelling along has just steepened; he's accelerating downwards, out of control. He must get out of his room, he needs air.

As he crosses the road a pizza delivery bicyclist swerves to avoid him. He stumbles to a bench in the gardens, feeling giddy. At the far end, the old man in his green woollen hat drinks from a bottle of cider. Albie sits, head bent, gasping for air; a weight is bearing down on his chest and he struggles to breathe. His hands tingle painfully. Two children died as a result of what he did; he murdered a colleague and has just ruined another to justify that. He pulls off his tie and opens his collar. Every step he has taken had a logic at the time but he can't remember it any more; he's gone too far to turn round now. There is no alternative but to battle on, plunging deeper and deeper into the forest where the trees grow closely together and it's impossible to see the way out. He breathes as slowly and fully as he can but his lungs feel restricted, the giddiness is worse. He leans further forward; his face runs with sweat, the drops falling on the paving at his feet. He can see tiny cracks in the stone, fissures branching out in a fine network too small to notice from a distance. They must be flaws that occurred since it was placed here, or perhaps when cut from the quarry years ago.

'Okay, mate?' The drunk has manoeuvred himself down the bench and is next to him, proffering his bottle of cider. The stench of stale urine is strong.

Albie waves him away and the man backs off,

looking scared. The movement shakes Albie free. This is a panic attack, that's all. He forces himself to breathe more slowly. The sound of birds in the square begins to filter through the noise in his head. A panic attack, he has diagnosed plenty. He walks slowly around the path that skirts the grass; the quiet tread of his feet leads his thoughts back into order. Under his stewardship the laboratory will become a centre of excellence. He will employ the right people: workers, not mavericks like Bruce. He will direct the research to bring new vaccines to market. Hundreds will benefit. Thousands. He will plough the money back into research, safeguard the lab with cameras and locks and invite people he trusts to look after the animals, Skuld, for instance. He sits again, this time on an empty bench. A pigeon by his feet begins to strut, staking out its little circle of pavement, watching, assessing danger. The purple feathers on the neck shimmer in the sun. Police sirens sound nearby; he hears the familiar rumble of taxis arriving at the hospital. The normal noises of a normal-seeming day.

With Bruce out of the running, only Ed remains as a contender for the leadership – conceivably he has made his bid already. The pigeon at his feet comes close, cocking his head to one side, listening to every sound. Ed might have been discussed at the most recent consultants' planning meeting, favourably perhaps in view of the six months he'd already been in charge. Skuld could have been helping at that meeting if it had taken place before she left; she might have picked up something he could use to assess the threat Ed presents and then oppose it. He stands at the thought and the pigeon flies away; panic spreads quickly and the air becomes full of the clapping sound of birds' wings as he hurries towards Great Ormond Street.

Gita turns to him with a little cry of relief. She looks different from the pretty woman at Ed's party; her face is drawn with worry, her eyes dark with tiredness. She is cradling Billy who is grizzling and kicking wildly.

'Are you all right?' Gita asks, kissing Albie. 'I can hardly imagine how dreadful it must have been for you all.'

'Thanks, Gita. Tell me about Billy.' He indicates the chairs. Billy quietens as they sit; the room is peaceful, despite the medical equipment banked against the walls, and the clashing colours of the toys in their red and orange plastic containers. The atmosphere is innocent. Albie hasn't slept properly for days; his limbs grow heavy, his eyes close.

'. . . blocked shunt maybe? He's so unsettled.'

His eyes snap open. Gita is studying Billy's face; she didn't notice Albie's second of sleep. Just then the child gives a little snore.

'He seems settled enough now,' Albie comments; they both laugh.

'Isn't that always the way?' She sounds irritated and

relieved at the same time. 'He was up most of the night.'

'And as you mentioned, you are on your own—'

'That's nothing new.' Her voice hardens. 'Jake's driven Ed back to Jura to collect Ted's things. My husband takes his role in that family very seriously, more seriously than his own, sometimes.' A short laugh.

So that's where Ed has gone. Grief could make him ineffective but Jake is sharp, professionally curious; he might pester Beth with questions and she could let something slip. He needs to get them back, especially Jake. With Billy in hospital, Jake will feel obliged to return and Ed will have to accompany him in the only car.

He examines Billy, his fingers gently exploring the child's head, two centimetres above, two behind his right ear. He finds the small silicone dome implanted under the skin, a reservoir connected to two tubes, one from the ventricles in his brain, where the cerebrospinal fluid is produced, the other to the inside of his abdominal cavity so it can drain away. When he depresses it, the dome refills, albeit slowly; unlikely then, though not impossible, that the shunt is blocked. He slips a finger round the silky little wrist to take his pulse. The child screams and struggles. Gita holds him still while Albie looks at the back of his eyes, already reassured. A protesting child is not one who needs immediate action. He turns to Gita.

'His pulse is a little raised but he feels cool and the

optic discs are normal. He's not sick enough for an infected or blocked shunt and the dome refills, which supports my judgement.' Gita nods, her face taut with concentration. 'The nurse at your clinic could be right,' he continues. 'It might be a viral infection, usually upper respiratory. We'll keep him in for monitoring for twenty-four hours just in case. In the meantime, get that husband of yours back. We can discuss further treatment and any investigations when he arrives.'

Her face lightens. 'Thanks, dear Albie. You are being very kind to us.'

He talks to the nurse in charge; they can stay in the ward overnight, he is promised that Billy will be carefully watched and any deterioration reported immediately to the registrar on call. Albie takes leave of Gita who is settling him into a cot; he's quieter now and she looks relieved.

'Say hi to your lovely wife,' she says as she kisses him goodbye. 'She was so sweet to Billy.'

He walks towards the lift. He must be more tired than he thought; her words make him want to cry. His lovely wife. The wife he loved. Please don't lose control, Beth, he tells her silently. Wait. I'll fetch you, soon. We'll come back together. There'll be time to talk, understand. Forgive. Heal.

He glances at his watch; he's due in clinic and begins to walk so quickly he's almost running. There isn't time now. Beth will wait, she'll understand. In the few moments he has in the lift, he sends a rapid text.

Jake and Ed coming back to Jura. Stay.

He hurries from the lift to the clinic. She's used to waiting, after all; it won't be for much longer.

26

Jura. Summer 2018

Beth is weeding in the hot afternoon when Albie's text comes through; she reads the message then, after a moment, deletes it. *Stay.* What you say to dogs.

The weather has been perfect since he left. The air ripples with heat, even the birds are quiet. At night the scent of warm hay rises to the window. She walks slowly back to the house. Jake and Ed are coming back. They'll collect Ted's clothes but they'll want to search for the vials, they'll ask questions. After the brightness of the garden, the air in the house is as dark and cool as water. She stands in the sitting room, tapping her fingers on Albie's desk. She has looked everywhere but she's forgotten to search this desk. She opens it quickly. Science prizes and certificates are jumbled together. She picks out Albie's school-leaving photo; his face was fuller back then, the hair much longer. His expression is serious but there is a glow under his skin, as though lit from inside. When he left two weeks ago he seemed full of darkness. She turns over books full of maths, physics and chemistry, but no art or music. To progress in his world, you had to focus on fact. Toughen, push distractions aside. She's done the same, but tough fibres have a breaking point; in fact they fracture more easily. In the last few days it's as if the strands holding her together are snapping one by one. She piles everything back and slams the lid.

Harris begins to whine then bark loudly; she's forgotten to feed him and now can't remember when she last did. Tin in hand, she rattles through the knives in the drawer for the can opener. When the door opens she crouches down in blind panic, pulling Harris to her. She hasn't thought to lock the doors, even at night.

A tall figure blocks the light. Ted. The same height, the same slant to the shoulders. Ted as a young man, tall, clear-eyed and back for revenge. Her mouth dries; she can't move; her legs are paralysed by fear. It's too late to beg for forgiveness. She opens her mouth to scream for help, though there is no one who could hear her across the miles and miles of moorland; no one will come to her aid. A second later the figure dissolves into Ed. Jake pushes through the door behind him. Harris runs to greet them, tail wagging. Beth stares, her heart banging, unable to speak.

Ed halts, he looks surprised, a little uncomfortable. 'Oh, you're still here. Sorry to barge in. There's no car, we thought you must have left.'

She stands up slowly. 'Albie took the car, he had to go back to work. How are you?'

'Fine, thanks.' Ed's reply is automatic. He is not fine, of course, he looks ill.

'It's good to see you both again.' She is lying as well; they loom large in the kitchen and the past has entered with them. She will have to be very clever, more careful than she's ever been. 'Would you like some tea?' She turns on the kettle; her hands tremble. 'You must be tired after the journey.'

'We're here for Dad's things,' Ed says, staring around at the room as if he expects to see his father, slumped and sleeping in a chair.

'Of course.' She warms the pot and spoons in tea, adds the water. The little ritual is soothing. She can get through this; they'll go to his room in a minute, take his case, and then disappear. She'll call Albie, he can fetch her, together they'll go home.

'Everything is upstairs, ready for you to take.' She hands Ed a cup of tea and gives one to Jake.

'The coroner returned an open verdict at Ted's inquest.' Jake accepts the cup but his eyes watch her face as though he were a lawyer and she in the dock. She was wrong to hope. He wants far more than a case of clothes; Jake is after the truth. Her heart begins to race uncomfortably. Meanwhile Ed is staring at the chair where Ted had sat at supper on the last night of his life. He grips the table, his eyes fill. Jake pulls out a chair, tugs him to sitting and then stands near as if on guard. 'The coroner was unable to reach any other conclusion; there was insufficient evidence for accident or suicide.'

'I'm not really sure what an open verdict means.' She plays for time, marshalling her thoughts.

'That the inquest can be reopened if new evidence is found and presented to the coroner,' Jake replies.

'So . . . evidence of suicide?'

'Not necessarily. There could be evidence of death by misadventure, for example.' His voice drops. 'Or evidence of murder.' He is motionless, staring at her as if he expects a reply, but words like these need space, a framing of silence.

Ed looks up. She reads sorrow rather than accusation, he is deep in grief. Jake is the danger, the friend but not the son. She says nothing, but Jake rebukes her angrily as if she had.

'There is nothing concrete to suggest suicide. No note.'

'I suppose there are cases when that kind of decision is reached suddenly, a desperate, last-minute thing . . .' She is walking along an invisible tightrope, everything has to be balanced – too much weight on one side or the other and she will fall.

'The coroner said that in a surprising number of cases, a note of some kind is found.'

She mustn't point out that no note is not in itself evidence against suicide. She must place each step one in front of another with infinite care; the chasm on either side yawns.

'You mentioned death by misadventure; a loss of

balance near the edge of those cliffs – is that the sort of thing you mean?'

'I've thought about that,' Jake says. 'I've thought about that a lot. I know he'd aged, but I've never seen him stumble, his balance was excellent.' He has an answer ready for each point, like a tennis player who returns every ball, the kind that wins in the end.

'He seemed so tired; less fit than he used to be . . .' she says. Jake looks at her sharply, a glimmer of triumph in his eyes. She's made a mistake; her words imply past knowledge, and maybe an agenda. 'Albie told me they used to play squash, but that's a while ago now,' she adds. Her palms feel wet.

'He was fine that morning, Beth. We were with him, he walked for miles to the whirlpool and back.'

'He was drinking later, that might—'

'He's used to alcohol. I've never seen it affect his judgement. Have you?'

'I wouldn't know, I only saw him at a distance at parties, once a year.'

Jake allows a smile to cross his face, the kind that says you are lying You know far more than you are saying. You knew Ted by heart.

'He didn't drink much that evening.' Ed looks up suddenly. His cheeks are wet with tears. 'And he was happier that day; he'd cheered up a lot in the last few days before he died. He'd found these small bottles in the lab which he thought would clear his name.'

'Small bottles?' Beth turns to him with a puzzled little frown.

'Vials containing the solutions that were used in those experiments; he thought they'd been tampered with. He said he could see where the tops had been got at but I didn't bother to look.' His voice breaks. 'I didn't listen, it's my fault. It's all my fault; if I hadn't been in Berne when the trial began I might have seen something—'

'It's not your fault, Ed,' Jake interrupts. 'We've been through all that.' He looks at Beth. 'We need to find those vials.' His voice is sharp with suspicion.

'Of course.' She nods, gesturing to the room. There is nowhere that she hasn't looked.

'Having the vials would have given him a reason to stay alive, you see.' He comes a little closer. 'Why kill himself if he thought he could clear his name?'

'So many ifs.' She stands quickly, a little giddily. 'We seem to be going round in circles, with no real answers.' Circles that are getting smaller, like an animal trap that tightens round the struggling victim. Jake doesn't say any more. He has had enough of her now; she sees she is meant to get out of their way. 'Search wherever you want, I'll be upstairs if you need me.'

Her case is open on the bed where she began to gather her things days ago. Now Ed and Jake have come, she can finish packing. She'll call Albie once they've gone. The silky underwear is still in its cellophane packets, bought when she thought her body could console Albie. That hope had evaporated as quickly as the mist off the sea on a hot morning. Through the open window the cliffs are a brilliant green against the sky, the almond scent of cow parsley comes up through the still air. As she folds a shirt, a high-pitched mewing unfurls in the silence like the distant cry of a baby. She half falls, half runs downstairs, turning her ankle, then hurries limping through the kitchen. Ed and Jake are rifling through Albie's desk and don't look up. She jogs painfully into the garden, searching the undergrowth, looking under trees, her breath hot in her throat. A baby here somewhere, alone and desperate for its mother. She stops to listen again, but the crying isn't coming from the ground. Above her head two large buzzards float in the air, pale circles under each wing. Their calls are high-pitched, more like a cat than a baby. What madness overtook her? She puts a shaking hand to her mouth and limps slowly back to the house, meeting Ed and Jake on their way out.

'Off already?'

'To the hotel, we booked rooms,' Ed tells her, his hand on the car door. He has been crying again, his eyes look sore. 'Jake's tired, he drove through the night. We'll be back tomorrow.'

As she watches them drive away, she texts Albie:

Ed and Jake were here, looking for vials; coming back to search again tomorrow.

She replaces the phone in her pocket and returns to the house for a drink of water. She should eat as Albie said, but her left molar hurts when she chews. She used to look after her body as a soldier his weapons, but now she can't remember when she last saw a dentist. There is a strange taste in her mouth, sweet, stale. Her teeth feel gritty, as if she had stuffed her mouth with rotten cake crumbs but was unable to swallow them down. She should go for a swim to clear her head, but the ocean encircles the house, a glittering army laying siege. She sits by the window while outside the buzzards slide in the hot air, watching and waiting for prey.

27

London. Summer 2018

There is a wood on the stage now; real-looking trees and a man stumbling about as if lost. There are no signposts and no one to guide or command. This man is on his own, for better or worse than he could possibly imagine.

He's left the safety of his lair; a dangerous thing to do. Ask any animal.

Albie has a good view of the doors with his back to the windows. He's waiting for Skuld in the lower-ground-floor café at the Royal Free Hospital. On a nearby table, a group of white-coated students lean together over cans of Coke. Their pockets bulge with pens and torches. They are eager and untidy; that stage where you think knowledge opens the world like the pages of a book. He watches where and how they sit, who talks and who listens, the little signs that indicate who the alpha male and female are, though in the end none of that will matter. They are destined for the same cages, the same wheels. They will have orderly lives; their dramas will be contained. They won't pursue glory or revenge; when they sleep, their dreams will be pleasant.

Thunder rumbles. Beyond the large windows, the sky is black. Thunderstorms are predicted, unusual for July, but the weather has been unusual all summer. A group of nurses enter the café, the air rings with chatter and the clash of cutlery. The receptionist he spoke to yesterday promised to pass on his message; Skuld should appear soon. He'll buy her lunch, she might tell him what she heard at the last consultants' meeting if she was there. His mobile rings while he is scanning the queue by the canteen for a blond head, the slight figure.

'Mr Shaw is up, he is feeling better and wants to go.' Suria is his new registrar, keen to please. 'Brian Thwaite's fine, his tremor's gone.' As he listens, the café darkens, rain has started.

'Good. They can go home now.'

'Billy's a little unsettled again this morning . . .' She is hesitant, as though the bad news is somehow her fault. 'He was fine overnight but his temperature rose in the early hours; it's thirty-eight point five now.'

'Pulse rate?'

'A hundred and forty.'

'Vomiting?'

'Not since admission. His discs are normal though he's restless, it's difficult to see them properly.'

'Look again. Does the dome refill on pressure?'

'Very slowly.'

'Is his father around?'

'Just his mum; she's really worried.'

As Albie listens, lightning scrawls through the clouds, the students whistle and exclaim. He makes his decision; antibiotics will buy time for Jake to return with the hook of discussing an operation to remove the shunt.

'Start an IV and take the microbiologist's advice as to the best combination of antibiotics. See if you can contact Billy's father, ask him to come in to discuss treatment options.'

'I could organise theatre,' Suria suggests eagerly. 'I'll put him first on the list and that way—'

'The shunt isn't blocked, Suria. Antibiotics will keep him safe for now. Contact Mr Valance please. I'll review Billy later.'

He ends the call. There is a scent of burning, doubtless from the kitchens, but he thinks of lightning across the sky, bridges incinerating behind him. He looks at his watch. He'll scan Billy in a few hours then remove the shunt if he's no better. In the meantime his plan is defensible; antibiotics could work on their own.

'Baird.'

He turns. A dumpy, white-haired woman carrying a cup of tea has approached from his left. The Scottish accent is familiar. A friend from home? A patient?

'Baird McAlister, that ever was.' Oblique hazel eyes behind pebble glasses scan his keenly. 'You've forgotten me.' She leans to kiss him, her cheeks as furred and wrinkled as overripe peaches. He catches the scent of formalin and chocolate and in that moment the nights in the Glasgow lab come back to him, the project on rat stress that he conducted despite the disapproval of the laboratory manager, who is standing before him now, a little fatter , but with the same quizzical gaze, a capacious satchel slung across her body like a shield. Hilary Jenks.

'Hilary. What a surprise.' He indicates the seat next to him. How could he have forgotten, even for a moment? Her reign had been trenchant.

She puts her tea on the table and sits, a plump cat, settling herself on her cushion. 'Not exactly a surprise; I run the animal lab here nowadays. I heard you phoned so I knew where to find you. Couldn't resist.' Her eyes travel over him rapidly, frowning as if performing a risk assessment. She always was forthright. 'Well, and what are you up to, laddie?'

'I've been appointed acting consultant at the National Hospital in Queen Square and acting head of the lab at the Institute of Neurology.' Acting. The understudy called in at short notice and still unsure of the plot. He manufactures a smile for his audience. 'I've been very lucky.'

'You've come a long way.' Her lips tighten slightly. 'As I suspected you would.' Ambivalent congratulations, but it had always been tricky to read her. She'd hovered over his student project, attempting to restrict the hours he spent shining lights on rats, counting defecation as a marker of stress. She opposed the endless repetitions but his thoroughness had paid off; he'd achieved the project prize for that year which had set him on the path. He owes her a debt.

'You've come a long way too.'

'The Glasgow lab got closed down. A fire, made national TV.' Her voice is almost proud.

More fires; memory stirs. Glasgow. Three years ago, flames leaping into the dark air, the drama of rescued animals relayed on the ten o'clock news; a researcher had died trying to salvage his work.

'I'm sorry, Hilary.'

'Don't be. It was time for a move. Oxford first and then here about three years ago. I've got a great deal more responsibility now.'

'And the family?'

'Sven and I divorced, so I moved near our daughters.' She smiles fondly. 'We still keep rescue dogs.'

He recalls the little girls who watched him while they chewed their mothers' brownies and waited for their father; the mongrel she kept under her desk.

'I'm sorry,' he murmurs again.

Oh, we're much better on our own, just me and my girls. And the animals, of course.' Her next glance is probing. 'I heard about those vaccine trials at the Institute. What happened there?'

'I know very little about it. Ed Malcolm was running the lab for his father at the time. I was on the wards during the whole period.'

'And the recent death of the Professor?'

'A tragedy.'

'He must have been under stress.'

He nods, glancing away. He's not yet ready to discuss Ted with those who didn't know him. They sip in silence before he leans forward. 'It's been good to catch up,' he says, meaning it, 'but I'm here because I was hoping to meet with your new lab assistant; her name is Skuld.'

'Why would that be?' The cat's eyes glimmer.

'The police are tracing everyone who worked with Ted for information on his state of mind.' Where do these lies come from? he wonders. They appear as if ready-made from a store he never knew was there. 'I promised I'd chat to Skuld on their behalf.'

'Well, you can't. She's gone swimming, half-day.' She pats his hand and rises. 'Don't look so woebegone, I'll tell her you called. She'll be in touch if she has anything to say.'

He kisses her, her cheek indents, more marshmallow than peach, a rough, sugared surface. She adjusts her satchel and waves him off.

It's still raining. He turns right out of the hospital and begins to jog down Pond Street. It had been interesting to encounter Hilary again, unmellowed since the days she patrolled the lab in his teaching hospital, more challenging if anything. He'd felt warned off from Skuld, but he can guess where she's gone for her swim. She told him she and her sisters swam in the ponds on the Heath and he can't see her in the chlorinated water at Swiss Cottage Leisure Centre somehow – too conventional, too crowded. He turns left down South End Road then right on to the Heath. The grass and summer trees glow lime in the periphery; as he jogs his shoes become soaked and stuck with beech mast. Thunder is rumbling distantly, the storm moving further away. Halfway up Parliament Hill he branches off to the left, runs down to skirt the men's pond and join the narrow gravelly path that leads towards Highgate. The light abruptly dwindles, filtering through meshed branches. The smell of wet earth is mixed with the metallic scent of pond water.

Three bikes are fastened together against the fence. The gate is locked. A notice, hung with rope looped over the post, states that no swimming is permitted in thunderstorms. He scales the fence awkwardly and jumps down, his landing muted by the pine needles which carpet the ground. Wet trees crowd close to the path, dark green water glimmers between the ivy covered trunks up ahead. He detects movement in the pond; heads floating as if disembodied: blonde, red and grey. A wildflower meadow runs alongside, partly hidden from the water by trees and bushes. He stands behind a willow tree, up to his knees in thin grass and wilting poppies, shivering in his wet clothes and feeling absurd. He should be at work, not huddled by the women's ponds on the Heath in the rain, but he's come too far to falter now.

It's impossible not to pace as he waits and not to feel as he paces that he is becoming increasingly like Ted. He can see him as clearly as if he were treading the grass ahead of him, tall and vigorous as he used to be, phone clamped to his ear, turning and turning again, pausing to mouth a joke or pull a face. The sorrow is physical, a punch to his abdomen; he hadn't accounted for this. In the heat of that night he hadn't accounted for anything. He holds still, waiting for the pain to pass. After five minutes, the women swim to the edge of the pond and climb out. Skuld is distinguishable by her workman-like gait at odds with the fragile body. Verdandi's movements are calm while Urth lunges abruptly for her towel. He watches as they shed their black swimsuits, an uneasy spectator of Skuld's white back tattooed with a curving snake, neat buttocks and small breasts lifting as she pulls on a tee shirt. They move off into the trees; he runs to the back of the meadow, pushing through brambles, his clothes hooking on thorns. By the time he has wrenched himself free, he is almost upon them where they sit on a rug in a clearing. They look round calmly, almost as if they'd known he was coming. He smiles; he's beginning to be familiar with these girls, the air of mystery in which they cloak themselves, as though they have secret powers of some kind.

'I hope you don't mind me arriving like this.'

Skuld points to the rug. Little piles of wilted leaves are heaped in front of them, rolls of dark bread, cakes, apples. He shakes his head but takes it as an invitation to join them and sits next to her. Verdandi's face glowers between the limp grey curtains of her hair, Urth's brown eyes are lowered to her clasped hands; following her gaze he glimpses white fur, then two naked tails thread through her stubby fingers. Rats, white laboratory rats. He is astonished and outraged in equal measure. Urth places them gently on the ground, a nose lifts and twitches, pink eyes half close against the glare. The rats turn and scuttle through the arch made by her lifted thighs.

'Jesus.' He scrambles to his feet and takes a step into the undergrowth, but the rats have disappeared. 'Where the hell did they come from? They won't survive half an hour.'

'Freedom,' Urth says triumphantly. The word in her voice sparks the memory of a pub two years ago, the sisters celebrating the end of the day, or so he'd thought. He feels sick with anger. Had they been releasing rats back then? Bruce's smug face flashes into his mind, the loss of his rats hits him with force. 'My God, rats went missing from the Institute recently, my rats. Was that you as well?'

'Your rats?' Verdandi regards him scornfully. 'Animals belong to themselves.' She leans to retrieve the swimsuits and Urth begins to fold paper around the remains of the food. They seem in a hurry. Albie senses a gap closing, time slipping away. If he scares them off with accusations he won't get the answers he needs. He crouches down near Skuld. He'd last seen her in the lab when he changed the vials; had she been there to steal some rats that night? He pushes his suspicions aside, he has to. 'Let's forget the rats for now. I came to find you because I was hoping you might be able to help me.'

She leans forward and pulls up a strand of ivy, running her fingers over the glossy leaves. Her sisters pause, they inch closer.

'Around three years ago, you let me know what had been discussed at the consultants' meeting, the very first one you helped at.'

He studies her face for a sign that she remembers but she doesn't look up. She might have forgotten but the moment is as clear for him as if he has just closed the door on her, has just met Bruce in the lift, has just encountered Ted on the steps of the hospital. 'What you told me back then turned out to be prophetic. I was hoping you might pass on what happened at their last meeting too.'

'What makes you so sure she was even at that one?' Urth demands fiercely, forestalling her sister's reply.

'Skuld said she served coffee for the consultants at their meetings on a regular basis,' he tells her, surprised. 'You'd asked her to.'

Urth frowns but she doesn't reply; he turns back to Skuld. 'The last meeting would have taken place about a month ago, just before you left.'

'What exactly is it you want to know?' Verdandi demands.

He pauses but they are unlikely to tell anyone about this conversation. 'Ted would have resigned around that time, appointments are discussed at those meetings. I need to find out if my name or Ed's was mentioned as his replacement. I'm in charge now; if I'm to take over permanently I'd like to make plans for the future of the lab.'

'I heard the Professor give that post to his son.' Verdandi's eyes shift over his face. He'd forgotten she was at Ed's engagement party.

'He held the post for a while, but Ted remained in control,' he replies. 'He'd already given me the strong impression that when he retired, the leadership of the lab would come to me.' He addresses Skuld again. 'I'm hoping you'll tell me what was decided at the meeting. There's so much I want to do.'

She lifts her head, her pale eyes gaze serenely into his, his thoughts crystallise. 'I share Ted's vision you see,' he continues. 'We worked together. I want to dedicate my life to making a cure for brain cancer in children a reality.' These words are, he realises, completely true. His ambition has become, if anything, more pure. The desire for money, houses, safety has faded. There will be no family to house, no children to keep safe. Beth won't want grandeur now. Her image, thin and tearful in the garden as he last saw her, flares then dims again. 'I'm convinced Ted would have wanted me, not Ed, to carry on with his work in the lab. I'm certain he—'

'Yes,' Skuld's lilting voice calmly interrupts. 'That is what he said in the last meeting.'

He stares at her, scarcely believing what he's hearing. He may be deep in the woods but perhaps he can still hack his way out.

'I was there with the coffee as usual.' She is more fluent than he remembers, much more confident. 'The Professor had resigned like you say, he was sad actually. He warned there would be difficult times ahead. He told everyone he had asked his son to step back, and let you take over—'

'So now you have the information you wanted.' Verdandi's voice cuts sharply across Skuld's.

So Ted had trusted him after all; more than he did his own son. A soft clattering sound breaks the silence as rain begins to fall on the leaves above them. The air turns colder. He could weep. Ted had made good on his promise in the end, but he never breathed a word; he must have meant it as a surprise, a gift, secretly planned.

The girls stand. Urth crams the food into a rucksack. Verdandi folds the rug, her lean white arms flashing in the air. Skuld is shivering; none of them are wearing warm clothes. They are more vulnerable than they realise; with their misplaced notions of freedom for animals, they are drifting into danger.

He turns to Skuld. 'I won't mention those missing

rats to anyone, but you need to take care. The woman you work for is an old acquaintance; if she knew what you were doing, she'd call the police.'

Verdandi smiles and Urth chuckles. He stares, confused. Perhaps they think themselves beyond the reach of the law. He has warned them, that's all he can do.

Skuld throws a broken roll towards a couple of mandarin drakes swimming beyond the water lilies. There is a splashing rush as they paddle close, their eyes naked as beads. The larger one puts his webbed foot on the other's back, pushing him under.

'We should go. Come, Urth, hurry, Skuld.' The strange Norwegian names fit these women, he should look up what they mean. Verdandi weaves her way rapidly through the ivy and stinging nettles, closely shadowed by Urth. As Skuld turns to follow he puts a hand on her arm. 'Thank you for letting me know what was said at the meeting.' He smiles at her; if she hadn't been interrupted by her sisters, she might have shared even more. 'To be honest, I'm surprised that the consultants are so free with—'

'What they say in front of me?' She wrenches her arm away; for the first time her voice lifts in anger. 'It's very simple. I don't talk so they don't see me. They treat us like they do their animals; if you don't speak as they do, you don't exist.' She spits neatly on the ground and, with her side-to-side stride, hurries after her sisters.

'Goodbye,' he shouts but she doesn't turn round. He

wipes his forehead and cheeks with the cuff of his shirt; it's as though she had spat directly at his face. He feels shaken and stands by the pond staring at the ducks as they swim away, their quarrel forgotten. He can't tell which was the aggressor now and which the victim.

Back at the fence the bikes have disappeared; he swings himself over the gate and begins to jog towards Kenwood House. His damp trousers flap uncomfortably against his legs. The pain in his abdomen is back, he feels racked by sorrow. Ted had cleared the way for him at the last meeting, regardless of what had happened before that point. He'd been appreciated at the end, trusted by the man he killed. He's on the edge of an abyss scrabbling for a handhold and then he has it. Ted's words come back in time, the ones he quoted whenever Albie regretted an operative decision or a faulty diagnosis. *You make a decision based on the information available at the time, that's all you can do.* Ted gave the lab to his son; Albie's decision to hijack the trial followed that. How could he have known then what would ensue?

He enters the gate to the grounds of Kenwood and the vista opens up. The rain has stopped. He pauses by the sloping lawns in front of the great white house to turn on his phone. He ignores a voicemail from Beth, scrolling down to the text from Suria: 'Billy seems stable.' Another from Bridget asking him to call in urgently, which he can do on the way to see Billy. Beth's message can wait until he has more time; she is slipping below the surface of his thoughts, while Ted has emerged as if dripping from the deep. A couple of runners speed by, startling him, their faces sweaty, feet thudding on the path, oblivious to everything but their own efforts. He follows them, picking up speed. He feels released. The way ahead has opened up.

Bridget then Billy. A list; he is used to dealing with lists. The abdominal pain has receded. He sprints towards the Highgate exit.

28

Jura. Summer 2018

Early each morning the deer stand in a group of six, watching her. They position themselves on the green-grey bluff above the house, their delicate heads outlined against the sky. The fawns are spotted, their hooves a polished black; they seem to have stepped out of a fairy tale, too perfect to be real. The boldest runs a few paces towards her then away. His antler buds are visible already. The hinds keep very still; there are no stags but the group seems complete. They observe her as if from another, more ancient world, waiting to see what she will do, this female on her own with no young. She sits cross-legged on the grass outside the gate, hoping the brave fawn will come close, maybe put his soft nose in her hand for the salt. Deer tracks are everywhere on the island, in the mud, on nibbled grass and printed on the beach, thick exclamation marks pressed into the damp sand. She fastens the gate open for them at night but they never enter the garden, or if they do, they leave no footprints. The grass is longer now, turning silky, threaded with sea campion, pink thrift and clover.

Today she is too late to see the little herd. She had lain awake most of the night, waiting for a call from Albie, incoherent terrors flaring like summer fires on the heather, one thought lighting another. The sky was pale by the time she slept. When she wakes she is sweating, the sun across the bed and the phone in her hand, her neck stiff from lying awkwardly against the pillows. The tooth in the back of her mouth is hurting again. There are faint sounds in the house that could be voices, low mutterings, her name amongst them. She lies still, her heart beating so hard the sheet over her chest moves with the pulse. Is it her imagination or could it be burglars? Most likely the police. They said they might return; she must have forgotten to lock the door again. By the time she has dressed and crept downstairs, they have disappeared, leaving no trace. Harris is whining to be let out, his drinking bowl is nearly empty, the water looks green. Outside the grass looks tired and yellow in the midday heat. The deer have long gone to the shade of the wood.

The fridge is still crammed with bacon, cheese and butter. Two chickens stand in a pool of pale pink blood, the grey skin studded with the tips of feathers, dark splinters, digging in. She jams the bacon in the freezer. In the bread bin, patches of mould have spread, blue starbursts through the loaf. There is wine, though; the bottles stand in the pantry on the lead sink, a round-shouldered group, gathering dust. Albie must have planned for drinking every night and at lunchtimes as well, anticipating laughter, clinking glasses. Convivial chat. That's what would have happened, would still be happening if she had confessed nothing of the past. She has to hold to a doorway as the thought arrows through her mind, leaving a track of fire. If she is to blame she is being punished now. Albie might leave her as Ted did, as her parents did; he might have left her already. She pours a glass of wine and drinks it quickly, it's midday after all; her parents had been drunk at breakfast. She pours another then another, the toothache begins to fade. She rinses out the dog bowl, scrubbing the slimy base with her fingers, running fresh water in, slopping it over. In the garden the noise of the birds and the sea beat against her, louder than usual. There is no message from Albie. She phones him but he doesn't answer, she leaves a voicemail. 'Be careful,' she whispers into the phone. 'Very careful. Don't talk to anyone, don't trust anyone. The police were here, snooping around.'

The patch of nettles growing by the trees has doubled in size. There is a trowel in the outhouse but she sits instead, already tired out; her back against the wall of the house, wine glass in hand, trowel on her lap. She sleeps in the sun until a cold fall of shadow wakes her. She opens her eyes to see Ed, back again after his night in the hotel. He looms over her, suitcase in hand, blocking the sun.

'Hi there.' He sounds impatient, he looks hot already. 'Okay to start searching again?'

She stands slowly, fuddled with sleep and wine, and leads him inside. He disappears upstairs. Jake is up there already, shouting something inaudible, cupboard doors are slammed. The loft hatch slides open and the ladder thuds down. She retreats to the garden again with a newly filled glass of wine. The nettles under the tree are difficult to dislodge, the roots are deep. After an hour she has made little impression. Despite gloves, her hands and arms are covered with weals, which burn and itch. She retrieves her glass, but coming in for camomile lotion, sun-blind, she trips and falls. The glass shatters against the floor and the fragments lodge deep in her palm. They must have caught a vessel; the blood seeps out very quickly. Whimpering with pain, she pulls out two jagged pieces of glass and wraps her hand in a tea towel, then begins to sweep the fragments up before Harris gets a splinter in his paws. Ed comes running downstairs.

He inspects the wound. 'You'll need stitches.' He sounds angry. 'And a tetanus jab.'

'No.' She can't face a doctor or questions. She backs away, shaking her head. 'It'll heal on its own if I keep it clean.'

'Don't be ridiculous.' Ed pulls car keys out of his pocket. 'Besides blood loss, your hand function could be compromised. It looks deep.'

Blood has soaked the tea towel; Ed binds another more tightly round her hand and shepherds her towards the door, picking up his case as he goes. Jake's still upstairs, she hears him moving furniture. He calls out as they leave, but Ed doesn't bother to reply. Once they are on the road he drives very fast.

'About you and Dad,' he says after ten minutes, his eyes on the road. Her heart begins to beat wildly, like the wings of a bird that's been caught by a hawk. 'I never really knew when it ended.' He looks sideways at her then back at the road. 'I couldn't tell Jake, he worships Dad; I didn't want to let my father down. All the same, Jake picked up on something between you and Dad, so now I'm not sure if it ended after all.' His voice is quiet; his face has become very pale. He's near to tears. 'I can't bear the thought that you were keeping him hanging on.'

'Jake's wrong.' So Jake had worked out a connection, but in grasping for one truth he'd missed the darker one. She had been bound to Ted by hate, not love, but if Jake thinks she was still involved with Ted when he died, the net might begin to close around Albie, the jealous husband. 'There was nothing going on between me and your father. We were over years ago, long before I was married.'

'He lost everything: Naomi, Mum, you, his career.' Ed wipes his eyes, an angry swipe. 'In the end he lost his life.' He glances at her again, the car veers and he rights it quickly. 'I'm glad Jake was wrong. To be honest, I've always wondered if it was you who ended it and whether he was still unhappy because of that.' His fingers grip the wheel so tightly that the tendons on the back of his hands jump out like thin yellow ropes. 'I can't stand the thought that he suffered over you as well as everything else.'

The opposite, she wants to say, Ted discarded her. She'd been hurt, not him. But she needs to be careful, or he might guess it was she who'd had her revenge, she who made him suffer in the end.

'He called time, Ed, but there were no hard feelings. It had run its course.'

He nods, seeming glad to accept what she says. He'll let Jake know, it might lessen his suspicions. She feels sick now, her hand throbs badly. In Craighouse, Ed calls at the shop to ask where the surgery is and the shop owner comes to the door to point the way, the same blonde woman she saw on their honeymoon. She looks neater now, slimmer. She wears her hair up and holds a toddler by the hand. Her life has gone forward, not backward.

They arrive at a wooden building in time to catch the GP, who is turning his car in the forecourt. She recognises the bearded doctor who had been chatting to Albie by the shop a lifetime ago. Close up he has bulging eyes that give him an air of surprised enquiry. He introduces himself as Dr McAleer, his patients call him Andrew. He unlocks the surgery and ushers them both inside. The surgery smells of disinfectant and new carpet. They walk into his room, a spartan place with a brass-rimmed photo on the desk of a happy-looking girl in jeans on a beach, a baby strapped to her chest. Beth looks out of the window to the sea, a line of blue in the distance between the roofs; she can't remember when she last felt happy.

Ed gives the details of what happened, and his name as a contact along with his mobile and email. Beth is now registered as a temporary patient. The doctor nods, tapping the keyboard. He glances up when he hears where she is staying.

'I heard what happened. I'm sorry.' He must say this many times a day but it sounds genuine. Her eyes fill, as though she has a right to be sad and is deserving of compassion. Ed's fists are balled in his pockets; his head is lowered.

They are taken into a room equipped as a small operating theatre; there are high lights, a beige couch with a neatly folded blanket and wrapped instruments on a trolley. Andrew takes off his jacket and washes his hands at the little sink.

'I need to go soon if I'm going to catch the Glasgow plane. The ferry leaves in fifteen minutes.' Ed stares at Beth as he rattles his car keys; does he think she has done this on purpose?

'I can drop Beth back at the house; you won't have time.' Andrew doesn't look up; he is absorbed in positioning her hand on a towel and then swabbing the skin around the injury with pink disinfectant.

'You'll have to catch a later ferry anyway, won't you?' she mutters to Ed through clenched jaws, sweat trickling down her back as the stinging liquid seeps into the wound. 'You need to pick up Jake.'

'He's gone already.' Ed turns to go.

'When? He can't have done.' Grief must be making him forgetful. 'I heard him rummaging about upstairs earlier. He shouted something as we left; if you don't go back he'll be stranded.' Like me, she adds silently.

'Beth, I saw Jake off on the ferry last night,' Ed says. 'He organised car hire on Islay and left me his.' He exchanges a glance with the doctor. The noise of paper being ripped as the packets of equipment are opened sounds loud in the moment of silence. Beth stares at Ed, certainties tipping like instruments on a tray.

'His son's ill, he left in a hurry.'

'Billy's ill?'

Ed nods and walks out without replying; the door closes behind him.

It must have been the police she'd heard, then, returning to comb through the bedrooms alongside Ed. Why didn't Ed tell her that? Does he know more than he is saying? Fear beats in her throat; she shivers although the room is hot.

The doctor slides a needle into the edges of the jagged wound, which puff up with the local anaesthetic. He probes for pieces of glass with a fine pair of forceps; the tips grate as they find fragments. Red stained, they shine like jewels as he holds them up to the light.

'It's deep,' he murmurs after a while. 'But I think I've got all the pieces. It should really be X-rayed. I can organise that for you tomorrow.' He looks up; his glance is kind but searching. 'So you fell with a glass in your hand?'

'I was drinking.' He will judge her for that, but she doesn't care, though if he knew why she was drinking, he would finish what he was doing, lock the door and call the police.

'Hence the smell of alcohol,' he says calmly, as if it's normal to drink in the morning, drink so much you are unsteady on your feet and your thoughts begin to slide. He cleans the wound then pushes his threaded needle through the torn muscle, sewing in silence. The quiet room, even the uncomfortable tugging sensation deep in her hand, adds to a sense of safety, of being looked after. She leans back in the chair.

'If it wasn't Jake, it must have been the police,' she murmurs. 'They said they might come back but I don't know what they hope to find.' In the following silence she stares at the bent head, the thick, wavy hair and glinting specks of dandruff at his parting, unease growing. Were they searching for the vials right now? 'I'm frightened.' The words slip out before she can stop them.

He cleans the skin again and begins to suture the edges together. 'Don't be, it's going to heal beautifully.' He pauses, his voice becomes more gentle. 'But you must be mistaken about the police. There are none on the island today.' He loops the thread into a neat knot and cuts it with the scissors. 'They come over from Islay when necessary, but the ferry boilers were serviced in the early hours so the first boat docked only ten minutes ago.'

He's implying that she imagined the noises she heard upstairs. A low chuckle takes her by surprise. She stares at the doctor; is he laughing at her now?

'Almost there.' His voice is kind. Her head begins to bang; she puts her free hand to her face, it feels wet.

'The days following a death can be very difficult,' Andrew continues. 'How much longer will you be alone?'

'My husband is fetching me tomorrow or the day after.' She doesn't explain that they haven't settled on a day, that there are no definite plans for her return, or none she can remember. Panic begins to creep along her skin like the first crawling sensations of flu.

'Can you manage till then, with one hand? Have you food in the house?'

She tells him she does, far too much food. She doesn't admit she has eaten nothing for two days, that she feels light-headed as though floating unanchored. After he has finished, he draws up the fluid for the tetanus injection. As the needle pierces her skin, she begins to shiver uncontrollably, unable to stop her teeth chattering. Andrew wraps her in the blanket from the couch and, shrugging on his tweed jacket, helps her into his car. He drives slowly, waving to people as he passes, two capped old men leaning against a wall, a woman with a wide pram walking slowly in the centre of the road. He seems well known, liked.

'Sleeping all right?' He is driving a little faster now they are beyond Craighouse.

She nods; she has been sleeping a scant hour or two each night, but there is little point in telling him this.

'Eating?'

At the thought of the chicken and slabs of cheese in the fridge she wants to vomit. She opens the window as they pass the lake and with a shock she sees a child between the road and the water, a little girl standing very still. Her dark hair and white dress look incongruous against the soft greens and browns of the landscape. She is looking straight at Beth, smiling as though she recognises her, and then she lifts her arm to wave, the small fingers stirring as if in a slight wind. Beth smiles and waves back, noticing as she does there is no one else in sight, no picnic rug, no car, no parents. She feels the clutch of panic and turns to Andrew. 'There's a little girl over there by herself, she's only about four. We should stop.'

'I've never seen such a young child out here on her own.' He brakes. 'Show me.'

She turns back to point, but the shimmering grass is quite empty apart from the ragged balls of bog cotton that glow in the grass like white flags.

'She was over there, right there, waving at me.' Beth's voice wavers. She must have been imagining things, there is no one there at all. She puts her hand to her mouth, frightened. The child seemed so real, so familiar. She shivers again. The boards she nailed down are breaking up, something is seeping through.

Andrew drives in silence for a while and then starts speaking again. 'Sadness and shock can affect us in different ways, making us imagine many things.'

His voice is gentle, the hands on the wheel look kind; in his warm car she feels sealed against the outside, protected from real life. It's as though the world doesn't exist, and she can tell him whatever she needs to. Doctors are sworn to confidentiality; he will keep her secrets if she shares them. It would be a relief to open her heart to someone she can trust.

'It's all my fault,' she whispers.

His eyes are back on the road. He nods; her confession doesn't seem to surprise him. 'Guilt is a normal part of grief.'

'I mean I was responsible from the very beginning. I'd had the idea in my mind for a while, I persuaded Albie to go along with it.'

The car goes over a pothole; her hand is jarred against the side of the door. She winces but he doesn't notice. 'You inspired him? Gosh. Your husband's a great man, I follow his work.' He sounds in awe of Albie, as Albie did once when he talked about Ted.

Andrew smiles at her. 'So you had this idea; where did it come from?'

She feels sick now. Her forehead is sweating, her vision darkening at the edges; she gropes blindly for words. 'The vials, I think; yes, that's how it began, with the vials.'

'Sorry, Beth, what vials are these, exactly?'

She will have to begin at the beginning. She wipes her forehead with the sleeve of her shirt. Andrew's right, she needs food; the facts are slipping away. 'The ones Albie changed; Ted found them – evidence, you see. We had to do something then.' She stops, surprised; that's the story, the short version. There's a longer story hidden behind the first one, about love and betrayal and loss, but the details slither from her mind. What was it that she lost? She glances at the doctor in panic.

'It's okay. I think I understand.' Andrew's voice is reassuring. 'It was a collaborative effort, your husband followed your initial idea and adapted it. Ted backed it up with evidence. Something like that anyway, impressive teamwork. Well done, you.'

She turns away. How stupid he is. She shouldn't trust him. He can believe what he wants, secrets should be kept anyway. She let Albie know hers, and look what happened. Her hand throbs, there is an answering pulse of pain in her tooth.

'Can I get out now?' She puts her good hand on the door handle, pushes it down. 'I'll walk the rest of the way.'

'Watch out there.' He presses a switch and the locks of the car clunk in unison; she feels a beat of alarm but his voice is matter-of-fact. 'I'll take you to the house. You're not in a fit state to walk; you've had a tough time.'

She leans her head against the window; she is tired of him now. She might have made a mistake about the noises this morning and about the little girl just now, but if she imagined them, perhaps she is imagining this too. Perhaps nothing is real; she'll wake soon and find herself back in London, in bed with Albie. She smiles. The phone will go and it will be Ted, asking Albie to meet him for a run or discuss a patient he is worried about. Albie will comply; he always does exactly what Ted wants. She tries to hold this picture carefully; the fingers of her sore hand flex and the pain flares. Her hand opens, the images slip away.

The doctor has seen her smile and smiles too. It's easy to see he likes her. When they arrive at the house, she doesn't ask him in and he looks disappointed. He drives away and she goes inside. Harris runs to her, wagging his tail joyfully. She feeds him, pours herself a large glass of whisky and drinks it as she leans against the door to watch Harris trundle round the broken trees. She feels better already, she just needed that drink. She checks her phone but there are no more messages; instead she sends Albie one.

They didn't find the vials. Billy's ill, Jake's coming back to London.

His returns in a second.

Good, as I planned.

What does he mean? He planned Jake's return? How? She walks into the garden but stops abruptly, as though a trapdoor has opened in front of her that leads to deep watery blackness. The only answer that fits Albie's text is one that terrifies her. Albie has enticed Jake home, using Billy's illness as bait. Her hand is throbbing badly and she goes back into the house. If Albie is hurrying down a path she couldn't have foreseen, she had opened the gate for him herself, she pushed him to the starting point, but they didn't set out to harm those other children. They were accidental casualties; this is different. Billy might be in danger. Billy, whose head had smelt of toast, whose warm weight had rested so comfortably against her side. There is no reply to her phone call.

Don't play games she texts instead. This is a child's life, Albie.

A text comes back immediately.

Don't worry. I won't let anything happen to Billy.

She takes the whisky bottle and sits down on the kitchen floor next to the stove. Illness can catch you out. Gita will be frantic. Harris puts his head on her legs. She rests her sore palm on the dog's warm skull and closes her eyes. Her tooth is banging in her mouth so she swigs from the bottle. The whisky warms her, hunger disappears, and after a while the pain slips away with the worry. She closes her eyes.

29

London. Summer 2018

Bruce is still there. The downloaded material must have escaped the computer monitoring system. The relief Albie feels is intense; he took an unnecessary step he can still retrace. Bruce is heading away down the corridor in the centre of a group of lab workers, his dusty hair and purple jacket unmistakable amidst the white coats of his colleagues. Bridget, flame-haired and noisy, is bustling along next to him.

'Bruce!'

The lab is safely his; he must unravel the harm he has done to his friend before the images are tracked. He can pretend that he himself has been the victim of dubious images downloaded to his own computer, advise Bruce to check his files and delete what might be there before they are picked up.

'Wait up.' He runs down the corridor, but when he reaches the group Bruce is nowhere in sight. The lab workers stare at him, their faces blank with surprise; he feels giddy as though the world is tipping the wrong way.

'Sorry,' he manages to say, his cheeks stinging

painfully. 'Stupid of me, my mind must be playing tricks. I've been working too late. I could have sworn . . .' He stops talking; there is nothing to say. The apparition had seemed so real from a distance. He shakes his head self-deprecatingly; a ridiculous mistake. The strain is telling on him, he needs to get a grip.

'Carry on. I'll join you folks in a minute,' Bridget says. The little knot of workers move off and, motioning Albie to follow, she walks down the corridor to her own room where they sit either side of her untidy desk, littered with photos of cats and piles of paper. A bobbly mauve cardigan is slung over the back of her chair.

'Thanks for coming in so quickly, Albie. I sent you that message urgently because I wanted to tell you before you saw it on the news. I wasn't sure if you knew.'

'Knew what?' This could mean anything; he aims for an expression midway between bewilderment and concern.

'Bruce was arrested yesterday.' Bridget speaks calmly but the hand on the desk trembles. 'They took his computer, his laptop, his phone. All his books, everything really.'

'Bruce was arrested yesterday?' he repeats, truly astonished. Bruce's downfall was far swifter than he'd envisaged. 'There must be some mistake.'

'I went to see Mike Foster, the IT chief.' She sounds bewildered too, her normal clipped delivery softened with dismay. 'He wasn't supposed to tell me and I'm not supposed to pass it on, but I know how close you were.'

Close? Perhaps that's how they seemed to everyone: good mates supporting each other, chatting in the coffee room, discussing research. It might have been difficult to detect the rivalry between them.

'Bruce has been downloading illegal material. Images from the net.'

'He's always looked at porn, we knew that. Is it illegal now?'

'This wasn't porn, Albie. These were pictures of children, abuse images.'

It's easy to look appalled; the words, spoken aloud in Bridget's unassuming office, with her cardigan and pictures of cats, seem grotesquely out of place.

'What will happen to him?' he asks, sidestepping the discussion about how people surprise you, how you never dreamt the person you knew or imagined you did was capable of such deceit.

'Bail initially. Prison possibly, after a trial. One thing is certain, though . . .'

He watches the struggle between sorrow and anger on her homely face. She is used to managing schedules and work sheets; faced with depravity, she is out of her depth.

'He won't work here again. His career as a clinician is over and he'll be barred from all research in labs which deal with children's diseases.' She rises from the desk. 'Ironically, Bruce was keen to head the lab.' She shakes her head sadly. 'He told me once he was a little jealous of you, Albie. He thought you had your life so well sorted with the locum, your marriage, the holiday house, all those things. You seemed so steady to him. You may not know this, but he admired you. He mentioned you'd helped him considerably with his research. If we feel betrayed, you must feel worse.'

He walks down the corridor to the exit beside Bridget. She continues to talk; a stream of words he hardly hears. Remorse burns. He is incapable of reply.

'. . . so come in next week.' Bridget has stopped by the door to the lift. 'Things will have quietened down. We'll need to chat. I'll provide the committee with an up-to-date reference, and after your appointment we can discuss future directions for the lab. Despite everything Bruce had some good ideas; some may be worth taking forward.' She squares her shoulders as they round the corner and hurries towards the little group that is waiting by the water fountains.

There it is after all. Bruce will leave his mark. Albie enters the lifts but turns to peer back down the corridor, half expecting to see the curly haired figure of his colleague, leaning against the wall, his face puckered in amusement as if at a private joke.

Billy's hand lies open on the sheet, a starfish of fingers and pink palmar curves. Green vomit lines the cardboard pan on the bed. Gita raises her head from the bed as Albie enters, relief in her eyes. Her hair is flattened on one side, the skin of a cheek has been scored into creases where it rested on the sheet. Billy begins to wail, a thin, high-pitched noise ending in breathless sobs.

'He was fine overnight and okay-ish till the last couple of hours,' Gita says, picking him up. 'Since then he's been getting worse; it's happening so quickly.'

Albie rests his palm on the swollen forehead; the little boy jerks his head back. The renewed yells are deafening; he calls the nurse. A tall African woman comes in, bringing with her an air of stately calm.

'I need to look at the back of his eyes, Judy. Can you hold him still for me?'

He angles the beam of his ophthalmoscope into Billy's eyes. Immobilised in Judy's hands the child quietens. Gita stands at the window, her hands clasped against her mouth. The normally flat optic disks are bulging with the pressure transmitted from the brain; the engorged vessels that run with the nerve are distorted as they lip over the pronounced curvature at the edge of the disc.

'What? What can you see?'

'The optic disc is swollen, Gita.'

'I knew the pressure was up.' Her knuckles are white bulges of bone. 'So there's an infection somewhere in the system?'

'Possibly, though he's been on antibiotics as you know,' he replies as he feels Billy's scalp. The silicone dome empties under pressure but this time doesn't refill. His heart sinks.

'The shunt is blocked now, and the block is in the brain,' he tells Gita quietly.

'What makes you so sure?' she asks as Judy puts Billy into her arms; he stirs and grizzles quietly as though exhausted.

'The dome didn't refill this time. That means fluid is getting from the dome to the abdomen but not from the ventricles to refill the dome; the shunt must be blocked in the ventricles,' he explains carefully.

She stares down at Billy who has lapsed into sleep. 'Will it unblock itself if you double the dose of antibiotics?' she whispers.

'It's not quite as simple as that. Whatever the cause, if the shunt is blocked I need to operate. I can simply replace the catheter if it is not an infection. If it is, the whole system needs removal: the catheter, the dome and the peritoneal shunt.' He forces himself to smile though the regret rises like bile, bitter in his mouth. He could have removed the catheter or the entire system hours before.

'The last blockage was caused by an infection.' Her mouth trembles. 'What else might be blocking it this time?'

'The little side holes in the shunt can just silt up with protein.' He puts a hand on her shoulder. 'Rarely, the very tiny blood vessels that actually make the fluid can get sucked up in the end of the tube and block it.'

That would be the worst scenario, but there is no need to frighten her; the chances of that happening are minute.

'So in any case you need to replace the tube in the brain?'

'You've got it.' His voice is deliberately cheerful; the least he can do is not share his worry. 'It's a straight forward procedure but there are risks, like every operation. We'll need your consent.'

'No problem.' She is more relaxed now that Billy is quieter; he doesn't tell her this kind of quietness is a bad sign.

'We'll need a scan before operating. Can you help me wheel him to the scan room, Judy?'

'Jake should be here too, he's downstairs somewhere, phoning work.' Gita takes out her phone.

'So he came back in the end.'

'Not quickly enough.' She stabs at her phone.

Judy moves the bedside table and grasps the head board, Albie pushes the other end, and together they manoeuvre the bed out of the room. The sick child moans quietly and guilt overwhelms him, a deep ache, like the descent of flu. His plan to make Jake return worked, and the wait that incurred was clinically defensible; all the same the sense of impending disaster is threaded through with dark strands of guilt. He hadn't needed to lure Jake back. Jake didn't find the vials, nor did Ed; they weren't there to find. The story of the lost vials has come to an end; this is the living story, unravelling fast.

Jake meets them halfway down the corridor; his face sags when he sees his son again. 'Jesus. He looks worse.'

'Hello there, Jake.' Albie continues to push the bed. 'We are taking Billy for a scan so we can see what's happening.'

'You should know what's happening.' Jake holds his son's hand as he walks beside the bed. 'The shunt must be blocked with an infection; you've got him on the wrong bloody antibiotics.'

'We can't be sure of anything just yet,' Albie replies, guiding the heavy bed around the corner.

'You would be, if you'd been with him.' Jake straightens and attempts to take Gita's hand as they walk, but she wraps her arms around her body, walling herself away from him. They sit in the waiting area, while Albie continues to the scanning room with Billy.

Owen anaesthetises Billy; his normally relaxed expression is tense with concentration, his eyebrows are lowered, his mouth a tight line. Albie cleans the scalp with chlorhexidine and inserts a tiny orange needle deep into the dome to withdraw the few drops of clear fluid remaining at the base. He injects this into a pot, a nurse hurries off to take it to the microbiology lab. The little team cluster around the child as he is placed in the scanner. Albie retreats to the overlooking imaging room; he stares at the computer screen as he waits.

A sense of doom is palpable above the silent machines in the scanning room and hovers over him too. If a scan of his brain, not Billy's, were to spring from the darkness of the screen, the limbic system might be warped beyond recognition, the amygdala diminished. He was a good doctor once, a good man, but it's too late now for repair or repentance. He looks down at his hand as if the twisting blue veins on the back were a map that might point to where it all began. But the veins are a network that doesn't have a beginning. They branch and circle. Where was the wrong turn? How far back should he go? He has made all the wrong choices, though perhaps they weren't choices but consequences of how he was made and who he already was. He knits his fingers to stop the trembling.

Billy's scan appears. The new, larger size of the ventricles is obvious. The cave-like spaces in the brain seem to fill it entirely. In addition, there are cracks of darkness within the surrounding white matter, radiating out from the lining of the ventricles – fluid under pressure being forced into the brain itself.

He brings Gita and Jake into the room; they are familiar with Billy's scans to date. Faced with the new image, Gita gives a cry of dismay. Jake pushes forward, his face almost touching the screen.

'The scan confirms that the cerebrospinal fluid is blocked, but from this alone, we can't see why,' Albie says.

‘So unblock it.’ Jake bounces on the balls of his feet. Albie can smell him, stale sweat and unwashed clothes. He is unshaven; he must have travelled non-stop, taking the ferry from Jura to Islay, then Islay to the mainland. The long drive to Glasgow then the wait for space on the next plane or the one after that. He’s done it himself, many times.

‘That’s exactly what I am about to do.’

‘Why the delay before investigation?’ Jake’s eyes are lit as if for battle. ‘He’s been getting worse all the time.’

‘His management has been systematic, Jake. I set up treatment as soon as a problem became apparent, and my team has been monitoring the situation since,’ he replies, wiping his palms against his white coat.

‘In your absence.’ Jake’s face is close to Albie’s. ‘How could anything be more urgent than a sick child?’

‘You weren’t here either, Jake.’ Gita’s voice trembles.

‘I was in Scotland, helping Ed. It was important.’

‘More important than your son?’ Gita turns away; she stares through the window to the scan room where Owen and his assistant are carefully lifting Billy from the trolley back to his bed. Jake slams one hand into another, a brutal movement. They will not survive this, whatever the outcome. Jake’s face is flushed, Gita’s tear-streaked. This is love, dying. A moment like the headache that presages cancer; destruction will follow, confusion and pain. Then, emptiness. He walks slowly from the imaging room to the corridor, trailing the anaesthetic team who are pushing the bed straight to neuro theatres. The bond between him and Beth seems broken too, as though in falling Ted pulled it down with him. He hurries to catch up with the bed. After this, when Billy is better, he'll think about Beth then. Fractures heal, wounds aren't always fatal. They'll knit back together, given time. Then he empties his mind of Beth, of Gita and Jake, even of Billy. There is no sadness, no regret and no tragedy; not even a child in danger. There is simply a blocked shunt that needs removal and replacement. He will have to muster all his skill.

Fifteen minutes later he is gloved up in theatre, Billy more deeply anaesthetised, the head cleaned and positioned against a padded horseshoe rest, the right side uppermost.

The nurse tells him the results from the pathology lab show that there is no infection.

He performs a meticulous C-shaped incision in the skin of the scalp around the silicone dome and then dissects it free from the underlying burr hole in the skull. Holding the dome with a pair of toothed forceps, he very, very gently exerts the lightest pulling pressure to extract the connected tube from the ventricle. Nothing happens. He pulls again with a small increase in effort, still nothing. He tries several more times, increasing the pressure by tiny amounts. His hands begin to sweat. He remembers a French exam at school, each question more impossible than the last. At some point he'd begun to scrawl rubbish; anything to have done, desperate to get to the end no matter what. He has reached that limit now. The dead children, Ted and Bruce cluster at his elbow. Beth is hovering too. He is in too far, he has done too much. There can be no going back. He presses his lips tightly together and pulls. There is a tiny ripping sensation, and the tube comes out in his hand. He inspects the end immediately. With a sickening sense of helplessness, he sees pink-red stringy fronds, fairy seaweed, filled with blood. The choroid plexus has been torn, that delicate network of vessels that lies in the ventricles had been drawn into the holes in the tube, the diagnosis he feared the most. Now the ripped ends in the ventricles deep in the brain will be bleeding rapidly and there is no way on earth to stem the flow. He calls for another catheter, but before he can insert it down the old track to drain the blood, the brain, under overwhelming pressure, pouts up through the burr hole.

He stares at the bulge of glistening grey jelly, threaded over with red vessels. The substance of life. *A child's life, Albie.*

'Fuck,' he mutters. 'Fuck. Fuck.' He senses Owen's glance; Albie is normally quiet, not given to expletives. He should have left well alone when he sensed the tube didn't yield; he could have inserted another shunt alongside, leaving the old one in place. The ghosts have disappeared, have they achieved what they wanted? He needs to be quick. There may still be a chance, another place where fluid could be drained. He pushes a new length of tubing back in along the approximate track of the one he has just removed, and positions it in the ventricles just short of where the other was. He withdraws the inner catheter: blood starts dripping fast from the end of the shunt.

His assistant wipes his face. In a calm voice he asks Owen to cross-match blood. In fifteen minutes the blood dripping from the tube slows to a standstill. He performs a burr hole on the opposite parietal bone, swiftly inserts another catheter, endeavouring to reach the ventricle that side, hoping that this will be successful, that clear fluid will begin to drip from the end to relieve the mounting pressure in Billy's brain, but nothing. No cerebrospinal fluid, not even blood. Dismay thickens at the back of his throat, he forces himself to breathe slowly to cope with the rising panic. At his request, Billy is taken for a scan by the silent team. He can see from the images beamed to the screen in theatre that the blood has at last clotted but there is a new horror. There is now a solid cast of blood filling both ventricles, set like clay, taking up the entire volume of the ventricles both sides.

The child is returned in minutes. Albie retracts the catheter slightly in the hope that around the edges of the massive clot some of the cerebrospinal fluid will leak away. Nothing comes back. He looks down; his clogs are in a pool of Billy's blood. The point of no return.

He gives the order for Billy to be taken to the Paediatric Intensive Care Unit. He helps Owen move the child from the operating table to the bed, and walks behind to the recovery bay. The small brain is now being forced downwards in the skull. Once the third nerve that controls pupil size is squashed, the pupils will dilate; death will follow swiftly. If he could pray, now would be the time. His thoughts jump wildly even as he walks out of theatre. Another burr hole, though how will that avail as the blood is set in a vast solid clot? Sucking out would achieve nothing. Excision of a skull flap and manual removal of the clot would mash the brain. If Billy is continuously ventilated on PICU there is an outside chance the clot might liquefy, it might be possible to drain it then. Please God . . .

Owen's quiet voice cuts across his spiralling thoughts.

'Both pupils fixed and dilated.'

The knot around the bed stands back. No one looks at him.

Owen touches Billy's hair. 'I'm sorry,' he says, though it is unclear exactly who he is talking to.

30

Jura. Summer 2018

The scent of earth close up; peat and smoke. Fungus. Wood. Iron. Blood.

An ant with many legs lies on its back, becomes two, one struggling with another, pulling it over the swords of grass, dropping, picking it up, dragging it. Aggressor or helper, a fierce instinct is at play; the tangled organism carries on, staggering out of sight. There are seeds down here, brown and cream pips lying on the dark soil. Fragments of wood. The stalks of grass gone yellow at the base. Her ear is tight against the soil, listening to the sounds that seem to thrum beneath the surface – unintelligible mutterings – angry, as if the earth itself is blaming her.

A yard away is a curved back of orange hide, sides blotched with white as if touched by a finger dipped in paint. A twitching ear. The fawn has been in the grass for hours, a night and a day at least. Both have been abandoned, though she has been waiting for rescue longer than he has. Three weeks in all? Longer? She swims in time, losing track.

The little animal struggled to get up at first, and

then gave up, looking at her as if she were a stone or a tree, a stain in the landscape. Pure regard, bearing witness.

The ears are long, pointed, lined with white. They flick backwards and partly rotate. She had wanted to stroke the tiny head, cup her hand at the furred angle of its jaw, but she knew not to. After a while, the neck relaxed again, extending forward, the long skull sank close to the ground. Green shines from the ring on her finger, the light could stab him in the eye like a blade. A ring should mean safety but hers feels dangerous; she doesn't need it any more, less fettered without. Its purpose has been spent, though thinking back she can't remember what that was. She pushes it carefully, stone side down, into the soil. The gold band follows. She lies still, like the fawn. She feels close to him now, closer as the hours tick by and the light softens. No one comes. They have been abandoned by their families, both their mothers have gone. The fawn's mother could be eating or mating or dead. Maybe she's watching from the shadows, waiting until Beth leaves, to fetch her fawn.

She rises to her feet at the thought, and the world becomes dark. She stays quite still until she can see again; the fawn doesn't move. The white flap of a sail beats beyond the trees, or the tail feathers of a large bird like a sea eagle. Gone in a heartbeat. Angled sunshine on rock perhaps. Her head aches as she walks slowly to the house. The garden watches her, indifferent to her plight. Inside flies rise buzzing from the dirty wine glasses on the table and the remains of a sandwich on a plate. Last night's supper or the night before. While chewing, a stone had rolled in her mouth; it became a tooth in her hand. It didn't hurt, though her mouth was filled with blood.

Grass and twigs are scattered on the floor, blown in. She tries to sweep them up but her hand throbs, the mutterings swell, she drops the broom.

Someone else's face looks back from the mirror. Wild hair, a leaf caught in the knotty black. Mud on her chin. Tears on her face. Blood on the collar of the shirt she is wearing. A man's shirt. She stands still when the car comes down the road. It stops, footsteps come to the door. Knocking. Louder knocking. She pushes herself to the wall; the stone is cold against her flattened breasts. There is a measured thump of feet walking around the house outside. She crawls upstairs and looks down from the window, careful to stay out of sight. The man has dark wavy hair. Tweed-covered shoulders. Familiar, though she can't place him. He walks from window to window, hooding his eyes with his hand. He doesn't look dangerous, but that might be a disguise. She lies on the bed; after a while a car door slams, an engine starts, gets fainter.

The voices are louder, clearer, though she can't hear the words. She understands they are blaming her for something, though she can't think what it is. When the bright light goes from the room, and the shadows are long over the bed, she gets up, looks out of the window. White is still flickering through the trees. Sail? Bird? Sheet? Shawl? Dress? She walks downstairs, feeling sick, holding on, going slowly.

Outside, the fawn is still lying in the same place. She mustn't touch him, though she wants to. If she touches him, he might die. A child has died; was it hers? An eye for an eye, a tooth for a tooth. She puts her hand in her mouth, her fingers come out covered in blood.

She starts to follow the white that is flickering beyond the trees, clearer now, a shawl for a baby. No, it's a dress, a child's dress. No, it's a child, the little girl; she has found her way here and is dancing ahead through the gate and over the stretch of grass; she disappears down the little path. Beth follows, dizzy and sick with the heat. On the beach she sees that the child has climbed the rocks to the side under the cliffs, too high. Her heart clenches, she starts after her, but the little girl jumps, her white dress fluttering. The light from the low sun dazzles. She puts her hands over her eyes, looks closely at the glinting water. The child is up to her neck, waving.

Beth takes off the shirt, surprised at her body in the daylight. Her breasts are smaller now. Her belly and thighs have shrunk. She climbs down the shelf of rock to the lower ledge then steps off that, going more deeply than she meant to. Her bones must be nearer the surface than they used to be, they hurt in the cold.

The salt finds the wound on her hand. A wave knocks her sideways and her ears fill. In a gap in the waves she glimpses the child. The white dress is floating around her; it will trap her. She needs to reach her and take it off, swim with her back to the rocks.

Silvery walls of water are in the way. She would see better standing, but when she lowers her feet to the ground, the ground isn't there. It occurs to her she should have told someone she was going in the sea, but there was no one left to tell. The water fills her mouth, colder than blood. The child has moved further away, out of sight.

Once someone was with her, whose face glittered in the sun. He swam through the water like a seal but he's not here now; in this moment of fear even his name has gone. A wave hits her in the face. There isn't a child in the water, she has made a mistake. Another wave hits and then the next one. The water is in her throat. She turns to go back but her way is barred by waves. They turn on her like animals.

The group of deer waits outside the open gate until dark. Their heads are high, they are listening, scenting the air. They approach the house gradually, feeding as they go, until a window bangs in the wind and they startle back, then they approach again, wait again. There is a noise of a dog barking for a long time, whining follows but then the noise stops. The largest female enters the garden. She walks stiffly and neatly to the tree. She bends her neck, noses the still form, licks it.

The skin twitches. The fawn lifts its head and, in a rush of unfolding legs, lurches to its feet and stands swaying. The mother turns and walks out of the garden and the small animal follows.

Act Four

31

London. Autumn 2018

The post lands where it falls. Leaflets from local restaurants, political pamphlets, pictures of chained dogs and animals in cages, bills in brown envelopes, some with red type. Who cares? Albie kicks the whole lot out of the way.

Nowadays he starts early and stays late on the wards or in the laboratory. He has been promoted to consultant surgeon and official head of the lab. Both Ted's jobs are now his. His appointment to the lab was uncontested, Ed didn't even apply. Owen told him Ed had a place on the Nottingham rotation as a junior registrar; their paths are unlikely to cross again.

He was given a month off but refused, agreeing instead to bereavement counselling. Sometimes he looks in the mirror in the operating theatre and sees Ted as he had been in the last weeks, stooped, sallow and hollow-cheeked. Harris is looked after by a dog-walking team from early to late; he should sell him or give him away but lacks the courage.

He eats microwaved meals standing up, drinks bottles of wine. He focuses on the next thing and the next. It seems possible to stay on the surface; the mechanics of travel are helpful. Conferences in America, Japan and Australia, there are talks to prepare, airports to arrive at and leave from, checking in and out of hotels, sapping heat to endure, all useful. Four months in, he manages whole days without thinking of anything except work. Sometimes it's as though the last three years have never been. He treads around the chasm of her loss, never going near, and wonders if he can keep this up for ever.

On a late return from a Paris conference he has to force his way into the house; the front door is caught on wedged mounds of post. He tells Owen the next day.

'You need a housekeeper.' Owen's glance takes in his face and his clothes.

'I just need someone to pick up the post.'

'Your shirts should be ironed. You've lost weight. We got Natalie so that Elsa can be free for Gus. She does laundry and cooks. She'll pick up the post too.' Gus is now a demanding four-year-old; Asperger's syndrome has been recently diagnosed.

'It's different for me. My place is a little untidy right now but when things get less busy—'

'I'm asking Natalie.'

Natalie is neat, her jeans are precisely torn. She chews gum neatly. She irons the shirts, stacks the post on his desk. He finds meals in the fridge on the days she comes, labelled in a careful hand. He leaves her money every week, cash. Two months go by.

'How are you?' Owen and he are alone, the only ones left in theatre. The four American neurosurgeons who had been watching the operation have all gone to lunch. Albie feels sorry for them; it's harder to watch than to perform, much more tiring. People come every week, almost every day. He's becoming famous for his operations, for the use of viruses. They use different ones now. The university admitted no responsibility for the misleading trial results but regrets were fulsomely expressed to the bereaved families. Billy's death was reviewed by the coroner and found to be a result of his chronic condition; it was intensely regrettable that the unavoidable trauma to the choroid plexus led to frank haemorrhage; no fault was found or ascribed to the surgeon or his team. Owen must have sensed how the pressure had mounted that afternoon, but only Albie knew that the ghosts of the past had stood with him and that he took a wrong turn.

He started several letters to Jake and Gita but was unable to think of what to say or how to finish. He tried to phone them once but his call was blocked. They have never been in touch. Perhaps they are coming to terms with Billy's death in their own way, perhaps treading it down as he is, for now. What happened to Ted went largely unacknowledged, at least in public. The open verdict still stands, but if the parents of the children who died in the trial thought justice had ground appropriately fine, who could blame them? The final report summing up investigations at the lab revealed nothing untoward, but stringent new procedures are in place.

Bruce's fate was the subject of media interest for a while, his denials greeted with scepticism. Both his laptop and his hospital desktop had been used in the attempt to download the images; the odds were overwhelmingly against him. His lawyer was unable to prove it wasn't his crime. He escaped prison after a protracted trial, but the police monitored all his devices from then on; he was ordered to pay a punitive fine with community service on top. His career was over. He was occasionally seen in clubs, once or twice lurching on the streets, then he disappeared. Bridget thought he'd left the country, but for all anyone knew he could have died of an overdose at the back of a club. In Albie's dreams he sees Bruce sometimes, vomit-stained and unconscious, slumped against a toilet bowl on a stained floor. By day Albie blocks out everything with work. He is congratulated for his persistence, for his endurance against all odds, for turning the laboratory into an internationally respected centre.

'How are you, really?'

A diminishing number of people ask him that now, the questions fell away quickly. 'Fine' covers everything: the days he pushes blindly through a fog, the better ones when he can taste food, the bad ones when terror keeps him awake. The way the cliché turns out to be true, that money doesn't buy happiness. How much he misses Ted and even Bruce.

'Albie?'

'Sorry.' He looks at his friend's earnest face. 'I'm fine.'

'Come to supper tonight.'

He can't think of an excuse, so he goes, taking a bottle of wine. Owen lives in a flat in a converted warehouse in Brixton, it takes an hour to reach it. The spaces are large, a little cold. There are scattered pieces of Lego everywhere. Elsa has cooked pasta for Gus, the only food the boy will eat. Gus is leggy with large teeth and an uneven fringe of silky hair. There are layers of plasters over his knees. He glances up from the Lego he is laying end to end across the room then hunches down again, disappointment in his contracted silhouette. Albie only then remembers how Beth had sat with the boy at a lunch party, missing the meal, looking at a book, answering questions about plants. At the table, Gus pushes away his food. Elsa's shoulders droop with tiredness. Owen brings her drink to the table, touching her shoulder; she puts her hand up to cover his, Albie looks away.

'I want Beth,' Gus whines.

Pressure builds behind his eyes. He was wrong to come here. He has worked out how to avoid her at home; here he has been ambushed.

'She can't be here,' Owen murmurs to his son, glancing at Albie.

'Why can't she be here?'

'She died, Gus. She drowned in the sea.' Albie's words are out of place in the bright kitchen with its jumbled pans and Lego underfoot. Gus begins to rock in his seat. Elsa puts her arms round him, resting her forehead on his head, she closes her eyes; the room is full of unspoken reproof. Albie would like to continue now he's started, blurt out that the police found her in the shallows. The weather had been bright and calm, a summer's day, the island at its best. Her body was being gently pushed this way and that in the surf, hair spread like dark seaweed. Naked. He would like to tell them that it wasn't her in the morgue with a bruised face and mauve mouth, stitches on one pale palm. Her rings had gone. She had gone. Nevertheless, he had put his mouth next to the cold ear, a trail of shining salt on its rim and a fingerful of water in the meatus; he had wanted to beg for forgiveness. He shouldn't have left her alone. He loved her, he thought she knew.

He says nothing. He doesn't know Owen well enough; he doesn't know anyone well enough. Elsa puts Gus to bed.

'I heard from Ed this afternoon.' Owen pours him more wine and sits down, leaning back in his chair.

Albie drains his glass; the wine burns his gullet. He has been drinking too much lately. 'How is he?'

'Busy,' Owen says. 'He asked for news about your research.'

'I'm glad he moved away, for his own sake.' Albie watches Owen. Does he ever wonder what really happened?

'I agree.' Owen puts his glass down and stretches. 'He needed to put some distance between him and his father's kingdom; yours now, of course.' He looks at Albie's empty glass, gets up to retrieve the bottle, pours and then sits down again. 'He told me Theo's staying with his mother for the present. She took Ted's death hard, harder than they thought she would. Theo's put his career on hold for now. I wasn't entirely sure from the conversation when he plans to resume.'

Jenny's recovery may not be possible, the grey landscapes of her paintings will darken. Theo has lost everything. Albie is scalded with remorse and leaves without waiting to say goodbye to Elsa who is reading Gus a story. He is relieved to reach home; he feels calmed by the extreme tidiness. The post has been stacked in two heaps on the desk. He makes coffee and sets himself to work through the night, sorting the letters of condolence, old parking fines and invitations to conferences. His thoughts become ordered; it's an hour before he gets to the bills. The one from Scottish Power is written in red print, warning they will cut off the supply in two weeks if the bill is not paid.

That was two months ago. It's November now. The house will be icy without warmth from the night storage heaters. The pipes will freeze, may have already frozen. He went back after Beth's post-mortem to pack up and collect Harris from Iona, but left again swiftly, neglecting the end-of-summer jobs. The water should have been drained down, the night storage heaters left on. Beds stripped. For all he knows there is still food in the fridge. He pays the electricity bill online and at lunchtime the next day Googles tourism in Jura. A picture of a stag on the beach comes up, water curling invitingly on the sand. He sends an email to *islandholidays.com*, a family agency who let and service holiday cottages. He asks for a house clean, and as an afterthought, enquires about letting the house out. He adds that spare keys are at the hotel. An email comes back that evening from a Mary Mackay, agreeing to service the house; her parents knew his. It is their quiet time; they'll go to the house in a couple of days. A letting contract is promised, the cleaning bill will follow when the work is done. The name is a familiar one, an old island name. When the contract comes he signs it quickly.

Three weeks pass; life has changed since the evening with Owen, becoming grey, shot through with black when his guard is down. He hasn't heard back from Mary Mackay, she must be busy, distracted by family. He sends another email. On Friday of the fourth week his operating list is cancelled to make room for emergencies; the day is stormy and he works from home, catching up. There are seventy emails to go through, including one from Scottish Power informing him the electricity has now been restored. In the afternoon he settles to write a paper, but as the hours go by the house seems full of noise and his concentration falters. Rain blows at the glass walls in diagonal sheets. Worsening gales are forecast. In Jura water will be crashing against the cliffs, the waves pounding the beach where they found her. He stands at the thought, the chair falling behind him, and walks outside, pulling his anorak from the hook by the door as he goes. The last time he was in the garden it was a warm evening in late spring, but now the cold day has darkened with the storm. The wind is so strong he can scarcely breathe. There is an old pot by the door he hadn't noticed before, rosemary straggling over the edge. Rosemary for remembrance. The lawn is covered with a blanket of dark leaves; the apple trees are bare. Behind the hedge, the vegetable patch is thick with weeds, foliage grown high, rotten seed heads and the blackened leaves of ancient potato plants. Her hand had been in his; she had been showing him a heaped row of freshly turned earth; new potatoes, your favourite, she'd said. He picks up the trowel on the grass; the wooden handle is soft with rain. A watering can is full of rainwater and leaves; he empties it and takes it into the shed. The light bulb has blown and he treads on grit. Some animal has torn holes near the bottom of a paper sack of fertiliser. Mice or foxes perhaps. A notebook, swollen with damp, lies on the bench, faded to brown though a flowery design is still visible. A torch is sitting on the side amongst the nibbled bulbs.

He switches it on and off, memory flickering. The ground is wet but he lies full length to angle the torch under the hut. The weak beam picks out stones, leaves, a pile of chewed paper, red fur, white bone. Small skulls: the remains of cubs.

The tears are hot against his face, unstoppable. On all fours, he is dimly aware that he is making noises like an animal. He loses track of time. The remaining light fades around him, the wind becomes more fierce, rain soaks his scalp. Gradually the cold penetrates his palms, Harris is whining by his side. He pushes himself to standing and walks slowly back to the house.

The hot water in the shower sluices the mud and the tears; he stays under the spray for a long time. When he switches the water off, he is conscious that the doorbell is ringing in long, impatient bursts. He dresses rapidly, pushes his feet into trainers, walks to the door, and swings it open.

It takes a second to recognise Jake.

32

London. Late Autumn 2018

Finale.

The theatre is dark. No movement, no music.

The audience hesitate – is it over? Should they leave? A voice in the darkness begins to recite a poem, part of a poem. Well, a line of a poem, with additions.

'*No man is an island.*

'He considers himself an exception, unconnected and enduring, like his island. Time and the tide win in the end though he thinks he still has time on his side.'

Rhythmic sounds fill the auditorium, like heartbeats or the breath sounds of a runner or waves. The sounds grow louder and louder and louder until there is a deafening roar as if a cliff face has been cleaved from the land. Then, silence.

*

Jake looks much older though it's hard to say exactly why. Larger but not fatter. His chest is bulky, his shoulders more broad. His hair has been shaved to a reddish stubble over his head. The odd-coloured eyes are blank; his hands hang loosely by his sides. Albie last saw him at the inquest into Billy's death; he had seemed young then, a youth bewildered by grief. He'd left immediately afterward, followed by Gita who was unrecognisable.

A wheelie bin has been tipped over by the wind, the contents scattered on the tarmac. Gulls are already at the rubbish, there are branches on the road.

'Jake. Come in.'

The wind blows into the house, carrying with it leaves and twigs, pieces of bark, they swirl down the hall. Jake steps across the threshold and then stands still. His clothes stream with water.

'Let me take your coat.'

Jake hunches his shoulders, shoving his hands deep in the pockets of his jacket.

'Well, let's have some coffee.' Albie shuts the door and the leaves on the floor lift and dance.

'I think I know how you might feel.' He reaches to touch Jake's shoulder but the man jerks away. 'I understand the place you are in.' Christ. He's beginning to sound like his own grief counsellor; the aggression in Jake's face is making him nervous. He leads the way into the kitchen and switches the kettle on. 'I hope you and Gita—'

'She's left me.'

'I'm sorry.'

'Fuck off.' The foxy face becomes wolf-like, the words are snarled. Jake walks closer to Albie, and for the first time, Albie feels a frisson of fear.

'She blames me for what happened to Billy. I blame me for not being there, but you and I know why he died.'

'He died as a rare complication of his chronic condition, Jake. You were at the inquest; the blood vessels were entangled in the tube before Billy even came to the hospital.'

The room had been hot, very crowded. He had told the judge that Billy had been admitted immediately, monitored, treated with antibiotics, scanned and operated on within hours once the situation began to deteriorate. What had happened was a chance event, a million to one occurrence that wasn't his fault. He didn't tell them he'd waited to operate until Jake's return – that wouldn't have made any difference anyway – or about the moment of despair, which had. Nothing would have brought Billy back.

'Fuck off.' It's louder this time.

Albie makes coffee, he concentrates on steadying his hands. Jake's instincts are honed; there is no way he could know exactly what happened, yet he senses the outcome could have been different.

'Ed's back.' It sounds like a threat.

The coffee slops into the saucer. 'How is he?'

'He's come for his job.'

'I'm told he is settled in Nottingham.'

'The job you're keeping warm for him.'

So Jake's here on Ed's behalf. Albie blots the saucer dry and turns to face him. 'I appreciate Ed might feel passed over, but Ted made it clear he wanted me to be in charge. Ed knew that.'

'How the hell do you make that out?'

'I was reliably informed that Ted advised his son to step back and make way for me. He made his views clear in a consultant meeting. We shared a vision, you see—'

'Fuck that.' Jake laughs, he moves closer still. 'You've obviously been sold some kind of half-truth. Ted knew his career was over after the children died; he warned Ed you'd stop at nothing to run the lab. Ted told Ed exactly what had transpired in the meeting: he'd advised his colleagues to let you take the flak from the trial and tidy up the mess – you were to be the fall guy – but Ed was the future of the lab. He'd told the consultants he'd advised his son to wait then apply a few months down the line. That time has passed, he'll be appointed soon.'

Where do you find the truth, the whole truth? How deep do you dig? How far back do you go? Perhaps it depends on where you stand and what you need, on who you choose to believe. Rain is pelting against the glass; Skuld's shuttered face seems to float in the green-grey light outside. Had he been purposely misled? Perhaps he'd only heard what he'd chosen to. Truth is like the sea, whose changing colours come from the weather at the time. What he told himself as a boy became the lies he believed later on. It's years too late for the truth.

'Well, Ed's ready now.' The menace in Jake's voice is clear. He has come to prepare the way for his friend.

'I think we're talking at cross purposes. There's no vacancy. Even if Ted did say those things, which I doubt, I can't be forced out.'

'Force won't be necessary. Ed has the evidence to bring you down.'

There's no evidence. It's a trick to make him talk, the oldest one in the book. He smiles. 'I'm sorry, Jake, you'll have to try harder than that.'

Jake returns the smile; he puts his hands into his pockets, seeming to relax. For the first time he looks almost friendly. 'You might have got away with it if only you hadn't contacted Mary.'

Who the hell is Mary? He stares at Jake as his mind scrabbles at his memories.

'About a month ago at your request, Mary Mackay took her cleaners into the house,' Jake continues conversationally. 'They were confronted with a pool of stinking water.'

So she went in after all, odd she hasn't sent a bill. He sees sodden carpets and ruined furniture, a small thud of worry lost inside the greater one. 'I'm not quite sure how burst pipes constitute evidence.'

'Don't worry about the pipes, they were fine. The issue was the fridge-freezer which had stopped working, the power had been cut. There wasn't much water, a couple of buckets at most. The problem was the contents. The smell of rotting food was terrible; Mary had to clear it up herself, her staff refused.'

Has Jake come to lecture him about the electricity bill? 'I paid what was owed weeks ago, the power has been restored now—'

'It must have been restored following her visit – just as well, or these might have been frozen in again and missed.' Jake pulls his fist out of his pocket. 'She found them when she emptied the bottom shelf.' He uncurls his fingers: two small vials clink together on his palm, like the faintest echo of some long-ago music.

'They were in a plastic bag behind some packets of bacon which were putrid.' He holds a full vial up to the light. 'Varicella vaccine extract for immunisation. Batch 82297X. From the batch used in the trial. Only they don't contain vaccine, do they, Albie?'

Albie waits for him to finish while his thoughts run to the corners of his mind like rats in a cage.

'The full one almost certainly contains saline; we know this because the contents of the other have already been sent for analysis. Pre-injected with saline, no rat would have reacted badly to subsequent injections. The results would have implied the treatment was safe, though as we all know it turned out to be deadly. Yes,' Jake says quietly, 'I know my immunology now.'

'Ah. So that's where they were.'

Jake has been very thorough, he'd have wanted to avenge his son's death as well as Ted's, but if Albie can only keep his head, there is nothing to link him to the vials. 'Ted told us he had found some vials; he was worried someone had sabotaged the trial. It seems he might have been right. He died before he told us where he'd put them. This is good news, Jake. If you're right, it will mean Ted can be exonerated. His family will be thrilled. I'll make you some more coffee, this one's gone cold.'

'Beth gave the game away in the end.'

'Beth?' He's brought up short, outraged.

'Let's go back to Mary; she was worried when she found the vials,' Jake continues. 'She knew medicines need to be disposed of properly, so she gave them to the island medic, one Dr McAleer.'

The bearded man who sought him out after Beth's inquest to murmur about the balance of her mind. Visual and auditory hallucinations. A depressive psychosis unveiled by stress. Albie had been scoured by guilt, it had been a struggle to hear him out.

'Beth fell, got glass in her hand. You probably know that part. Once he sewed her up, the doctor drove her home. She was rambling about some vials. He thought she was referring to your research but it made no real sense to him at the time.'

'She wasn't well.' He wants Jake to stop talking about Beth, stop using her name. He walks away but

Jake follows him, moving around so he faces him again, always standing too close.

'The doctor's thoughts entirely. He was so concerned about her mental state he went back to see her. When he couldn't find her, he wrote everything she'd said in her file. He felt she might need intervention; he called again the next day but gave up after that, assuming you'd taken her home, just as she'd told him you would. She was found on the beach the following day. When Mary showed him the vials months later and told him that she found them in your house, it rang a bell. He looked at his notes again and Beth's words began to make sense. Ed's name was in her notes so he was contacted; he's passed everything to the police now.'

He should have been there, she was frightened. He would have held her and calmed her and brought her home. 'She wasn't herself. Nothing she said can be taken as the truth.'

'Poor Albie. I should really feel sorry for you. It seems that the woman you married turned out to be mad as well as vengeful.'

This will be over soon if he keeps his nerve, there is no real proof. Jake's voice acquires a taunting lilt.

'She obviously wanted retribution. Ed told me how his father used her, then went back to Jenny. Beth was a woman scorned, Albie. A cliché. She used you to bring Ted down.'

'I understand you are grieving, Jake—'

'Ed's worked it out. You doctored the vials, didn't

you?' He comes closer still. 'Ted guessed they would prove his innocence, which means we don't believe he committed suicide.' His face is almost touching Albie's; Albie can see the pores in his nose, the dry flakes of skin at his hairline. 'Which means we think you murdered him.' Jake smiles, a bitter expression with no joy. 'That would have fitted in nicely with Beth's plan for revenge. Clever girl, your wife, patient too. She must have planned this for years.' Jake's mouth is still smiling, though his eyes are bleak. 'The things people do for love,' he says.

Love. Beth's soft face in the moonlight, her hand in his. The children they tried to make, the child she miscarried. Beth, floating in the waves, helpless. His mind crashes with grief.

'Iona filled me in when I went up with Ed to look for the vials. We stayed in the hotel. She gave us the back story.' Jake's voice has acquired a vicious edge. 'They say your father was a tyrant, your mother away with the fairies. Your brother's a wastrel. You were the ambitious one. Beth must have seen that, twisted it.' He laughs, a thin, yelping noise more like a howl than a laugh. 'She'd been waiting for someone just like you to happen along, so blind with ambition you couldn't see the facts. You've been had, Albie. Used.'

Rage drenches him like a wave. 'Ted was the one who used her. He wanted to carry on using her; he never gave up. The day before he died, he put his hands on her.'

Jake shrugs, watching him, waiting.

'Don't shrug, you bastard,' Albie shouts. Harris slinks whining under the table. 'She was mine. Ted was a thief, he stole everything from me: my ideas, my work, the kids I should have had. He wanted to steal my wife.' He is engulfed with fury, drowning in it. 'I'm glad I killed him. He deserved to die. I'd do it again.' He sees his spit land on Jake's face.

Jake smiles. 'So now it's just a matter of time. They're coming to get you, and time is running out. Tick-tock, you bastard.'

Albie stops listening. This has become an operation, an emergency one. He has to focus, empty his mind, attend to the detail. His anorak is behind the door; he lifts it off the peg, takes his wallet from his desk and mobile from the side. Jake's eyes follow every move. Harris is still under the table; he picks up the dog lead from the counter and, pulling the dog to him, clips it on. He opens the door; dusk has come early; it's still raining hard. In the distance he hears several sirens. It can't be the police coming for him already but he begins to run down the road, picking up the pace easily. Harris gallops beside him. The fierce wind is behind them, helping him. He feels fit and powerful. He will cross the Heath where the police cars can't follow, leave at the Highgate exit and make his way through the back streets to Victoria station, then the night coach to Glasgow. After that, an island. Not Jura, they will be waiting for him there;

the Orkneys maybe. Then Iceland. There will be time to think later.

The noise of sirens echoes up Haverstock Hill. He runs down Pond Street. On the other side of the road fire engines are clustered at the entrance of the Royal Free Hospital, blue lights flashing in the gloom. Uniformed men grapple with hosepipes, police guide lines of people out through the doors into the forecourt and car park, nurses among them pushing beds. Commands are being megaphoned. A bomb scare? Terrorists? He runs faster, scanning the building as he goes, catching black smoke behind glass on the top floor, looking again in disbelief, counting up the floors. The one that houses the animal lab is on fire. Hilary is somewhere in there, Skuld too. Any other day he would run to help, but this isn't any other day. Passers-by stream up the road, doubtless on their way to offer aid; they glance at him in surprise as he thunders the other way, but he is running for his life and if the world is going mad, he can't afford to stop. Hilary is resourceful, Skuld will be safe.

He turns left at the bottom; Harris keeps pace. There is a sign at the entrance of the Heath, warning of high wind and falling trees. If anyone is after him they will think he has gone into Hampstead Heath Overground station. The paths under the trees are obscured with shadow and running with water, slippery where the branches overhang. Up ahead a group of hooded women shelter under the tossing branches of a large pine tree. They are smoking, huddled close, seeming oblivious to the storm. They hold numerous dogs on leads, large mongrels, restive with restraint, who snap and growl at his approach. He moves to the edge of the path, giving them a wide berth, half tripping on the verge, glimpsing a hand on a lead. He sees stamped on the back of the plump and freckled wrist, the perfect tattoo of a small mouse.

He glances up into the rounded face of Hilary; she is talking. Skuld, Urth and Verdandi huddle close. Hilary is smiling at the girls as she talks; her eyes tilt like those of a cat. Skuld's eyes are identical, Urth's too, even Verdandi's. He sees the resemblance between them all and the truth slices through him with icy force. Everything makes instant, terrible sense, everything except his own stupidity. How could he have missed it until this moment? The young women and the old one are bound together by blood as well as the little tattoos; it's shatteringly obvious now that Hilary's little girls with their shining oval gaze grew up to become the sloe-eyed women who led him on with the half-truths that Jake has just laid bare. Hilary, his old adversary, is their mother. She gave them all her eyes.

The facts spiral though his mind like lightning; differently lit, everything is revealed. The attacks on the animal labs at Glasgow, Oxford, the Institute and now the Royal Free were all the places where Hilary or her children worked; all were set on fire in their turn. Bruce told him the police thought the Oxford and the Institute attacks were connected and still he hadn't guessed the link: Hilary and her girls.

The women are absorbed in conversation with each other and barely give him a glance. There is no flash of recognition from any of them; he is, after all, simply a mud-splashed figure running past, one of many every day. He finds his feet and picks up speed again, breath coming hard, running through the sheets of rain as the layers of his life dissolve.

What exactly has Hilary done? What has she done to him? Why?

It must have been the work of years, training her daughters up as she began to burn her way towards him, placing them to work their mischief in the name of animal rights. Mischief that was, for a while at least, aimed precisely at him. He claws at the facts that spin in his mind. Lined up like dominoes they begin to fall one after another in perfect order; he can almost hear the little clicking noise as they tip over: Hilary the scientist who helped with the family's catering business. She had been behind the scenes all the time, directing, coordinating her daughters and his downfall. Sixties, jolly-ish, Hilary had delivered the anniversary cake. Another domino falls: the anniversary – the day Beth last saw his notebook. Skuld would have told her mother what to look for; it would have taken a mere second to slip his book into her satchel on the way out; an invaluable guide to the appropriate equipment for burning, the appropriate rats to release. There's no proof, there never will be. She's far too clever for that.

Albie pushes on up the hill, his breath coming in ragged sobs. He's been a fool, a blind fool. How they must have laughed. He sees them in a kitchen, dogs under the table. Hilary serving cake, Urth chuckling, Verdandi smiling her sly smile. Skuld listening, not laughing, she'd always been more on his side than her sisters. She told him once to take care. If she hadn't been interrupted by her sisters by the pond, she might have revealed all Ted's words. Or perhaps not. He'll never know.

His feet slide on wet turf, tearing the grass, he almost falls. Why him? He knows the answer: vengeance for his experiments in Glasgow. Baird McAlister, a menace to animals, a man who could be tripped by his own ambition. Straightening, he stumbles on. Or was his involvement pure coincidence? Hilary might have sent her daughters out to weave a web that caught him by chance. Skuld's words could have been entirely innocent, and his ambition did the rest, setting in train the death of the children, Ted's destruction. Bruce's. Beth's.

Beth. He halts at the top of Parliament Hill, his lungs heaving. The view over London is hidden. He can't see the buildings or the streets, the skyscrapers or the tiny houses in between. Only the street lights remain, everything else has disappeared. There is no landscape ahead of him now, no gleaming touchstones.

The wind blows against his face, he is wet through. Beth and Ted: he loved them and destroyed them both, or was it the other way around? There's no one left who can tell him now. Harris is whining by his feet but he puts his face in his hands. He must decide where to go and what to believe, but he stands in the rain like a mourner by a grave.

At the sound of nearing sirens he lifts his head, looking to the trees behind him, where the cigarettes glow in the dark. Skuld and her sisters are huddling with their mother and their dogs. They look harmless from here, a group of women finding shelter from the storm. He could make himself believe that; make them into a family of animal lovers out for a walk, ordinary women whose path he happened to cross by chance. After all, there is nothing to prove this untrue. The fires might have been nothing to do with Hilary; the rats he saw released could have been the only ones they freed. He might have lost the notebook himself on the wards or perhaps dropped it in the street. Whoever these women are, whatever they've done, it would be better to think of them as incidental spectators to the course he'd set as a child, witnesses to his unfurling destiny but not part of it. Better, far, far better, to remember his beloved Beth as a loving wife and not as a victim out for revenge who had used him from the start. No one twisted his life to their purpose, it would have been impossible. His fate had been set in the stars.

Fate. Destiny. The old words burn through his body with their ancient power. He isn't finished yet. He takes the lead off Harris; the dog will run better on his own. He starts downwards, his feet picking up speed. He is still in control, strong, young enough; he can go on, he can win. Beyond the trees around him he hears two sirens blaring, though whether behind or ahead is difficult to tell because it's mixed with the noise of barking. He turns to look, stumbling as he does so. Over the brow of the hill comes a large pack of assorted dogs, bounding towards him, unleashed.

Acknowledgements

I would like to thank the publishing team at Michael Joseph, Penguin Random House, in particular my editor Jessica Leeke, whose rigorous attention to detail helped make the book what it is. Thanks are due to Clare Bowron, Sarah Bance, Nick Lowndes, Claire Bush, Jenny Platt and Matilda McDonald. I owe so much to Maxine Hitchcock for her skill, encouragement and the consummate care with which she has published all three of my books.

I am grateful to Eve White of Eve White Literary Agency for her generously given advice and friendship. Eve is a true ally, always working beyond the call of duty. Thanks to her team which includes Rebecca Winfield, Kate Prentice and Ludo Cinelli.

Heartfelt thanks to Tricia Wastvedt, who was my tutor on the Bath Spa Creative Writing MA five years ago and whose kind and perceptive wisdom has sustained me since.

Thank you to the members of my writing groups who have been generous with reading and feedback: these include Tanya Atapattu, Mina Bancheva, Alexandra Bockfeldt, Victoria Finlay, Emma Geen, Mary Griese, Diana King, Christine Purkis, Susan Jordan, Sophie McGovern, Peter Reason and Mimi Thebo.

Thanks to Dr Ally Bienemann and Marcella Wyatt at the Functional Neurosurgery Laboratory at Bristol University, who guided me around the laboratory and answered my many questions.

Thanks to Rebecca Burke, secretary to Mr Colin Shieff, Consultant Neurosurgeon at The National Hospital of Neurosurgery and Neurology at Queens Square, for the time kindly given showing me around The National.

Thanks to Mr Kristian Aquilina, Consultant Neurosurgeon at Great Ormond Street, for his time and patience in acquainting me with his hospital.

Thank you to Inspector Ian Smart and PC Nick Shaw (retired) for elucidating matters of internet crime and police procedures.

Thanks to Cath McCallum of The Jura Hotel, in Jura, Scotland, and to Alex Dunacchie, who gave us a unique tour of the island.

Thank you to staff and rangers at Dyrham Park in South Gloucestershire for acquainting me with their beautiful herds of deer.

Thanks to my family for putting up with me working during our holidays and on their tables: my sons Tommy Gill, for his calm wisdom on all matters IT and for his editing skills, and Henry Gill, for reading and encouragement. I owe Scott Gill, my brother-in-law, for reading the manuscript three times.

Finally, thank you to my husband Steve Gill – companion on adventures, book related and otherwise – whose work as a neurosurgeon and whose presence in my life is an inspiration, always.

Discussion Points for Book Groups

1. The themes of ambition and revenge loom large in Albie and Beth's marriage. Do you think these desires would always have been destructive, or could they have been a force for good in a different kind of relationship?

2. Did your feelings towards Albie and Beth change over the course of the story? Why, or why not?

3. Discuss the claim made in the Neurobiology of Evil lecture that early adversity leads to criminal behaviour. In your opinion, do Albie and Beth's unhappy childhoods excuse their actions, or not? Can any of the characters be classified as 'evil'?

4. Discuss the ethics of animal testing. Why do you think the author chose to put Albie's character in the lab as part of his storyline?

5. Ted seems to betray Albie in presenting his work as his own and lying to him, but he also took the blame when Albie's surgery went wrong and when the Viromex treatment caused deaths. Discuss whether you think Ted is more honourable or more manipulative.

6. Do you agree with Jake's assessment that Beth planned Ted's downfall for years, and that she was waiting for an ambitious man like Albie to enable this? Was there anything pure about Beth's feelings towards Albie, or not?

7. Albie refers to omens and dangers he can sense but not see. Do you perform any superstitious rituals (e.g. touching wood), and why do you think people do this?

8. What did you perceive as the role of Hilary, Urth, Verdandi and Skuld in the story? Were they the architects of Albie's downfall, or were they simply witnesses to the destiny he had already created for himself?

9. Did you see any parallels between this story and *Macbeth*? If so, how did this shape your understanding of the characters and themes?

10. What or who is ultimately to blame for the deaths in this book? Is any one person to blame, or is the responsibility shared?